THE ROAD TO THE WORLD'S END

SIGURD HOEL

The
ROAD
to the
WORLD'S
END

*Translated from the Norwegian
by Sverre Lyngstad*

SUN &
MOON

CLASSICS

75

LOS ANGELES
SUN & MOON PRESS
1995

Sun & Moon Press
A Program of The Contemporary Arts Educational Project, Inc.
a nonprofit corporation
6026 Wilshire Boulevard, Los Angeles, California 90036

This edition first published in paperback in 1995 by Sun & Moon Press
10 9 8 7 6 5 4 3 2 1
FIRST SUN & MOON EDITION
©1933 by Gyldendal Norsk Forlag
Published originally as *Veien til verdens ende*
(Oslo: Gyldendal Norsk Forlag, 1933)
English language translation ©1995 by Sverre Lyngstad
Published by permission of Gyldendal Norsk Forlag
Biographical material ©1995 by Sun & Moon Press
All rights reserved
The chapter "Death" was first published in
50: A Celebration of Sun & Moon Classics
(Los Angeles: Sun & Moon Press, 1995)

This book was made possible, in part, through an operational grant from the
Andrew W. Mellon Foundation, through a translation grant from NORLA
(Norwegian Literature Abroad), and through contributions to
The Contemporary Arts Educational Project, Inc.,
a nonprofit corporation.
The translator would like to thank the NEA (National Endowment for the Arts)
for a translation grant for this work.

Cover: Knud Knudsen, *Close to Nærødalen in Sogn* (c. 1888)
Collection Universitetsbiblioteket i Bergen
Design: Katie Messborn
Typography: Guy Bennett

LIBRARY OF CONGRESS CATALOGING IN PUBLICATION DATA
Hoel, Sigurd [1890–1960]
[Veien til verdens ende. English]
The road to the world's end / Sigurd Hoel ;
translated from the Norwegian by Sverre Lyngstad.
p. cm — (Sun & Moon Classics: 75)
ISBN: 1-55713-210-0 (pbk. : alk. paper)
I. Lyngstad, Sverre. II. Title.
PT8950.H58V413 1995
839.8'.2374—dc20
95-40296
CIP

Printed in the United States of America on acid-free paper.

Contents

THE GARDEN OF EDEN

Alone

A ND THIS was the first thing he remembered:
¶ He was lying in bed. He had slept—a long time, for
ever and ever. Now he was awake. He roused himself from
sleep and sat up, raised his head over the edge of the bed
and looked about him.

He was alone.

Light came in through the window. Light shone from a
spot on the floor. It wasn't dark in the room, but everything was strange and terrible, and being alone filled him
with fear. He was too scared to stay in bed by himself and
struggled onto the wide floor. Out there it was freezing cold
and he felt even more alone. Some strange, dark things stood
along the walls on four little legs, staring at him and casting long shadows after him. He called Mother. He cried. He
started walking through the cold room calling Mother. He
stumbled onto the bright spot on the floor and saw the
moon, a terrible sight, a dazzlingly white man with flapping clothes; and the man tried to grab him with his long
white arms, with his long white, thin fingers that reached
clear through the windowpane and tried to grab him. He
couldn't move. Out there the white thing was trying to grab
him and inside, in the shadows, the dark thing was glower-
ing at him. He stood still, couldn't move. He was alone.

Sunday Morning

How did he know it was Sunday?

He just knew. It was Sunday in the sunshine, in the clouds, in the dew drops, in the spider's web glistening between the blades of grass, in the breaths of wind smelling of flowers—everything was full of Sunday.

The church bells were ringing. He was holding Andrea's hand as they walked down through the pasture. He was far from home, farther than ever before. The heather was in bloom, it blazed red in the sun. The clouds moved slowly in the sky. Every now and then a shadow fell over the world. Then it was sunny again.

They walked down the overgrown green path. He'd often stood by the gate looking down this road, which went so far and got lost among rocky clefts and alder scrubs, and was dangerous because it went so far and got lost. Now he was walking here himself, between rocky clefts and alder scrubs, and it wasn't dangerous, for he held on to Andrea's hand.

"We're going to drop in on Tøsten Teppen," Andrea said. "He's clearing some land for a new potato patch."

A new potato patch, that must be something you had to clear land for Sundays.

The heather grew tall on both sides of the road. It smelled

of heather. Here and there among the heather stood tall stalks with golden heads. There was a buzz of bumblebees. A glistening of dew and spider webs. And the birds were singing.

They walked among tall trees. They waded through grass wet with dew. The tall stalks brushed his face. Then they came to the clearing and stopped.

There stood Tøsten Teppen, big and tall, chopping at the ground with a big hoe. He had cut down trees and trimmed them and stowed them in a big stack, dug up roots and thrown them together in a big bristling heap, and gathered stones into a big pile. Now he grabbed a root and pulled, took a big ax and chopped, then grabbed the root again and pulled it out, shook the dirt from it and went to put it on the heap. Then he turned toward them, big and tall.

"Well, now, who's this I see out for a walk?" he said. He bent down, caught Anders under the arms and lifted him up in the air. Higher than the heather, higher than the stalks, higher than the tree tops, higher than everything. Anders soared like a bird up there, high in the sky, and saw the whole world, the lake and the church and the sky and the whole world, and was dizzy and blissfully happy. Then Tøsten put him back down and he felt dizzy, fell on his fanny and saw everything from below again.

The new earth smelled damp and cool. It glowed like heather in the sun, but in the shade it was blue.

Now Tøsten was swinging his hoe again. The sun shone on him. He laughed. His eyes and teeth flashed. The hoe flashed high in the sky. Standing there huge in the sun and blocking out half the sky, he swung his huge hoe, turning up new soil.

Afterward Anders sat out in the clearing working the soil. He hit the big lumps of dirt with a big stick so they broke and turned into many small ones. He picked little stones and gathered them into a big pile. The earth gave off a good sharp smell and he took a bit of it in his mouth to eat; but it didn't taste so good and he spat it out again—he spat several times to get it out again. Some tiny animals ran in and out among the lumps of dirt, they were black and green and brown and had bright shields on their backs which threw back the sunlight. When he knocked a lump of dirt to pieces, the dirt fell on the animals and hid them; but in a little while they crawled out again and scurried on.

Up above, the sky was blue, with white, slow-moving clouds. Once in a while a shadow glided across the clearing, and then everything became a little quieter. Afterward the tail end of the shadow glided across the clearing, and the sun shone once again. Tøsten and Andrea weren't there, but he wasn't alone, he could hear their voices now and then all along.

The shiny little animals scurried in and out among the lumps of dirt. The birds sang. The voice of Tøsten murmured on. There was a smell of earth. The earth had a red sheen to it. Shadows danced along the clearing. Then he fell asleep.

Afterward they walked up the path again, among heather and spruces and alder scrubs. Light and shadow danced on the ground. He thought about everything.

"Is the world bigger yet?"

Andrea looked down at him.

"Yes. Much bigger."

The World

THE WIND whistles and blows. It comes from the world's end.

It bobs the blades of grass and tosses the branches of the birch tree and rushes off again on its wide wings. Anders can see it as it rushes by every now and then. It's going to the world's end. One night, long afterward, he wakes up— it's the wind coming back from the world's end. It whistles and blows and rushes by.

That's how big the world is.

Anders is at the center of the world. He is at the center of everything.

Around him are all the other things. Mother and Father, Gorinè and Embret and Andrea, Tora and Kari and Åse and Pussy, the bed, the pillow, the blanket and the potty, the fireplace, the stove and the folding table, and the big clock that stands by the wall in the kitchen all day saying, An-ders, An-ders!

Those that are closest are the biggest. When they go away they grow smaller and are gone, except Mother. When Mother leaves Anders cries, for he doesn't want her to leave. Then Gorinè comes and looks after him, and Mother grows smaller and is gone.

At the center of the world is the house.

The house is full of rooms. He knows some of the rooms, they are *his* rooms. The kitchen, the side bedroom and the middle bedroom are his rooms, and the hall and the front stoop and the back stoop. The other rooms are far away and strange and wish him no good; he doesn't like to be in them, and not at all by himself. Upstairs are rooms where he's never been alone, and doors leading to rooms where he's never been. That's where the brownie lives, Rolf Bluebeard and the big, black dogs. He's not allowed to go in there, because he could lose his way. When he sees those doors he wants to go in, but then he gets scared and screams.

Around the house is the rest of the world. There's the yard and the garden and all the outbuildings, the servants' quarters and the road and the pasture, the forest and the lake and the whole world.

The world is big and dangerous.

Near the house it's not so dangerous, but farther away it gets dangerous. Behind the hayloft it's quite dangerous, because he can't see the house from there. And down in the pasture it's terribly dangerous, for that's where the bull calf is.

The things he doesn't know are far away and dangerous, they threaten him. But the things he knows are nearby and friendly.

The dangerous things he hasn't seen are dangerous. But the dangerous things he has seen are even more dangerous. The most dangerous is the chimney sweep and Ol' Man North-Wind.

The chimney sweep is black and has chalk-white teeth

and chalk-white eyes, and will come and get him if he's naughty. When he's washed he's called Kerstaffer and isn't that dangerous.

Sometimes Ol' Man North-Wind comes in through the kitchen door, and then there is a gust of cold air. He has thin hair and a sparse beard, a snotty nose and a hoarse voice, and he gasps and groans when he talks, his throat gurgles and his eyes and nose are runny. He comes around in the work seasons, and then he's called Karl Norderud and drives a team of horses and sits by the kitchen table coughing, gurgling and eating. But at other times he is Ol' Man North-Wind and roams about outside, howls around the corners and nabs all the bad boys. Anders knows him again by his voice when he coughs and says, Whoo-oo-oo!

There are many other things that are dangerous. God is dangerous, and the devil, who is abroad when it's dark, and the brownie in the hayloft, the murderer who was beheaded behind the servants' quarters and haunts the place at night, and the black dog at Hoff and the mad bull at Berg and the big turkey at the parsonage and the big toad under the back stoop which comes out as soon as he turns his back. And everything that's far away and not so far away but unknown to him.

Almost everything is dangerous. But he often forgets about it.

At the center of the world is the kitchen. In the kitchen are Mother and Gorinè and the folding table, the hearth with a fire in it, the stove and Pussy and the clock up against the wall. The big ones sit in the kitchen at all meals.

The big ones come in with a thundering noise. When

they sit down the floor quakes. They stamp and scrape with their boots, shout in gruff voices, grin and laugh and eat. Their long shadows lie along the floor. They light their pipes; the smoke has a sour smell and hangs blue in the air. They talk and brag and tease Gorinè, slapping their knees and roaring with laughter. They get up and leave, making the floor quake. Then they walk over to the servants' quarters, to smoke and to talk about strong men, spirited horses and ill-tempered women. The kitchen remains, very quiet now. The table, full of cups and plates, casts a big black shadow, and the clock by the wall casts a long black shadow, uttering the only sound in the whole kitchen: An-ders, An-ders, An-ders…

Then Pussy comes out from under the stove.

The table top in the kitchen divides the world in two. Anders and Åse and Pussy are in one part, from the table top down. All the others are in the other part.

Every now and then one of the big ones grabs him under the arms and lifts him high up, close to the ceiling where the big ones are. It's so strange up there among the big ones—so high up and so far away from everything.

Under the table is in his part, it belongs to him. And the stool by the fireplace and the bottom step of the stairs and all the things inside and outside that aren't so terribly tall. The wagtail hopping about and the sparrows sitting on the horse droppings, the little piglets carried into the kitchen in a tub so their mother won't eat them, and the little lambkins which can barely walk but seem to roll on wheels—they all belong to his part, and he owns them.

He understands very well what they say. He understands

what the wagtail says, and Pussy and the piglets and the lambkins. He understands what the grass out in the garden says when he sits there and it blows a bit. But he can't explain it to the big ones, they don't understand.

Over by the garden gate there is a tree stump covered with moss. He understands what it says, and once in a while when nobody is watching he talks to it. But he doesn't tell anyone.

On the far side of the yard is the road. It leads out into the world. There are two roads leading out into the world, there's up the road and there's down the road. The road goes up the road straight to the top of the hill and then it gets lost. And the road goes down the road all the way to the turn, where it gets lost.

He can go as far as the road, as long as Mother isn't in a bad temper. But he must never cross the road by himself, for then somebody will come driving along and run over him. The little kitten was run over when somebody came driving along, because it crossed the road by itself though it wasn't supposed to. And it became flat in the middle and oozed out at both ends.

Below the turn he can't see the road. But it's there. For he's been there once and seen that it's there. It goes down the bridge-hill to the bridge and over the bridge and up the other bridge-hill. He has seen the bridge-hills only once. But they sit there all the time. And at night, when it's dark and terrible, they sit there all alone.

The world is days and nights.

The nights are different from the days. Usually he's

asleep and knows nothing about it. But once in a while he wakes up and everything is dark and dangerous and different; he can't see anything and buries his head under the blanket so he won't have to look.

But sometimes it's moonlight and he lies in bed looking about him. Everything is asleep and quiet in the room, Father and Mother are asleep. Outside is the birch—all its branches hang still, its leaves all shine, they hang their heads and are asleep. The bottom of the sky is such a long way off. The clouds sail along so calmly. He lies there looking, wants to remember it all and tell about it. But when morning comes he cannot remember, or tell anyone about it, for it was all so different.

But usually he's asleep. Then he travels far and wide and sees many wonderful things—but he doesn't remember it until daybreak, and then he has forgotten it.

He is sitting on Mother's lap. She tells him about the Garden of Eden.

"God planted a garden in a place called *Eden*, far away to the east. There he planted many trees and put a fence round about. In the middle of the garden he planted a nice big tree called the tree of life. Farther on he planted a tree called the tree of knowledge...."

She tells him about Adam and Eve and the ugly serpent that crawled in the dust, and about God who appeared among the trees and chased Adam and Eve out of the garden because they'd eaten apples from the tree of knowledge. "No, no, the Garden of Eden isn't this garden. The Garden of Eden is far away, and there is an angel with a drawn sword guarding the gate...."

They sit in his room. The window faces east. Outside is the birch. Farther down is the pasture, it goes down to the lake. It's evening. The birch and the pasture are in shadow, but the sun shines on the east side of the lake, the houses are red and white and the fields and meadows are green. The Garden of Eden is over there on the east side of the lake.

A white cloud sails across the blue sky. It's high up. It sits right over the Garden of Eden.

There is something in the world called *time*.

Time is something which comes and goes. It is morning, noon, evening and night, morning, noon, evening and night.

Time is a tall, thin old woman who stands still over by the wall calling his name: "An-ders, An-ders." She always has a different face, all day. She's time.

Time is his going to be big some day and get a long nose like Embret and a red beard like Father, and walk with a big stick like the Sheriff.

But he doesn't believe it. He'll always be the way he is now. It was only before that he was different. For then he was smaller and couldn't even walk. But *that* was before.

The world is full of riddles.

Why isn't it light at night and dark in the daytime? Why is it a sin to eat a lot of sugar and a sin not to eat a lot of oatmeal? Why is it a sin to pick your nose?

Why are there so many difficult buttons in one's clothes?

The world is full of buttons and riddles which only the big ones can figure out.

The wind whistles and blows. The wind is something big that roams about outside. He cannot see it. Or can he? He's never quite sure. But he can hear it. When he stands out on the stoop and follows it with his eyes, it's broad daylight and he can see and hear so many other things. And the wind is light and merry, like himself and all the other things.

But sometimes he wakes up at night and hears the wind. And he lies there awake and listens. He thinks about Ol' Man North-Wind, but this isn't him. He thinks about the daytime wind which passed so high up and grabbed the birch by the forelock and shook it, then moved on and was in such a hurry. But this is not him.

In the daytime there were so many things. But now, when it's night and darkness, there's only him and the wind. He lies inside in the dark, and the wind is outside in the dark. He can hear it coming from far away and going to faraway places. It's big and terrible and furious, and hoots and howls and threatens—and it's small and sad and whispers and weeps. He understands some of what it says, but not all. He lies in the dark room and the wind is out there, fiddling with the door and the window to get into his room; but it can't get in, and it sighs and moans out there in the darkness and the night and the wind. The whole world is in darkness now. And the wind comes from all over the world. What is it the wind wants to tell him about the world? What has it seen?

He lies quietly in his bed and listens to the wind from all over the world, sighing and puttering over by the window— sighing and moaning and weeping and wandering on, far, far away, weeping and moaning, to the world's end.

The Garden of Eden

ANDERS LAY IN BED and wouldn't get up. It was late, and outside it was sunshine and fine summer weather; but Anders lay wide awake in his little bed, blinking his eyes at the light and making no move to get up. It was so nice in bed. And besides he was thinking about something.

Gorinè was tidying the room. Her face was all covered with wrinkles, and on one side of her nose she had a wart with three long white hairs on it. All women grew warts like that when they reached a certain age and started getting mossgrown, Embret said. Where, he wondered, did that moss grow? He had asked Gorinè, but she'd gotten so angry he didn't dare ask her again. It must be on their backs.

Gorinè went around fretting and nagging. In the morning she always did. Now she nagged Anders because he was still in bed; but he didn't listen to her.

He was thinking about God.

God was higher than everything else in the whole world.
Well, perhaps there were several higher-ups.
First there was Mother. For she was so nearby and was almost always the highest. She stayed mostly in the kitchen and the bedroom, there she was the highest one. She had too much to do and grumbled because she had so much to

do. But once in a while when she combed out her long hair till it reached way down and set it in a big bun at the back of her head, and it was Saturday night and she sat down and told fairy tales about the Garden of Eden and the trees and the serpent and God, then she was nicer than anybody else.

Otherwise Father was the highest one. For he had a red beard and was the highest of all. He was very busy and didn't eat in the kitchen, and when he was angry there was a crash and a bang. You'd be safer keeping mum about many things with him. But when he had the time and was friendly and stroked Anders' hair, nothing else was quite so nice.

But Father was away so often. And then perhaps Embret was the highest, at least outdoors. Embret had a long nose, and an ax in the crook of his elbow. He chopped wood in the shed, threshed grain in the barn, and walked about the fields making sure that everything was in order.

But in the hayloft the brownie was the highest one. Anders had never seen him. But he'd been in the hayloft by himself and heard him shuffling about in the big pile of hay; and then the brownie was higher than everything else in the whole world.

Still, God was the highest of all.

God sat in a chair way up on a cloud looking out on the whole world. And the world was big. It stretched everywhere he'd been and still farther. It stretched across the side bedroom and the kitchen and the middle bedroom and the living room and the office and the stairs and all the rooms upstairs and still farther. And it stretched into the garden and through the garden and down the road to the wood-shed, and behind the woodshed down to the rock and the pasture and still farther. It stretched across the whole field and over the fence and across the field at Berg and up the hills all the way to the forest and still farther; and it stretched to the lake and across the lake and up the fields all the way to the forest on the other side and still farther.

And everything that happened in the whole world, God knew about it. God knew all.

Anders knew many things too, and each day he knew more. And Gorinè knew very much, Mother knew still more, and Father knew still much, much more, but it was so difficult to ask him. But Embret knew nearly the most of all, for he was even older than Gorinè and had a white beard and a drip under his nose, and knew nearly everything. But he didn't know as much as God. Mother had said so.

When Anders grew up he would be like God and know all.

Gorinè was getting more and more impatient. But she didn't quite know how to handle Anders, and Anders knew it, and knew that she knew he knew it.

She gave him a shake. That he wasn't ashamed to lie in bed so late, big tall boy that he was! If he didn't get up in the morning, he would stop growing and would never get big!

But she said the same thing in the evening when Anders didn't want to go to bed. And so Anders just flung his legs about.

Gorinè stood helpless for a while. But then she thought of a way out.

"What do you think God will say when he sees you lying like this? And your father!"

Gorinè always thought it carried more weight if she made two threats at once.

"Father isn't home!" Anders said, about to lie down again. But then he was struck by a new thought, that about God. It occurred to him that God knew about all that happened and everything people did, even if it was only taking a single lump of sugar from the dish in the cupboard. Mother had told him so. Unless it was just to scare him.

He asked cautiously, "Can God see me all day?"

Gorinè nodded, pleased. "God sees you day and night, he does!"

Anders thought a moment. That God saw him at night he knew quite well, because that he'd known a long time. It was dark at night, so then God and the angels had to look after all the children. But in the daytime? It was different then because it was light, and so it couldn't be that necessary, could it?

He shot a glance at Gorinè to see if she believed it herself. Well, yes, it looked like she believed it. Then it must be true.

But there was still something he couldn't quite understand.

"Doesn't God ever go to bed and sleep?" he asked, searchingly.

Gorinè sniffed disdainfully, the hairs on her wart quivered. God never slept, that much she could say. And right now he was sure to be watching Anders. Because he watched all the naughty boys lolling in bed all morning and wrote their names down in a big book. Because they'd get a spanking when they entered heaven.

Anders glanced at the window but couldn't see anything. Then he remembered that God was invisible, just like the wind. Even more invisible; for the wind he could hear at least, and catch a glimpse of in the trees once in a while, but God came and went without a sound so it was impossible to be quite safe from him anywhere.

He tried once more. "Can God see me if I crawl under the bed?"

But Gorinè held her ground.

Oh, yes, God could see him under the bed, too. And Anders had to admit that this was quite reasonable; for all he had to do was to lie down on all fours and peek. It was a bit dark under his bed of course, but God could see in the dark. Pussy also could see in the dark. Anders had often wondered if God had eyes that shone at night, like Pussy's. He'd sat up in bed at night a couple of times to find out, but he hadn't seen anything. God's eyes must be invisible, like the rest of God.

He looked about him but couldn't find a single hiding place that was better than under the bed.

So perhaps he'd better get up.

But he couldn't stop thinking. And a little later, when he sat on the potty while Gorinè was making the bed, he just had to start questioning her again.

"How old is God, Gorinè?"

"Well, er …," Gorinè hemmed and hawed. "He's awfully old. He's older than everybody, he is."

"Is he older than the old church bell?"

"The sort of things you ask!" Gorinè said, sounding uppity. "Let me tell you, God is older than a hundred church bells—."

Anders couldn't quite understand, because Embret had said that the big church bell was the oldest thing in the whole parish. It had been made for Olav the Saint by the troll in Vardåsen Hill, many, many years ago that was. There was troll silver in it, that's why it had a different sound from every other church bell. But Olav the Saint cast a spell so the troll turned into stone, and you could still see its big toe sticking out near the north end of the church, as tall as a grown man.

Anders wanted to ask Embret if it was true about God and the church bell. For Gorinè didn't always tell the truth, and there were many things she didn't know; but that was because she was only a woman. And she couldn't do anything about that, Embret said.

Anders sat a few moments minding his business, while Gorinè stood over by the bed shaking out the pillows.

Then he just had to ask another question.

"Who does God look like? Does he look like Embret?"

Gorinè tossed her head in despair. "Ha-ha. God, oh no, he looks nothing like Embret, that's for sure! Of all things—."

"Who does he look like then?"

"That's no way to ask."

"Does he look like Father?"

"He doesn't look like anybody, I'm telling you!" And Gorinè gave the pillow a mighty smack.

Now Gorinè had become cross, Anders noticed. Still, he couldn't let go.

"Does God have a beard, Gorinè?"

Gorinè didn't answer.

"Gorinè, does God have a beard?"

"Yes. Oh yes, he does."

Anders found this reasonable. Embret had a beard, Father had a beard, the parson had a beard that was trimmed crooked at the tip, and Karl Norderud, who was a farm hand every work season, had a thin gray beard that he drooled into. It was clear that God must have a beard.

"Are you done now?" Gorinè asked.

"No. Does God eat, Gorinè?"

No answer.

"Gorinè! Does God eat?"

''N-no. ''

"Why doesn't God eat?"

"He doesn't need to."

Anders thought a moment.

"Will Embret go to heaven?"

"Yes, I suppose so."

"Will he chop wood there?"

"No, there nobody chops wood. The angels do all the work there," Gorinè explained.

Anders had to think a moment again.

"Do the others in heaven eat?"

Gorinè busied herself with the bed.

"Do they eat in heaven, Gorinè?"

"Yes, I suppose so."

"Do they get prune pudding on Sunday?"

"Yes, those who like to."

Anders looked at Gorinè; she knew quite a few things after all.

"Does God ever sit on the potty?"

"Good Lord, how can you ask such ungodly questions!" Gorinè said, annoyed.

"Yes, but —"

"Get done now, will you!" Gorinè was really angry.

Anders realized he wouldn't get any more out of her today.

"Yes, now I'm done," Anders said.

In the afternoon that same day Anders stood out in the yard. The yard was wet and the water purled in small streams down toward the road. There had been a thunderstorm and showers. The thunderstorm was God, and then he was angry; the showers were God pouring water down on the world from a big lake. Sometimes he did it to water the fields, but at other times he did it because he was angry with people. Today, most likely, it was mainly because the fields needed water.

All this Anders had learned from Embret down in the woodshed. And Embret said that thunderstorms were more dangerous than any other weather. They were most dangerous of all for cats, because they attracted the lightning; but they were dangerous for people too. Today's thunderstorm hadn't been much of a storm, though. When Embret was a hired man at Rud there was a thunderstorm so big you could stand in the yard and see fires on seven farms.

When Embret worked at Rud everything was much bigger than now. But today's thunderstorm didn't seem to be so small either—certainly Embret didn't think it was small while it was going on. He came from the woodshed into the kitchen in the middle of the work period and sat down without a word, and Gorinè went to lie down on her bed and covered her head with the pillow. And all the others came into the kitchen one after another, and nobody said a word. The sky flashed and roared, flashed and roared, and it got darker and darker. God came nearer and nearer. It had been nothing but fun while he was far away. Then it was just a dark-blue cloud that came rolling over the hill, rumbling and bristling with bright flashes. And a blue curtain hung down from the dark-blue cloud, and behind that curtain was God. Everything was pretty and blue. But when he came nearer it was no fun. For then it was serious.

Anders sat on a stool by the fireplace. He sensed that God was near and his stomach felt funny. He would never go to the pantry anymore or pull Pussy's tail or sleep late in the morning. It got dark like at night. And then came a flash of lightning—it was as if somebody shined a light on their faces from outside. And they all sat so pale and quiet, moving their lips without a sound. Anders knew what they were doing—they were praying. He himself prayed,

> Now I close my eye
> O Father up on high—

but then came a crash that made the house quake and the panes rattle, and he gave a start on his stool and didn't get any further. Another flash came, he began once more and had time to say, "Now I close—," but then came a crash so sharp and angry you'd think God had cursed and hurled something at the mountain, and Anders could see the whites of his eyes. Everybody gave a start and someone whispered, "She struck something that time!" And in the next room Gorinè lay in bed bawling, "Whoo-oo-oo!"

Then there were no more crashes. It got brighter, something was over, everybody straightened up and started chatting and laughing, Gorinè came into the kitchen with grimy streaks down her face, and Embret went down to the woodshed again.

And now the thunderstorm had almost passed. God was on his way home, only a rumble was heard now and then, far away. Far, far away.

It was strange how quiet and peaceful it grew everywhere now that God went home.

Pussy lay on the stoop. He was quite still, looking straight ahead.

"Pussy!" Anders called. But Pussy let on he didn't hear. He just remained quiet, looking straight ahead with narrow yellow eyes; and sure enough, right in front of him was a wagtail. It bobbed its tail and bobbed its head and quickly thrust its beak into the ground and quickly raised its head and looked around. It looked at Pussy, but Pussy didn't move. And the wagtail hopped closer.

Anders wondered a moment if he should go over to help the wagtail. But if he did, he'd never see how it turned out if he didn't help it, and he was eager to see that too.

He hesitated, uncertain. But now the wagtail had come close enough, and Pussy arched his back and made a leap.

Anders also arched his back; but there was no danger— the wagtail was down by the cow barn already and Pussy stood there staring after it. He looked stupid and ashamed.

Anders grabbed Pussy by the back of his neck. From far away came a rumble, and Anders understood what it meant. It was God saying he ought to make a speech to Pussy.

He grabbed him firmly by the scruff of his neck and spoke to him:

"What are we going to do with you, jumping after little birds? You know quite well you can only catch mice and rats. Haven't you heard what happened to the cat who caught a bird? All the other birds came into his bed at night and pulled his ears, like this, and plucked his whiskers, like this, and pulled his tail, like this, and stroked him the wrong way, like this!"

Pussy meowed and Anders looked him straight in the eye to see if he was sorry; Pussy's eyes were a yellow slit, and they were green in the middle. But he didn't seem to be sorry.

Anders turned around to look for the thundercloud. But it was gone, and you couldn't hear a sound. God had gone home. If he hadn't been so far away, perhaps he would have let the lightning strike Pussy because he wasn't sorry. But now there seemed to be no danger of that.

Anders took Pussy on his arm and stroked him the right way. Pussy began to purr.

Anders walked into the kitchen with him. There was nobody there, but on the table stood a bowl of cream.

Just in case, Anders glanced out the window and looked for the thundercloud once more. But it was nowhere to be seen. And Anders looked at Pussy and at the bowl of cream and knew he was very happy that God had gone home.

And then came the evening. It had grown so quiet. The chickens had gone to sleep, the cows had gone to sleep. He too would soon go in and go to sleep. He sat out on the stoop. The sun had set. High up, the night came sailing on a cloud. Then the trees began to tremble and to flutter their leaves, whispering about something he couldn't quite understand. The trees were all solemn, and somewhere in the twilight God was waiting. Everything was holding its breath and waiting. The flowers were quietly waiting, the crow in the birch was waiting, black and silent, another crow came winging its way, alighted in the neighboring birch and began waiting, everything was quiet and the night was drawing closer, the dark trees far away were coming closer, and

God came wandering into the garden along with the twilight.

Mother came out on the stoop and took him in her arms. He was almost asleep. She carried him in and put him to bed. She helped him with his clothes and with his evening prayer. Then she left. He lay there alone looking out of the window. He could barely see anything anymore, but a big murmur passed through the garden, then a long sigh, several long sighs, and a big rushing sound. It was God who had entered the garden and was wandering up and down among the trees. They murmured and spoke to him, and he murmured and answered them. A stream of sound—whispers, talk, a faint roar—flowed into the room. Then he fell asleep.

To God to Complain

ONCE UPON A TIME everybody had been so mean to him....

He sat inside the spruce hedge between the garden and the road, where he'd gone to hide. Everybody had been so mean to him and nobody loved him. Åse had pushed him and Tora had pulled his hair and Kari had laughed at him and Gorinè had been angry. And Tora had told on him and Gorinè had hit him, and when he rushed out into the yard and couldn't see a thing because he was crying, he ran into a pail of slops Gorinè had put there, just so, overturned the pail and hit his leg, fell and made a big bump on his forehead, and nobody came to help him, for Father and Mother weren't home, and nobody cared about him, and Gorinè came out on the stoop and yelled, "There you are again, you naughty brat! I'll teach you, just you wait!" And Tora and Kari shouted, "Boo to you, you naughty brat! Boo to you, you naughty brat!" and so he slipped away and hid in the spruce hedge.

He heard Tora and Kari and Åse on the stoop. Tora had gotten the water out of her shoes. Gorinè said, "Sure, they're dry. Bad boy. You go now, and be nice girls!"

They walked down toward the pasture, laughing and

hollering. They were going to the strawberry patch to eat all the strawberries. It was he who'd thought of it, but they wouldn't let him come along.

And Father and Mother were far away.

Pussy came walking up the road. He called, "Pussy! Pussy!"

But Pussy walked by and didn't want anything to do with him.

He couldn't help crying again, because nobody wanted anything to do with him. But his crying sounded so lonely here where nobody could hear him; frightened, he quieted down, just sniffling as the tears continued flowing.

Then he happened to look up at the roof of the barn, where the sun was shining behind a big cloud. And the very same moment he knew what he had to do. He had to go to God to complain.

God was far away. He lived in the sunset, Mother had said. And that was far away, behind the barn, and there he'd hardly ever been, and never by himself. But now he didn't know of anybody closer.

He got up at once and started to walk.

He walked and he walked. Across the road and toward the barn and the sunset, toward God. He sniffled and cried. But not aloud, for then Gorinè might hear him and come. And God was sure to hear him anyway.

He walked and he walked. But then he got into a big shadow and understood he'd taken the wrong road, for the shadow was coming from the roof of the barn. And he understood it wasn't possible to get to God by walking straight ahead, he would have to go back again, make a big loop around the pigsty and the pigpen and around.

He turned and walked back again in the direction of the upper corner of the pigsty with the pigpen. A big, pretty buttercup was right in front of him, he could have picked it. If he held it under somebody's chin, he could see if they'd eaten much butter recently. But he left it alone, mustn't let himself be stopped, because he was going to God to complain. And besides, he had nobody to hold it under the chin of, for everybody was so mean to him. And thinking about that, he began to sniffle and cry again.

"Oink, oink!" said the big sow, rubbing her sides against the wall of the pigpen. "Oink, oink!"

At first he could barely hear it, because his mind wasn't on it. But then he heard it. She asked him to scratch her a bit behind the ears. And of course he would have liked to, for she was so nice when she was contented and gave out her little grunts: Oink-oink-oink-oink! But he didn't have the time, because he was going to God to complain and mustn't let himself be stopped by anything and mustn't forget to sniffle and cry.

Around the pigpen grew some sorrel, big bunches of it. That was one of the best things he knew, because his mouth filled with water when he chewed it, and it tickled him and tasted sour in his mouth, forcing him to laugh. But he merely looked at the red sorrel standing there, without stopping to pick any, and went on—he couldn't take the time because he was going to God to complain.

A strange cat was coming toward him, it was gray and striped like the tiger in the book. It poked the stalks of grass with its jaws and asked him to scratch its jaws a little. He stopped to say he certainly would have liked to, because it was such fun to hear cats purr. But he didn't have the time, for he mustn't let himself be stopped by anybody, because he was going to God to complain.

And now he was almost on the other side of the pigsty and the pigpen, and soon he would be on the other side of the barn and would walk straight toward the sunset and God.

He had to decide what to say to God.

He would say:

"I'm only a little boy and everybody's been mean to me. Åse pushed me and Tora pulled my hair and Kari laughed at me and Gorinè was angry. And Tora told on me and Gorinè hit me, for Gorinè is a woman and sides with the girls against me, and when Father and Mother are away she always hits me...."

It occurred to him that he would have to tell the truth to God. And actually she might have hit him only once before. He repeated it again, "...and when Father and Mother are away from home, she often hits me and says I'm naughty."

He stopped for a moment.

But perhaps God would ask him, "Why did you pour water in Tora's shoes?"

And then he would answer:

"I did it because Tora was naughty. For she wouldn't take me to the strawberry patch because she said I'd been mean to Åse. That's why I poured a little water in her shoes, just to tease her a bit. I hadn't figured she would put them on, I had only thought she'd find them and see the water in them, and I would sit watching her when she saw the water in them...."

Now he felt safe, and was sure that God would side with him. And so he went on.

The field was thick with clover. It was full of clover and

the fragrance of clover, and full of bumblebees flying about, each humming its own tune. He remembered he'd known it, but now he'd forgotten it. He stopped in order to recall it again. But there were so many bumblebees, all singing at the same time. He couldn't catch the tune. And then he remembered he had to get on, for he was going to God to complain and mustn't let himself be stopped by anything. And he would say to God:

"I'm only a little boy, nobody loves me and everybody's mean to me. Åse pushed me and Tora pulled my hair and Kari laughed at me and Gorinè was angry. And Tora told on me and Gorinè hit me, and all of them stick together against me and eat up the strawberries for me. And Pussy wants none of me, and Father and Mother are far away...."

He walked and he walked. He had reached the other side of the pigsty and the pigpen a long time ago, now he was coming around the barn and saw the sunset and God.

God shone with such a strong light.

God shone with such an awfully strong light that it couldn't be the sunset yet, so he didn't have to hurry just yet. For God shone much too strongly. So he thought he'd look around a bit first.

The grounds were wide here, with cultivated fields and meadows. There were lots of bumblebees all over, one of them buzzed right past his nose and he nearly caught the tune, but then it was gone again.

He came to a ditch and had to cross it, for there were so many pretty flowers on the other side. And God too was on the other side.

He looked about him, but there was nobody to help him across. Then he understood he was supposed to help himself.

He stepped down into the ditch.

It was a bit wet and muddy at the bottom of the ditch, but there was quite a lot of grass, and many flowers. An old dung beetle sat there looking at him. It was so old that it had a green back. Maybe it was an old sorcerer or a bewitched prince. Or perhaps it was only an ordinary old dung beetle. He asked to find out, but it didn't answer, just sat quite still, and he couldn't tell for sure if it was looking at him or not.

Then he happened to recall something Embret had said about the dung beetle. The dung beetle was the strongest animal there was, Embret said. The flea was one of the strongest, for a flea could jump so high that, if we jumped that high, we could jump higher than the church steeple. But the dung beetle could carry on its back a piece of lead bigger than itself. Embret had read this in a magazine once.

He looked about him for something he could test the dung beetle with and noticed a big earthworm that had its home underneath a big wet lump of dirt. It was big and pink and the same at both ends like an earthworm should be, and had a lot of pink rings all over its body like an earthworm should have. It stretched and coiled and seemed to be looking around but wasn't, because earthworms are blind.

Right beside the earthworm grew some big, pretty plantains, which were almost as big as a tea bowl and almost as round. He would take the earthworm and put it on the plantain, then put the plantain on the dung beetle's back to see if the dung beetle could carry the earthworm. It might not be as heavy as a piece of lead that was bigger than the dung beetle, but it would certainly be quite heavy and much bigger than the dung beetle. And besides he didn't have a piece of lead.

He took the earthworm, put it on the plantain and talked to it.

"Now you must be a sensible earthworm and not get scared for I won't do you any harm or put you on a hook and fish with you, but just place you on the back of this dung beetle so we can see how strong he is."

It almost looked as if the earthworm understood him, stupid as the earthworm no doubt was, without a head and all, because it coiled up in the middle of the plantain to make a fine load for the dung beetle. But the moment he was going to put his fine load on the dung beetle's back, the beetle raised its body shield, let out a pair of clear wings, fluttered them a little, turned and buzzed them a little and flew off.

He just sat there, staring. He'd never heard that dung beetles could fly. Then maybe it wasn't even a real dung beetle. Then maybe it was a sorcerer after all, or a prince perhaps....

He took the earthworm and put it back. It immediately stuck one end under the lump of clay, as if it wanted to hang on to it and never touch the plantain again. He stuck the plantain in the ground close to where it had stood, for when it was called plantain it could no doubt be planted again where it had grown. And he began to look about him for other things.

A bit farther down the ditch was a nice big puddle. It glittered green and brown and bright, almost like the wings of a pretty butterfly. He walked over to the puddle and pulled off one of his boots and the stocking. The other bootlace had a difficult knot he couldn't untie, so he'd better wade with that boot on.

The water splashed briskly around his foot and gave his stocking a good cold soaking. Some nice rings formed on the surface of the puddle, and the bright green layer came apart, turning into shimmering dust like on a real butterfly wing. Then something yellow surged up from the bottom, and the whole puddle became yellow and muddy. He sat down at the edge and rowed in the water with a stick. The puddle looked like a big yellow lake with muddy yellow shores, without a house as far as the eye could see. But perhaps there were trolls and big animals on the bottom of the lake, and if he stirred it up even more perhaps the troll would pop out of the lake with the water pouring off it and look at him with big, glittering green eyes—"Boo! Now I'll come and get you!" said the troll.

He became so scared he dropped the stick and screamed. But the same moment Pussy came walking up the ditch, and that meant the troll wouldn't be coming, for there was no lake anymore but only a puddle, and now the mud was settling again too, and in the tiny cove the green stuff began once more to form a layer on top.

When Pussy saw Anders this time it accepted him at once, came over to him, poked him with both its jaws by turns and began to purr. Anders scratched its jaws. Pussy purred; afterward it shook its head because Anders' hands had been wet and shook its paws one after the other because the ground had been wet under it. Then it rubbed its cheeks against its paws awhile and licked itself a little. Now it was nice and clean and climbed up on the edge of the ditch, lay down on its side and lazily snatched at a butterfly with its paw.

But Anders had noticed something. Right beside the

puddle was a lump of clay, and it looked exactly like Gorinè. That is, actually the only likeness was the wart on its cheek, the rest wasn't very alike. Anders set about making the rest look alike too, and little by little there was likeness in everything.

He had meant to drown Gorinè in the pool as soon as she was finished, because he was so angry with her. But then she was such a fine likeness that he grew fond of her and couldn't make himself drown her right away. It occurred to him he could simply take another lump of clay and make Tora, who had been very naughty, and drown her in the pool instead. He found a nice lump of clay and began to make Tora. That was much more difficult, for she didn't have a wart he could start with—actually she had nothing he could start with. But in the end he discovered he could start with her mouth, which she opened wide when she said, "Boo to you, you naughty brat!," and then he caught her likeness at once. Afterward he made Kari and Åse, and now he'd become so good at it he could do it like nothing. Kari and Åse were only a bit smaller and still a bit smaller and opened their mouths wide and said, "Boo to you, you naughty brat!"

He planted them one after another along the edge of the puddle.

Now he really ought to drown them in the pool. But they'd become so pretty he didn't really want to drown them; rather, he felt like calling every one of them and asking them to come and look at all the pretty things he'd made.

But Tora wouldn't sit straight, he had to support her with a stick. He had to run the stick clean through her before she would sit straight.

When he'd done this he thought he might as well put a stick through Kari too, since Tora had a stick.

Now they were both dead, being run through with a stick. But he didn't put a stick through Åse, for she was so small. Not through Gorinè either, for she was so nice and had a wart on her cheek with three hairs on it, and he was afraid she'd break if he put a stick through her.

When he'd done all this he happened to look up. Then he noticed that God had gone into hiding behind a big blue cloud. Perhaps he'd gone to bed. Perhaps God was angry because he hadn't come at once.

He felt a little scared. But he felt a little happy too, because he'd certainly been quite scared of what God might have to say about Tora's shoes.

Perhaps he would have asked about that cake of Åse's too—but that was really much too big for Åse, who was so small.

Now it had gotten too late to go to God today. It would have to wait until some other time.

Suddenly he felt so proud and happy.

He was so happy that he had to shout something. He stood up and shouted,

> Tora, Tora, boo!
> Go put on your shoe!

For that was what he'd wanted her to do.

It sounded so pretty, so after shouting it once he had to shout it once more,

> Tora, Tora, boo!
> Go put on your shoe!

And once more,

> Tora, Tora, boo!
> Go put on your shoe!

He shouted it again and again, so loud that it echoed back from the wall of the barn. Each time he felt more and more happy and proud. And suddenly he could hear it was a song he'd made. One of those that rhymed. Like

> Old Man Joe
> bit his toe.

Or like

> Little Peter Lassen cried and cried
> for his fishing boat swept out by the tide.

He called as loudly as he could,

> Tora, Tora, boo!
> Go put on your shoe!

He had never known anything like it before. He felt as if he was growing moment by moment. He owned the ditch he was standing in and the field around it, the fence over there with a magpie on it and the brown horse and the yellow foal on the other side, the big dark hill and the sun yonder behind the bank of clouds—he owned it all because it was in his song. The words seemed to change every time he called them out, they meant everything and he owned it all.

He felt so happy he wished Tora and Kari could be there, then he would share it all with them.

He called and called,

> Tora, Tora, boo!
> Go put on your shoe!

Pussy had gotten up and was looking at him in amazement with its narrow, yellow eyes.

Finally he had no more strength and no more voice and sat down in the ditch. In a moment he was asleep.

He woke up from Gorinè standing over him.

She was quite beside herself.

"Thank God I've found you. I've been so worried about you. I've been everywhere—but then I heard you call and understood you were scared, poor little darling!"

She looked more closely at him.

"Oh but—phew, phew, the way you've been rolling in the dirt!"

The Trolls in the Hedal Forest

EVERYTHING had become different.
¶ The days weren't the same anymore. People were often angry and ill-tempered and went early to bed. The sun went into hiding, it rained and blew. The birches along the garden fence shivered and trembled, and Ol' Man North-Wind tore off their leaves as he swept past.

The evenings were pitch-dark, and around the corner a mournful dog howled and howled.

It was the fall, said the grownups. They coughed and hawked and blew their noses, and looked for the sun with sullen eyes. It was the fall, they said.

For quite a while fall was rather fun all the same. That was when the grain was harvested. There came many more people than usual then, and some of them were new. One was named Anton, and that was strange, for in the haying season there was also someone named Anton, but he was much shorter and had red hair, not brown, and many freckles in his face. So there were two named Anton.

Afterward the sheaves were put on poles to dry. And during the day it was fun to play hide-and-seek behind the grain poles. But in the evening, when dusk came, the field was full of big, dark, shaggy goblins who were quietly watching him and listening; but when the fog came drifting in, all the goblins began to move, to walk and walk, getting bigger and coming closer in their big hairy hides. Then Anders went in.

One day some birds were seen high in the sky, flying south in wedge formation.

"The graylag geese!" said the grownups, standing still for a moment and following them with their eyes. Way south the wedge shape was lost in the sky.

It was the fall, they said again. And they stood for a moment before bending over their work again. Anders saw they were sad and became very sad himself.

But there were still many days of fun, for lots of people came back to the farm to dig potatoes and stayed out in the potato field all day. The weather was cold and fog lingered in the tree tops, but they made a fire out in the field. And when their hands got cold from the wet, cold earth, they came over to the fire and held them over the smoke, talking and laughing. Anders stood watching Anton. Now it was the one from the haying season again, but his freckles were almost gone. He was the nicest Anton, because he had tufts of hair in his ears. A moment later Anders found himself alone by the fire, all the grownups were digging on the slope again, and Anders could only see their legs, and their rear ends pointing skyward. Still higher in the sky, there flew a couple of crows.

But one day all the potatoes had been dug up and all the grain poles gotten under cover. The fields were empty. Only Embret walked around in the grain field and the potato plot, gathering rakes and poles, hoes and empty potato crates. It rained on him, so he got wet. And everything was more lonesome than before.

It wasn't so nice outdoors anymore now. What had been fun wasn't so much fun any longer. It was no fun to crawl under the hayloft looking for eggs, for the ground was damp and cold and it was dark, and there weren't any eggs anymore. It was no fun to jaywalk in the roadside ditch and get his feet wet, because it was so cold and much too wet. It wasn't even fun to run and make himself fall on the leaves in the yard, because they were so sticky and nasty and his fanny got wet and cold right away.

He was alone. There weren't any birds to be seen in the yard anymore, only a crow now and then, but it was so gray and black and screamed so loud that it almost didn't count as a bird.

Anders clearly remembered fall last year. It was dark then too, and the wind blew and the rain splashed against the windowpanes. But, somehow, last year's rain wasn't as wet as this year's rain, and if he slipped on the leaves then, his fanny wasn't as cold as now.

Yes, in the old days fall was better, he thought.

But in the kitchen it was nice. A fire burned in the stove and on the hearth. Under the stove lay Pussy, his eyes narrow and green. And the strange thing was that when he lay under the stove there was a green light in his eyes, but when Anders pulled him out so he could look at the green light, it was gone.

Every now and then Anders and Åse would sit quietly in their chairs. For Gorinè had such a knack for telling fairy tales. She told them about the little boys who ran into the trolls in the Hedal Forest.

Once upon a time there were two little boys from a small

cottage a bit north of here, and they were so poor they didn't have a morsel of food but had to tramp around with bag and pail and beg their bread. One fall they wanted to cross the Hedal Forest to the Hedal Valley and lost their way in the thick of the forest; they were overtaken by darkness, and a wind was blowing in the forest. Whoo-oo-oo! said the wind. They settled down under a crag. The elder had his little ax with him, and he lopped off some pine branches and gathered moss so they'd have something to lie on. And there they were, cold and shivering and both hungry and weary, they hadn't tasted food or drink all day. And it was so pitch-dark around them that they couldn't see their own hands in front of them, and the wind roared in the forest. Whoo-oo-oo! it said.

All at once they heard shuffling footsteps in the forest, so heavy that the ground quaked and thundered. Then they understood that the trolls of the Hedal Forest were roaming around. The trolls began to yowl and carry on.

"Whoo-oo-oo!" said the trolls. "Here it smells of Christian man's blood!" they said.

Gorinè didn't get any further, for Åse became so scared she began to cry and couldn't stand hearing any more. That was because she was so small and only a girl. And so she had to go to bed.

Anders wasn't scared. For he was bigger and a boy. He looked about him—the corner behind the big kitchen counter was quite dark, and it was even darker behind the cupboard, and the windows were very dark and terrible. But scared, no, that he wasn't, and so Gorinè had to tell the rest. And Anders heard about the trolls who had only one eye among them, but it was the size of a windowpane and shone like seven moons. And then he heard about the boy who cut the hamstrings of the hindmost troll with his little ax and took the eye away from it, and about the pail of gold and silver the boys brought home to their mother. But deep inside the Hedal Forest the trolls hobbled about looking for their eye and wailing.

"Me oh my! Me oh my! Whoo-oo-oo!" they said.

Then Anders wasn't at all scared anymore. For when it ended so well, then he wasn't scared. And when he turned five he, too, would get an ax; Father had said so.

But after a few moments had passed, he was perhaps a little scared anyway. For the flames fluttered on the hearth, the shadows leaped and danced around the walls, and outside it rained and blew to make the house quake. Whoo-oo-oo! it said. The door opened with a bang and it was pitch-dark in the hall, the front door was open and it was even darker outside, and the trees whistled and roared.

Anders thought of the tall trees down the hill on the way to the store. That was the Hedal Forest.

No, the Hedal Forest was the pine grove behind the potato cellar, because there it was so dark when it was dark.

And the dense spruce copse down in the pasture right behind the fence, that was the Hedal Forest.

Anders sat snug in his chair by the fireplace, and he wasn't scared. But he would never step out of the kitchen anymore.

Anders sat under the kitchen table. He and Åse were playing hide-and-seek. It was the easiest thing to hide from Åse, she was so afraid she didn't dare look for him where it was dark. He could have hidden in the nook behind the kitchen counter, for there it was quite dark. Or between the cupboard and the wall, there it was even darker. But it was darkest of all under the kitchen table, now that both flaps were down. It was the Hedal Forest.

Anders sat stock-still. Åse padded about pretending to look for him. She clearly knew where he was, but she would never dare search in the Hedal Forest itself.

It was very dark.

Outside the wind blew. Whoo-oo-oo!

If he hadn't been so much bigger than Åse, and a boy and much less afraid, he would have been quite scared.

Now and then one of the grownups crossed the floor, he could glimpse a bit of their legs under the edge of the table. That was nice, because then they were *there*. But they made a thundering noise when they walked, and everything trembled. The ground thundered and quaked.

The fire flickered on the hearth. The floor went light and dark, light and dark, and the shadows leaped and danced. It was the moonlight coming down among the trees in the Hedal Forest. No, it was the light from the troll eye, and the shadows—the shadows came from the trees swaying in the wind.

Whoo-oo-oo!

Anders sat still. Behind him were the shadows. Perhaps one of the shadows would stretch out a long arm and grab him. He didn't dare move, because then it might come and get him. And he didn't dare turn around, because then it would quite certainly come and get him.

He clenched his fist as if clenching it around the little ax. In a year he would be five, then he would walk with the little ax in his hand and never be scared.

"Ollie, ollie, home free!" Åse called. Then she'd lost. She couldn't find him and had to be *it* again.

When Anders had to find a new hiding place, he thought he'd rather not crawl under the table anymore tonight. Not that he was scared. For it wasn't dangerous, it was only the kitchen table after all. But he'd rather find some other place.

Gorinè was preparing supper by the stove. He could hide under her skirt, then he would be closer to people. Strange that he hadn't thought of that before.

"May I hide under your skirt, Gorinè?" Anders whispered.

She looked at him. She laughed, but then she nodded. Anders crawled under her skirt. It reached all the way to the floor. Now Åse couldn't see him.

"Go look then, Åse!" he heard high above him. It was so far away.

The heat from the stove was coming at him clean through the skirt. It was dark. Darker than under the table. He only glimpsed something red through the cloth of the skirt; it must be the air hole in the stove. He was uncomfortable but couldn't move. He shouldn't have done this. Under the table it was light and cozy. He moved a little, for he was so uncomfortable, but he touched something right away, so he gave a sudden start and kept sitting there quiet as a mouse.

What was it? Something was coming with heavy steps, making the floor boom and quake. He felt a cold draft sitting there, heard a whistling and a roaring, a clumping and a stamping, then a deep voice saying something, coughing and hawking, yowling and carrying on. "Whoo-oo-oo!" it said.

He didn't dare breathe. This was the Hedal Forest. It was pitch-dark in the forest, he couldn't see his hand in front of him. He was locked in. The troll's hamstrings were right behind him. The ugly troll eye had a red glow. It kept looking and looking at him. *Now they were coming to get him!*

What was that booming and thumping in the forest?

It was his heart, going thump, thump.

"Whoo-oo-oo!" it said behind him.

It wasn't true that he wasn't scared. He was terribly scared, and if he got away this time he'd never lie any more or make himself more brave than he was.

"Ollie, ollie, home free!" he heard. It was so far away.

"Well, Anders, you can come out now," Gorinè said, high above him.

He crawled out.

And then it was only the hired hands who'd come in and sat down at the table. He had known it all along. After all, it was threshing day today.

They laughed when they saw him. They laughed and laughed.

"Well, now, where have you been?" Anton said.

Then they laughed.

"So you get under Gorinè's skirt, eh?" Anton said.

They laughed. Anton became more and more cocky.

"You start early, I'd say!" Anton said.

Then they laughed again. Anton laughed the most. He laughed so much that the tufts of hair in his ears wiggled and wiggled.

Everyone laughed. Embret laughed. Gorinè laughed. Even Åse, who was so small and scared and only a girl, she laughed too.

Anders shrugged it off. He didn't look at Anton. Once when Anton was asleep he would pull those tufts of hair out of his ears. He didn't look at Åse. Tomorrow he would take Åse and plunk her smack on her fanny among the wet leaves. And Gorinè—. Anyway, it didn't matter about Gorinè, for Gorinè was old and had moss on her back. And now he was *happy*. For now he sat safely on his stool by the fireplace, and nobody was coming to get him. He hadn't been very much scared, for it had all been just in fun, and he'd known that from the beginning; but he would never, never go into the Hedal Forest again.

The Snake

H E   S T O O D in the north attic. Outside it was daylight, but in there it was dusky, as always. That's where the dusk came from in the evening, it rolled like a dark fog down the stairs and filled all the rooms on the ground floor.

The shadows had their home there.

There were two windows, with many panes in them. But they faced north and all the panes were full of dust, and the whole attic was full of things that cast shadows. There were old chairs on three legs, an old cabinet without a door, a lopsided chest of drawers, two black mangles, a broken hanging-lamp full of cobwebs, a pile of cracked old bowls and troughs, two rusty candlesticks, a tattered Bible, masses of mouldy old Sunday clothes hung up in rows on long rods—they fluttered in the draft, coming alive. There were some old black spinning wheels and yarn reels and a large red-painted loom. There were old skin rugs, a large sheep-skin coat and a sledge apron of brown dog's hide. In the corners lay heaps of old boots, gaping with black toothless mouths, or with mouths full of yellow eyelets and fangs.

All this was something he knew from before. For the north attic was a fun place when they were many. But now he was alone, he had been put in there for punishment. The door closed behind him with a bang.

He didn't dare to move, didn't dare turn around and look,

because behind him something sat quietly watching him. He didn't dare to scream. He didn't dare close his eyes, didn't dare keep them open and look.

Then he saw it. Way back in the darkest corner there sat something dark and stared at him. First it was a boot with two red eyes; but then it moved a little when he moved and was a rat which sat staring at him in the corner behind the gray chest.

His heart skipped several beats, as if pondering. Then it beat fast, fast. Then it stopped again.

Had he moved anyway? Suddenly the rat hunched down in the corner. It hissed. Then it darted across the floor toward him, looking like a big ball of brown thread with the end of the thread trailing, and it hissed and hissed as it rolled toward him, its body flush with the floor, without feet.

He screamed a short scream and jumped a step back. That was enough. The rat got scared and swerved around him, then rolled on, fast, fast, reached the other corner and was gone. His legs gave way under him.

He sat quite still. Not a sound could be heard up there in the big shadowy attic. It was so quiet that his ears were ringing, so quiet it made you think you heard the dust falling and falling, quietly and invisibly, slowly covering everything in there. Now and then an almost inaudible snap, from a chair or a cupboard, a rustle in some corner. Almost inaudible, a dusty cobweb of a sound.

Somebody came in. Who was it? He couldn't remember afterward.

"You'll be a good boy now, won't you?" she said.

Then she must have noticed something in his eyes—she lifted him up and carried him out with her.

He was out in the open, far away from home. Andrea had taken him along. It was a Sunday at dusk.

Spring was on the way; the sky was as it is in spring, but there was still a bit of snow on the ground. Some snow must have fallen overnight, it lay fresh and white. But underneath was ice and it was bumpy and uneven—the weather had been mild and the snow had melted to slush, which had frozen to ice with tracks after many boots.

They stood in the yard at Berg. It was a vast yard. A regular crowd was gathered there, tall and grown-up all of them, except him.

The yard was white, but all the paths were gray with ice, and wet. The snow was still sticky from the sunshine earlier in the day, but now it was turning cold, someone said. From every roof in the yard streamed a trickle of water, as happens on Sundays in early spring. Down where he stood, among all those grownups, it smelled of wool and water and sticky snow, and of wet leather from all the boots. The grownups stood in a circle, talking and laughing. There were men's feet and women's skirts on every side of him, he heard talk and laughter over his head, the water trickling from the roofs far away, and the crunching snow nearby when they shifted their feet. Without noticing, some man stood with one boot in a puddle of water—there was a splash whenever he moved his foot.

A voice rang out, *The bull has broken loose!* And suddenly he was alone.

It was like in a dream. He stood still, unable to move. But he could see everything, and he saw everything at once.

He looked in all directions at once, and the things he saw cut across each other and got mixed up, being all there in the same moment; he himself was in the middle and yet he wasn't there. He saw all the grownups running away from him, one dense throng of backs, one big black living spot against the white snow; skirts flapped, heel plates twinkled and boots clumped. The bull was coming, a dark spot far off, way down by the cow barn, he roared and roared and grew bigger and bigger. Between him and the bull lay the white yard with its gray paths, empty and tremendously large but smaller and smaller as the bull came nearer and nearer. In the middle of the yard was a black square amid all the white, that was the well—the well-pole looked like a long black line running slantways up the red wall of the barn, up the white roof and way into the gray-blue sky. A thin black cord hung from the end of the pole, tracing a line down the gray-blue sky, through the white snow, across two of the gray paths and down to the handle of a bucket hanging straight over the well. Now the bull roared louder, he'd reached the well. What if the well barred his way—; what if the well-pole went down and blocked his path—.

Something detached itself from all those backs and turned, it was Andrea; she jumped back, got hold of his arm and almost pulled it off him—he swept through the air, his ears ringing, a door was opened before them and slammed behind them with a crash that made the house shake; they were in a dark room full of people, the men braced their backs against the door, the door crashed and crashed, the house shook, and the girls pressed together around the window in order to look, cried and didn't dare look. A man's voice was heard outside, it was the dairyman, someone said—there he got hold of the nose ring. Afterward they all pushed their way out of the servants' quarters and saw the dairyman leading the bull far down the yard—it was all over, everyone was talking at the same time and laughing, and there hadn't been any danger at all.

Then they went home. Andrea carried him part of the way, for he wasn't very good at walking, his legs somehow refused to carry him; but he'd been very plucky, had neither screamed nor cried, and if he kept it up he'd be very plucky when he grew up. And when they got home he'd better not tell about any of this, for there hadn't been any danger at all. Andrea's cheeks had broad streaks from crying.

He didn't say anything at home and Andrea stroked his hair, gave him a cake and whispered that he was very plucky. But how strange—he had no desire to play that evening, and every once in a while he would stand stock-still; he felt as if he stood in a vast empty yard and *it* was coming at him—the well was so still and cold and the well-pole rose slantways up the sky, quiet and cold.

Bedtime came and he was put to bed. He slept and dreamed. He stood alone in a vast white yard, deserted and empty, and *something* was coming at him. Everybody had left him. The well looked cold and still and didn't move, and the well-pole looked cold and quiet, pointing up at the sky like a long finger and not moving. It turned its long, cold back on him and didn't move. He was alone, and a slow dread, cold and quiet, came over him. It pressed down on him, pierced his clothes, crept coldly down his spine, settled coldly around his chest, wound itself slowly about him so he couldn't breathe or walk but had to stand still while it kept coming toward him. "What's wrong with you, child?" Mother asked and woke him up. "You're moaning so terribly. Are you sick?"

He was very plucky and didn't say a word, only trembled a little; and Mother got scared and took him out of his little bed and into her own. There it wasn't dangerous, for it was so nice and warm there, and when *it* came from one side, Mother was on the other side, and she turned around, made a jump back and got hold of his arm, and he swept through the air into the living room and there was no danger.

"You're spoiling the boy!" Father said one evening. "He can't sleep in the same bed with us forever, you know." So Mother had to put him back in the little bed again. He was scared but very plucky and didn't scream or cry, he didn't dare to when Father said something. He fell asleep and dreamed the dream, and nobody turned around to help him. He woke up from moaning and from Father and Mother bending over his bed.

"Something must've happened to him," Mother said.

Father didn't say anything. But he patted his forehead. It was odd, as if he patted something away. The well-pole didn't stand there anymore, cold and quiet, turning its long back on him. He fell asleep and slept without dreams.

Afterward he was able to sleep without dreaming for many nights. But then the pat on his forehead seemed to wear off, and what Father had patted away returned. Once more he stood in a wide, vast yard. *Something* was coming at him—he woke up from screaming, and Father and Mother were bending over him. Then he knew that if Father patted his forehead, the evil thing would go away; but he couldn't ask him to do it.

Had it happened, or was it a dream?

He stood in the yard, it was evening and he was alone. The grownups had forgotten him outside. He wanted to scream, he wanted to run inside. Then they came jumping. Out from under the stoop, from the wall, past the corner, out of the roadside ditch—large, dark-brown toads with big warts on their backs and everywhere. Even their eyes were like big warts; but if you looked more closely, only the upper part of their eyes was a wart, a big fat wart; the lower part was a human eye, calm and blue. Then it wasn't a toad but a bewitched human, and the witch was waiting behind the corner, she would come forward in a moment and turn him into a toad.

Jump! The ground gave a little smack with each jump they made. They came closer with each jump. They spelled rain and were poisonous, had warts on their backs and big yellow bellies, and they edged closer and closer and wanted to get him. They came to get people who'd been mean to them, climbed into the house at night, clambered into people's beds and lay down on top of them, crept up the coverlet and into their mouths and suffocated them. That is, if you'd killed one of them.

Jump! They jumped closer. There were lots of them, the whole yard was full of them. There were two, three, many. But sometimes there was only one. And that one was bigger than all the other toads and jumped and jumped toward him, looking at him with big eyes under its big warts and jumping closer and closer, big and silent, with its swollen light-yellow belly. Then came somebody who'd heard him scream and helped him inside. Or he woke up, trembling and sweaty, and had only dreamed it all.

He sat on the rock putting sticks into a pine cone. It was the largest cone of all and would be the new big bull when he'd put horns on it, the old big bull would be a bell cow.

A loud, ugly scream came from the yard. It sounded like Andrea. Then he heard an angry man's voice, and afterward there were many excited voices all mixed up. He dropped the cone and ran around the house into the yard. When he got there, all the big ones were gathered in front of the washhouse. Andrea, Embret and Gorinè stood in the middle. Nearby sat a water tub, with its pole in place. Andrea was pointing here and there and talking in a shrill voice, "We were carrying the water tub and I walked first. Then I saw him right in front of my feet, I screamed, and Embret—." Here Embret cut in, talking in a loud, angry voice and pointing, "I was standing by the barn bridge setting teeth in this rake. Then I heard Andrea scream and I turned around sharply and saw him—." Andrea and Embret talked at the same time in loud, piercing voices. "He raised his head and hissed, I was about to step on him—I turned around, right where I am standing now, and—"

"Just then Embret turned around, grabbed the rake handle and—"

"He'd raised his head and was ready to strike. Then I gave him a blow on the head with the rake handle—"

"We came walking along where the water tub is sitting; I'd just told Gorinè—"

Suddenly Andrea began to cry and couldn't go on.

There was nothing to be seen. All the big ones stood in a tightly packed circle, bending forward and sticking out their behinds so you couldn't see anything.

Then all were gone except Embret, who kept pointing, and Father, who hadn't been there before. Anders stepped closer.

It wasn't a bit big. It looked just like a black stick. Anders felt they'd fooled him. He stepped closer.

It moved. It was all alive. Embret had killed it with the rake, and yet it never stopped twisting and turning. Anders felt a cold shiver all over and became terribly angry. He wanted to turn around and run away. He stepped closer.

Then he saw the three-cornered head.

"Nothing to cry about," Father said. "It's dead, it isn't dangerous anymore. It'll just have death spasms for a while, as long as the sun is shining on it."

Right then the sun passed behind a cloud, and it appeared to be a little less alive. Father opened its mouth with a stick and showed its fangs. Then he pointed at its eyes. The eyelids lay like a film over its eyes and were transparent like glass, the snake could see right through them and never blinked.

Embret said, "I stood over by the barn bridge setting teeth in this rake. Then I heard Andrea scream. I turned around sharply. His tongue was going in and out of his mouth and he was about to strike, and Andrea was barefoot and just stood there screaming. I swung the rake handle and hit the back of his head."

Anders didn't want to look at the snake anymore.

He looked and he looked.

He'd never seen anything so alive as the dead snake. He didn't want to look at it any more.

He looked at the three-cornered head and knew that he'd never seen anything so ugly and disgusting and dangerous before.

The snake was like nothing else in the whole world. Still he recognized it. It came crawling out of a bad dream.

He stared and stared at it.

The snake stared back at him, crawling and slithering.

Its eyes were evil, reddish and furious, and it was alive in every part even though it was dead. It stared at him, making him feel utterly alone. It didn't blink. It wasn't ashamed. It could see right through its eyelids. It saw right through him but pretended to lick the dust before him. It was ugly and disgusting and knew all.

He drew back step by step. Step by step. Finally the snake was nothing but a dark moving stick down by the washhouse. He heard the loud, angry voice of Embret: "I grabbed the rake this way..."

He turned and ran. When he had reached the stoop he turned around sharply. But the snake wasn't coming after him, it was only a little stick far down the yard.

When he grew up he would kill the snake.

When he grew up—. But he felt that deep down he didn't believe he'd ever be big enough to kill the snake.

A carriage turned into the yard one evening in late summer. Everybody knew the yellowish-brown horse with its black falling mane. When it came galloping along, with a clatter of hoofs and a rumble of wheels, its mane like a black cloud behind its head and the dust like a white cloud behind the carriage, everybody knew that Svartbekken was on the road. His horse was called Sorrel. Svartbekken drove around the parish buying up cattle for slaughter. He had a farm, also called Svartbekken; but it was far away, and there he did nothing but drink.

The carriage turned into the yard. In the carriage sat Svartbekken, big and broad. His nose was gnarled and blue. He had small, pale, red-rimmed pig's eyes. He didn't have a beard but was unshaven, his stubble stood out like pig's bristle. He had a crooked pipe between his teeth, and the spit had run down along the mouthpiece till it formed a yellow brook in the stubble.

He waved a greeting with his long whip and called to Father, standing on the stoop, "Well, are we going to do any trading today?"

"Hm—I don't know…," Father said.

Svartbekken stepped heavily down from his carriage. Father and Mother and Svartbekken went down to the cow barn.

Anders walked up to Sorrel and looked him over, as he'd seen the grownups do. He was soaked with sweat and foaming at the mouth, the foam dribbled from the bit onto the ground. His eyes were wild as if he didn't know anybody; and when Anders tried to stroke his muzzle, as the grownups used to do with horses, he became quite furious, tossed his head and showed the whites of his eyes. Anders got scared and ran to the cow barn.

They were standing beside Skoglin's stall. Svartbekken pushed his finger hard into Skoglin's side. She turned her large head and looked at him with her heavy eyes. He grunted and turned to the calf pen. There stood Anton, the bull calf. Åse and Anders had played with him all summer. They could remember him from the time he was newly born, staggering on his spindly long legs and being dumb and droll. Now he was much bigger but just as much fun and as droll. They'd called him Anton because he had such hairy ears.

Anton came to the front of his stall at once, tilted his head and wanted to play. Svartbekken poked his thick finger hard into his side, as if he wanted to pierce a hole and pull out something. Anton thought he did it to play and bent his head sideways with a gentle look in his eyes, trying to butt his hand; but Svartbekken didn't look at him any longer, he was talking to Father about the price, waving his arms and yelling. They were enemies. But suddenly they were friends, and Father had sold Skoglin and Anton. They walked out into the yard again, and Svartbekken went inside with them. Then he came out again, cracked his whip and drove off—he had to take another spin before nightfall and would pick up the cattle in a couple of days. Father kept walking back and forth in the yard, he had a queer look in his face and strange eyes, and was angry. Suddenly he stopped, shot out his fist as if trying to hit someone, turned red in the face and cried, "I should've asked twenty kroner more!"

"Twenty kroner at least!" he cried. Anders crept quietly into the shadow, around the corner and away. He saw that Father was dangerous, for him and for everyone.

The same evening but long afterward, perhaps an hour, perhaps more, he heard a rumble down the road. He was still sitting where he'd gone to hide, in the ditch between the garden and the road. Some birches there had branches that almost touched the ground, and nobody could find him there.

It was Svartbekken coming. But now he drove much faster than before. Sorrel was dark with sweat and running with his head against his chest, for Svartbekken held the reins so tight; the foam streamed from the horse's mouth. And Svartbekken sat in the carriage, his face red like raw meat, his nose blue like entrails; he hissed and cursed and squirted spit, and the spit trickled down his bristly beard.

He kept throwing his body from side to side in the carriage, lashing out at Sorrel's head without pause, and the whiplash whistled, winding itself like a snake around his muzzle, and Sorrel ran with upturned, bloodshot eyes blind with terror. It was twilight. A heavy thundercloud had rolled up above the edge of the hill; it had made a couple of rumbles already, far away, and when Svartbekken snapped his whip driving past, his red face seemed to drive clean through the menacing blue cloud. Anders threw himself forward and prayed: God! Strike him! God! Strike him! But then he was gone, the cloud was still, nothing happened, God had turned his back; and Svartbekken was hissing and snapping far off yonder, with a rumble of wheels and a cloud of dust behind him—there he vanished at the turn of the road. The dust slowly settled on the flowers and grass on both sides of the road. Long afterward there came a harmless delayed rumble from the cloud, it was like an old man walking around by himself, humming and grumbling. Now he didn't hear the rattle of the carriage any longer. The forest, the fields and the meadows were darkened by the heavy shadow of the cloud.

Anders sat and sat. It was getting dark. He was scared of the dark but continued to sit there, afraid to go in. He'd seen Father's eyes as he walked back and forth in the yard and knew that Father would sell him to Svartbekken for twenty kroner.

There was a country that was not a dreamland, nor a wide-awake world. Sometimes he would find himself there, unable to sleep or wake up, he just lay still; he tried to sit up but couldn't, he wanted to scream but couldn't. *Some-*

thing was coming toward him. It came rolling along the floor, it came riding across the yard, it came crawling toward him out of a dream, it was like God with transparent eyelids and evil eyes and *knew all*. He looked at the snake, which was God, and at God who was the snake, and he couldn't move, or tell if he was asleep or awake, until he woke up from screaming and heard Father talking angrily to him from the big bed, as if he'd been disturbed. Then he knew he was awake and, wonderfully relieved, lay down to sleep.

The grownups talked about the devil, and they talked about death. They often spoke gaily about the devil. He was lame, had a horse's hoof on one leg and was really a kind and stupid man. But about death they spoke cautiously and in subdued voices. He was a skeleton with a scythe over his shoulder and walked around mowing down everything living, like grass. He was an old man with a rake gathering everything living, like hay. He was an old woman with a broom who swept up everything living, like straw. He walked through closed doors and placed himself at the head or foot of the bed when somebody was ill. One and all became strange when they talked about him, their voices sank and became shadows of voices, and the fire on the hearth sank and became the shadow of a fire.

But to Anders death and the devil were one and the same. And he was not a skeleton with a scythe over his shoulder nor an old woman with a broom. He was Svartbekken, red in the face like raw meat, blue around his nose like entrails, with small, angry pig's eyes and a beard like pig's bristle, and jaws that hissed yellow spit and ugly words. That was how he drove across the earth with his whistling whip, under a mutely threatening sky that still didn't strike him down— and an evil three-cornered head with evil eyes without eyelids stared, mute and calm, at all the evil that happened, and let it happen. He had seen it this way once—or dreamed it, he wasn't sure.

The Fox

I T WAS WINTERTIME. Everything was white outdoors. A bird sat in the birch by the garden gate, wagging its long tail and chattering. It was a magpie, they said. He was standing in the yard. The sun shone, the birch sparkled and the magpie chattered away, but you couldn't make snowballs; the snow was just cold and white and slipped between your fingers like sugar, and something was nipping at his ears. He ran inside—it was a Saturday, but he'd forgotten about that. They'd just washed the big, dark, cold entrance hall, and the wet floor had frozen over and was covered with a thin layer of ice. He came at a run, slipped and fell, and his left ankle hurt terribly. That was because he'd wanted to throw a snowball at the magpie's head, he thought. Mother had told him never to throw anything at birds. He lay on the floor, unable to stand on his leg. He was crying, but nobody felt sorry for him or came to help him up. He had to crawl across the floor to the door.

They said he was naughty. He cried in the morning when they put on his stockings and shoes. He cried in the evening when they pulled them off him again. He cried in the daytime when he made a false step with his foot.

He cried to make them understand his foot hurt. They said he was naughty.

The doctor came and looked at him, talked fast and squeezed his ankle, making it hurt terribly. He didn't dare cry, because it was the doctor. But the doctor saw that it hurt and told him to lie still for a few days.

He lay still for a few days. Outside, in the birch, sat the magpie, tilting its head and wagging its tail.

One day he heard the clamping tread of a stump in the kitchen. Then he heard a sweet woman's voice and knew it was Mari Bakken, the one they called Mari with the Leg. For she had a stump instead of a foot on one leg and supported herself on a big stick with a lump of lead at the lower end when she walked. She carried a bag over her shoulder and was always sweet, with a smirking face. She came to see him in his room and felt so sorry his leg hurt so badly. She wagged her head and talked about her leg, and about that day up in the woods when a large stone fell on top of it. Cocking her head, she cried and dried her eyes with the back of her hand. Then she turned around to talk to some other people, her voice was sweet and she didn't cry anymore. Turning to him once more, she felt so sorry for him and cried a little again. She had a kerchief on her head that fell over her forehead, and a big woollen scarf over her shoulders; it was crossed over her chest and tied in the back, and from behind she looked exactly like a magpie. But her face was sweet and sly, even when she was crying at her worst, and in front she looked exactly like the fox in the picture book. He wanted to ask them to take her away, because she wished him only harm and would cast a spell over him and take away his leg. But he couldn't utter a word, she had already cast her spell.

His foot didn't get any better. The doctor came to look at it, talked fast and squeezed his ankle, making it hurt. It hurt more and more each time. In the end he dared to scream, because he couldn't help it.

Then one day the doctor came and said, "It's all been arranged, you can take him and go now."

He sat aloft. They were riding in the carriage. Father held him on his lap. He was covered up to his neck by the leather mudguard. They were on their way to the station, and from there they would go to the city and on to the hospital. He was scared but not only scared, for he was at the center of everything, was taking a long journey and was talked about by everybody; and he'd seen Mother cry because of him and Father with a strange look in his eyes, and now he had a new hat on his head; it was a handsome hat made of brown straw, with large brims turned up at the edges so he could use it for a boat when nobody was watching, and it had a broad blue band hanging down behind. They drove so fast that the wheels spattered mud. The ground was thawing, there were deep wheel tracks and water and slush on the road. It was a sunny day, with a biting wind. They had come a long way and everything was strange, there were fences on both sides of the road and flat fields behind the fences. The fields were yellow and gray, with a bit of green. Here and there in the fields were pools, in a couple of places patches of snow. A gust of wind came along, stronger and more biting than before, it snatched his hat off his head and blew it over the fence, straight into a pool lying big and blue in the yellow meadow on the other side of the fence. There it was, sailing along like a fine boat, its bands trailing behind on the surface of the water. It was all because he'd thought of using the hat for a boat. The pool didn't feel sorry for him. It had gotten in the way on purpose and lay there clear and blue, with little blue waves moving across it, and it threw back the sunlight and laughed at him. Sailing along, the hat sank deeper and deeper, and the blue bands became darker and darker. Embret stopped the horse and climbed down from the back seat. The hat lay almost still—the wind couldn't push it any further, heavy with water as it was and sitting so deep. Embret took a long stick and tried to reach the hat but couldn't. He climbed the fence, the stick in his hand. Walking down the meadow, he sank deep into the ground with each step, and the gray mud stuck to his boots so they got bigger and bigger. Now he reached the hat with his stick and pushed it slowly ashore. The water poured off it. A new gust of wind came, pulling and shaking the horse's mane and Anders' hair. Embret brought the hat. Its bands were dripping wet. It was all because he'd wanted to use it for a boat.

Father opened the suitcase up front and took out a big white kerchief, which he tied around Anders' head as if he were an old woman.

"You'll have to sit like that for a while. You can't be bare-headed in this cold wind," he said.

Anders cried. But Father laughed, Embret laughed, and the pool back there behind the fence laughed. Then they drove on. The hat was drying on top of the mudguard up front. Anders thrashed with his fists and cried, but Father laughed and held him tight; Embret had taken his seat in the rear and said gee-up to the horse.

"Now you look nice. You almost look like an old woman now," Father said, laughing.

A crow took off from a stake in the fence. Farther on it turned into a magpie.

They drove past a cottage. On the stoop stood a witch with a long nose and a kerchief that fell over her forehead. She wanted to take away his leg and turn him into an old woman.

He thrashed with his fists and cried.

He had no voice left when they reached the station. He didn't look at the train, which he'd never seen before. For now they would drive him to the city and the hospital and turn him into an old woman who looked like a magpie behind and a fox in front.

He woke up in the morning and was in the city. Everything was strange. A woman came in and gave him milk and Christmas cake in bed. He didn't like her. She had a friendly face. A picture of a fox hung on the wall. He didn't want any Christmas cake. Later, Father took him on his arm and carried him out. Everything was strange and different. There was a moose head with big antlers over one door, he recognized it from the picture book. He looked at it, but seeing a fox in the next window, he screamed and didn't want to see any more.

Afterward he was in a bright lofty room, lying in a tall bright bed in the middle of the room. Father had gone away, because he didn't want to be with him any longer. There were only strangers standing around him. One man and many women. The man was dressed in white like the miller, but he looked like the butcher. He didn't have a beard like the butcher and wasn't bald like the butcher, and his clothes weren't greasy or shiny or black, and he was different in everything. But he looked like the butcher.

The man smiled, said something to him and smiled. And

all the women smiled. That was because they were scared of the man. Anders smiled at the man. Then he got a mask over his face, like the one they put on the pig, and couldn't see anymore. Something had a sickening smell. He saw the head of a fox.

He awoke and sat up in bed. Then he wasn't there any longer but somewhere else. It was a strange room. It was big and dark and had many beds. One wall had several tall windows where a bit of light came through, enough to make them much lighter than the wall. There were long curtains before the windows, the beds made two white rows, and in between it was night, dark and awful. Some people were sleeping in the other beds. He sat up in bed without saying a word and was far away and alone.

Then he was home again. It was strange. Home had become so far away; but suddenly he was home again, and suddenly all the other things were far away. The big room with all the beds was far away, and the white man and Sister Else, who was white and blue, everything was far away all day and only came back at night every now and then. Then he awoke and sat up to look at the beds in two white rows and the long curtains before the windows. But he was home, and through the panes he saw the shadow of the birch. He fell asleep.

During the day he sat in a chair, but soon he would be all right again. It had gone so well and he ought to be so glad, and so grateful to the man at the hospital who'd been so clever. For the butcher was not a butcher but a fine doctor, and he hadn't become an old woman, for after a while his leg would be as strong as ever and he would run like the others, play like the others, play hide-and-seek in the garden like the others and sit under the apple tree like the others. And he had a nice scar on his ankle, no one else did.

He was different from the others. They didn't have a scar on their ankle like that, not one of them did. When visitors came he sometimes had to show it, and then he got cookies. Åse and Kari and Tora had nothing to show and didn't get any cookies.

The others had to be good to him, for he wasn't well yet. He had to take a green medicine and a yellow medicine. He liked the yellow medicine, because it was thick and sweet, but he didn't like the green medicine, because it was green. He always remembered to take the yellow medicine but forgot sometimes to keep track of the green medicine.

Åse and Kari and Tora didn't take any such medicines. No one else took such medicines.

No one else had been as far away as he. He had traveled. He had traveled to the station and to the city and had seen a moose head with big antlers hanging over the door.

Åse and Kari and Tora hadn't been to the city and hadn't seen a moose head. For they were only girls, and when they grew up they would only be women, and when they got old they would only be old women with kerchiefs on their heads. Åse wanted to be a boy when she grew up, but that was out of the question, no matter how much she cried. For once you were made to be a woman, you would always be a woman. Nothing could be done about that, Embret said.

He was much better off than the others.

He didn't have to fetch firewood. Kari and Tora had to. Åse got out of it because she was so small, but when she became bigger she would have to fetch firewood.

He didn't have to run errands. Kari and Tora had to. He, too, could easily run errands, like bringing the farmhands something to drink when they were out in the field, calling them for dinner, or going to Neset with the mail, because there he always got a waffle with butter. But there was that bad leg of his. It was Kari and Tora who had to run. Kari and Tora flung taunts at him, especially Tora. Others, too, flung taunts at him sometimes. Gorinè, even Andrea. Only women, all of them.

He took it calmly. He could take it calmly because they got nowhere with him. He knew it, and that was why they got nowhere. Father and Mother were worried about him. He got the best of everything. Everyone had to be good to him.

"Anders must get the best piece, because his leg has been hurting," Mother said.

Then he looked calmly at Tora. He always looked at Tora, for she was the biggest and strongest and angriest. Kari was never really angry, she only cried when they were mean to her, and if somebody was good to her she became sweet and happy at once. But Tora was angry and smart and dangerous, therefore he was angry with Tora. He looked at the good piece and looked calmly at Tora. And Tora looked at him and was angry because he was looking calmly at her, and got angrier and angrier because he was looking calmly at her. If she became so angry that she said something, she got punished.

He looked calmly at her. But she didn't say anything.

"You poor thing. Here's a cake for you!" Mother said.

Mother was baking. Kari and Tora had asked for a cake but hadn't gotten any. He didn't have to ask, he got it anyway.

The summer was well under way. He was healthy. His leg didn't hurt anymore, he only limped a little.

Kari sat in her room playing with a doll. He wondered if he should go and share his cake with her. Kari was good. Yesterday she'd given him a piece of candy she'd gotten at the store. And his leg didn't hurt anymore. It was only Mother who thought his leg hurt and who gave him cake.

"You poor thing!" she said.

When he had been miserable they said he was naughty. Now they said poor thing. But then they said he was naughty.

He felt sorry for himself and ate the cake.

Later that summer Mother had a baby and forgot about him a little. He was mostly together with Åse; for Kari and Tora were so big, and Tora said he was much too small, and a poor sort of company for girls because he limped.

His foot was getting better and better. Everybody said it was getting better and better, and he must be so glad. He could walk and he could stand and he must be so glad.

It didn't hurt any more; but it wasn't quite as fast as the other. It wouldn't run, and therefore he couldn't run. He had a slight limp. He had to walk a bit slowly and be a bit careful, and he couldn't take part in all the games. He couldn't play tag or run, goose, run, trample hay or jump around in the hayloft, play hide-and-seek in the garden or run about the pasture, play stickball or go with wet feet or catch a cold, run bareheaded or barefoot or bump his ankle, because then it might start hurting. Father and Mother were constantly nagging him, he mustn't forget these things for a moment.

Summer and fall went by. Then late fall came and the ground was frozen. The birch glittered in the sunlight. The magpie sat on a branch wagging its tail and looking at him. Right in front of his foot lay a nice stone, but he didn't bend down or try to pick it up. Then the magpie flew away and he went in. There stood Tora and Kari holding their skates. The lake was frozen, and they were allowed to skate if they stayed near the shore. Mother would watch them from the window.

He didn't have a pair of skates. He hadn't gotten the skates Father had promised to give him this fall, for he couldn't go skating yet. But he could come along and watch Tora and Kari. He would get a shawl to sit on, and so he could help Mother look after Tora and Kari.

They walked down to the lake. Tora and Kari didn't speak to him. They didn't like to take him along. They didn't like to have anyone come along to look after them. Once they were at the shore, he put the shawl on the ice and sat down on it. Kari and Tora put on their skates. He sat as if the shawl were a fine chair, looking out across the whole lake.

"Remember to stay close to the shore, will you!" he said.

Tora sniffed.

Tora was a good skater. Kari wasn't so good, her legs ran away from her so she was left sitting on her fanny. The ice was clear and hard. Other kids were skating in the other coves, they looked like little black spots far away on the ice. Some of them came racing up. They rushed like the wind along the shore. The ice creaked and crunched and their runners left white streaks behind them. Tora was almost the best skater of them all. Kari fell and got up again, fell and got up again, and fell again. She had tremendous fun when she forgot to be scared.

It was great fun to skate. Some other time he, too, would skate perhaps. That was no problem, everyone could skate. He sat on the nice shawl looking across the ice and minding all the others, king of the whole lake.

Ole Sand came racing up to them right away.

Anders called, "Be careful now and stay close to the shore!"

Tora sniffed, wheeled away with Ole Sand and was gone. Kari stood for a while, then she set off after them.

"Be careful," he called; but she was gone already.

Knut Neset came whizzing up to him.

Anders sat on his shawl.

"Poor thing, so this is where you're sitting?" said Knut. Anders felt warm and glad. Knut was the tallest and strongest one in Tora's class.

Knut looked about him. "Hey, Lars, come here!" he called. Lars came up to them.

"Let's give Anders a little ride so he can have a bit of fun!" Knut said.

They took him by the hand and dashed off. He just stood still while the air whistled past, he'd never had so much fun before.

They headed right out on the lake. He wondered if he should ask them to be careful and skate along the shore but couldn't bring himself to do it—they were so tall and so nice to him, and so tall.

Suddenly they let go of him.

"The ice is giving way!" they shouted, dashing toward the shore. Anders slipped and fell, got up again and ran a little, fell and hit his face on the ice. He got up again. Far down, by the shore, Knut and Lars stood doubled up, laughing. "Look at him! Look at him!" they shouted. "The ice is giving way! The ice is giving way!" They laughed and hollered.

"Come, we'll give you a little ride," Knut said again. And before he could say or do anything, Knut and Lars had grabbed him and dashed off again. "The ice is giving way!" they shouted and let go of him. He continued gliding outward, while hearing their runners crunch the ice toward the shore. He got up and ran, slipped and fell, hitting his forehead on the ice, got up and ran again. He noticed he slipped less and moved faster if he took it a bit easier and allowed himself to limp. Knut and Lars laughed and hollered. "Look at him! Look at him! Look, he's limping!"

Again he fell, and was still lying there when Tora and Ole came up. He didn't see them but heard how quiet it grew down there—he raised his head and saw them, got on his feet but slipped and fell once more. Tora didn't stop but skated straight up to Knut and slapped him, one, two, three times. Nobody said anything. She came and helped Anders to his feet. Then Kari came. They took his hands and led him ashore. Tora went to pick up the shawl. Then they walked him up between them.

"Pooh! That was nothing!" Tora said.

"You lame duck!" said Tora.
"You lame duck!" said Kari and Åse.

Kari said it because Tora said it. And Åse was so small and stupid, she didn't even understand what she said.

"And you don't even limp!" Tora said. She thumbed her nose at him: "Your foot doesn't even hurt anymore!"

"...not even hurt anymore!" Åse echoed.

They were behind the barn. They'd played in the ditch and picked coltsfoot and white anemone. But then they'd quarreled about who owned the birch-tree stump over by the fence, which you could sit on and which had a little hole in the middle.

It was true. He didn't limp anymore and his foot didn't hurt anymore. But he didn't say it did either. He said it only when somebody wanted him to fetch wood or run an errand. When visitors asked him he always said it didn't hurt anymore. Still, Tora was envious of him.

"*You* pull Kari's pigtails!" he said.

It occurred to him that perhaps he did, too; but so did she. He thought for a moment and said, "And you kicked Åse out of bed because she cried! And you've gotten a brooch from America! And you'll never let anybody else wear it! That's why I want the birch-tree stump. You've got the brooch, haven't you!"

"Yeah, you've got the brooch, haven't you!" said Kari and came over to him. She was thinking about her pigtail; and she'd love to have that brooch.

"Yeah, you've got the brooch, haven't you!" said Åse and came over to him. For Kari had already gone over to him. And now she remembered that Tora had kicked her out of bed.

So he had won and owned the birch-tree stump.

Tora and Kari were envious of him and he often quarreled with them. Especially with Tora. And he usually won. Because they were two, while he was alone, so he became much more practiced and more clever and beat them.

And they were always afraid when they quarreled with him. Because Father and Mother had asked them to be nice to him, for what if his foot started hurting again! Therefore he knew that when they were angry with him, deep down they were afraid. And so he was strong when he quarreled with them, beat them, and felt like a man.

And therefore he didn't mind quarreling with them, for he knew he'd win. They, too, came to know it little by little and weren't very eager to quarrel with him. Sometimes he thought it was almost as if he ruled over them with his foot. Before, he had felt like one of them. But it was as if it had made him different. It had made a man of him.

He was quite aware that he got too much of all the good things. And every now and then, when he hadn't quarreled with any of them in a long while, he felt a little embarrassed accepting a good thing if they didn't get something too.

But then he thought quickly: how could he help it if Father and Mother…Anyway, he'd gone through more than enough bad things for the good things he was getting now…So he must somehow have deserved it, since he was getting it…Maybe he was smarter and more spunky than the others…In any case he wasn't to blame that it had turned out this way.

If he'd quarreled with them he thought: Maybe he was getting a bit too much—but the others were so angry and so envious because he was getting so much that it served them right.

And in the end he thought: They're only girls. I'm a man.

"You know, I think you are a little fox," old Mari with the Leg said one day. She'd been listening to them without their noticing her. He and Tora had quarreled and he'd won.

He looked at her and didn't say a word. Then she hobbled down the road in the dusk. When she turned her back, she looked like a big magpie hobbling down the road.

Suddenly he grabbed a stone and threw it after her.

He missed. He'd waited till he felt sure she was far enough away.

Death

THEY COULDN'T SEE MOTHER for several days in a row. Strange folk came and went. In the kitchen they were all putting their heads together, and Gorinè and Andrea didn't answer when they asked something.

One morning Gorinè came up and told them to hurry and get dressed, because now they could come to Mother's room. She helped them, but one of Anders' shoes was gone and it took him a long time to remember he'd used it for a boat in the wash basin yesterday. It wasn't quite dry, there was some water in it, and he had to put on his old shoes from way back. When they got to the bottom of the stairs they had to stop and keep quiet; Gorinè went ahead and was gone for quite a while. Åse crept up to the door and listened, but Anders just kept looking down at his old shoes. An idea had occurred to him, but he wasn't sure. When he straightened up, he saw a gray, angry day staring at him from the window next to the front door.

"What can it be, you think?" Åse asked.

"She's having a baby," Anders said.

He couldn't say *r*. So he didn't say *Mother*.

"A baby," Åse said. And as if Mother were going to have kittens, she began to jump and dance, shouting, "Mother having a baby! Mother having a baby! Mother having a baby!"

Åse couldn't say *s*, even if her name was Åse, with an *s* in it. *Åte*, she said when someone asked what her name was. But she mostly cheated and said *Tulla*.

She jumped and danced.

"Hush, kids! Mother is sick!" Gorinè said, coming from the kitchen. She took them into the bedroom.

There lay Mother, very white and strange, seeming to smile at them; but she almost didn't smile. Anders looked mostly at the strange woman standing there, the one who'd come yesterday, and realized it was the midwife. The midwife always had to lend a hand when babies were made. She was dressed in black, with a cap on her head and a brooch, and an ugly long nose crooked at the tip and small pig's eyes with gray eyelashes; she pretended to smile sweetly, but behind it all she was cross and ugly and wanted only to do harm.

"Now you've got a little brother," said the midwife.

He lay in the cradle beside the bed. He had a small red face, which stirred and twitched. Now he screamed "Baa! Baa!," like a little sheep. The midwife hurried over to tend him, and then he quieted down again.

"You must be very glad, both of you, now that you've got a little brother?" the midwife asked, smiling crabbily around her sharp, crooked nose. Mother didn't say anything but just lay in her bed and smiled; she looked pale and barely smiled. Anders didn't say anything. It seemed to him he'd gone through all this once before, a long time ago.

"You are glad, aren't you?" Gorinè too asked. Åse was glad. Anders didn't say a word. Then Mother looked at him and asked, in a small voice he almost didn't recognize, "Aren't you glad, Anders?" Then he checked how he felt and knew he was glad.

They couldn't stay very long, for Mother felt poorly, and only the midwife with her long, sharp snout and gray pig's eyes could be in there. In the kitchen Åse was glad that she'd got a little brother. Anders walked away from her and went down to Embret in the woodshed.

It wasn't gray and cloudy outside after all, but sunny. And Embret stood behind the long chopping block that spanned the entire width of the shed and chopped wood, making the chips fly. He placed one end of the log on the pile of chips before the chopping block and the other end on top of the block. Then he gave a blow, the log split, and a drop squirted from his nose and swept through the air in a long arc and fell way over in the pile of chips. But a new one began to form right away. There often hung a drop at the tip of Embret's nose, because he was old and had a white beard and a long nose with a bump on it, almost like the roof over the kitchen steps. Drops would form there, too; at night they turned into icicles, but in the daytime water trickled from them. But that was a long time ago, early last spring that was. And the drops under Embret's nose were something quite different from what Anders himself had under his nose now and then, for with Anders it formed at the root and had to be gotten rid of, but with Embret it hung at the tip. When Anders grew up, he would also have a drip at the tip of his nose perhaps; but you could never be sure, because Father never did, so Anders wasn't sure he'd have it when he grew up.

The pile of chips before the chopping block quivered at every blow. Embret hadn't looked up even once. Then he'd better be silent.

At last Embret looked up and they began chatting, as Embret stood leaning on his ax.

How long did someone have to stay in bed after a baby?

"Oh well," Embret hemmed and hawed, wiping his forehead and his nose with the back of his hand, "it can differ quite a bit. Maria Teppen, now, had a littl'un recently, and she was up the fifth day, she was. But it can be more or less, depending."

Where did such babies come from?

Embret stared at him. "You know that, don't you, big boy like you? A big bird brings 'em at night. Hmm."

Oh yes, Anders knew.

Embret busied himself with the wood, stacking it. Then he took a new chunk, chopped it up and put the wood on the stack.

Anders stood watching him. "Her tummy will get smaller now, right?"

Embret looked sharply at him. "Yeah, perhaps so," he said. Then he bent down, grabbed another chunk and began to chop without looking up. The chips went flying on the pile. Anders turned and walked up to the house again.

The sun shone brightly, the wagtails darted about in the yard, and the cat sat on the stoop. It was summer now and lots to do. But Anders was deep in thought and didn't look at the world around him. He limped a little on one leg when he walked.

She didn't get up again the fifth day.

When she didn't get up the sixth day either, Anders went to her room and told her off. Maria Teppen got up again the fifth day. Why wouldn't Mother get up again? It was a shame that she should be poorer than Maria Teppen.

They laughed. They didn't even understand what he meant. He'd noticed it many times—the grownups didn't understand very much. They seemed to think it was all right for Mother to loll in bed day after day while others got up again the fifth day.

She didn't get up again until the ninth day.

Mother almost never had time to be with Anders and Åse anymore. She had to be with the newcomer at all times. If she wasn't with him he cried, "Baa! Baa!" He had blue eyes and thin red hair all over his head. The grownups said he was pretty.

Lots of people came visiting, they got coffee and cake. Anders and Åse often got cake. The Master Builder came with his big red nose, bringing Mrs. Master Builder, who was laced more nicely than everybody else and looked as if she'd been turned on a lathe from her stomach to her armpits. She was his godmother and he often thought about her. He'd gotten a silver spoon from her—he ate with it on Sundays. She patted his hair, saying he must be very glad now that he'd got a little brother. Anders felt so queer, with her being so nicely laced, having such soft hands and smelling so good; he wanted to hide in her skirt and to run away. He just stood still without saying a word.

Many others came to have coffee, patted his hair and said he must be glad. And little by little Anders realized he was very glad he'd got a baby brother.

If anything, Åse was perhaps even more fond of him than Anders was. Her new brother was almost like a doll to her. She wanted to tend him. She wanted to take him out of the cradle and lull him to sleep. She wanted to press his eyes to see if he could close them. She wanted to put a pine cone in his mouth when he cried.

Anders might have been even fonder of him if he'd been all right. But something was wrong with him. The doctor came to tend him many times, but he was still ailing almost all the time and would cry terribly, and Mother had to be around him every minute. Maria Teppen's little boy was fit as a fiddle.

It turned out that the newcomer was a heathen without a name. Then he got baptized, cried awfully and wet himself in church. They called him Harald and gave a big party, where Harald wasn't allowed. But Anders could come into the living room and sing "Little Peter Lassen cried and cried/ for his fishing boat swept out by the tide," and everything was fine except that he couldn't say *r*, there were so many *r*'s in that song. But many said he did very well, and Harald wasn't there. He lay asleep in the bedroom, was a Christian and was named Harald.

The summer was going by.

It was a long summer. Mother couldn't spend so much time with them as before and wasn't as nice to them as she used to be anymore, because Harald was so naughty. And Anders' leg wasn't quite well and he couldn't run as much as usual, and he often had to sit on the stoop while the others were running around. So the summer often seemed quite long.

It was this summer that Anders learned to say *r*. And Åse learned to say *s*—but that was later. Afterward her name was always Åse.

Anders would hit Åse once in a while, when nobody was watching, because Åse was naughty. Åse cried but seldom told on him, because Mother was mostly too busy to listen.

Most of the time he and Åse were good friends. They stuck together. For Kari and Tora were going to school and were so much bigger, and his leg hurt and he couldn't run, and Mother had so little time. Somehow, Anders and Åse mostly had each other, and Pussy.

And then they had the play rock behind the house. There they had cows from spruce cones and sheep from little spruce cones and goats from pebbles and a bull from a large spruce cone with two big horns. They had a horse of wood that Embret had made for them. And they had a cow barn, a stable, a summer cow barn, and a main building. But later that summer there was a big storm. It rained and thundered and there was a flood, and the water carried away all the cows and sheep, leaving only the goats and the horse. From then on it wasn't that much fun on the play rock. Åse wanted to rebuild it, but Anders wasn't very eager to. He knew it was God who'd made the whole thunderstorm, and how could they have expected anything else than that God would come and destroy this play rock they were so fond of! For Anders had noticed that God was often out to get him. But he'd fooled God all the same—for, truly, he had never been terribly fond of this play rock. And now it didn't matter anymore. Anyway, they'd better not tease him. For then it might end up like the tower of Babel Mother had told him about—that God came down and confused his and Åse's mother tongue so he wouldn't be able to say *r*.

Little by little Anders forgot about this and helped Åse rebuild the play rock. But it became her play rock now, not his, and he only gave her good advice and was the vet for her cows when they were going to calve and rubbed the horse with ointment when it had the strangles. He himself had grown too big for such things. He was nearly five years old.

Anders and Åse were much by themselves. Often next to nothing would happen, but off and on something did happen anyway. It was this summer that Anders was allowed to bathe in the lake for the first time. It was this summer he saw his first adder, was at the summer dairy for the first time, was allowed to come along to the islet in the lake to pick lilies of the valley, was in the parsonage garden stealing forget-me-nots and at Grandmother's eating too many strawberries and throwing up, went to sleep in church and fell down from his pew, and spilled chocolate on his white blouse at the Sheriff's, got a scolding, started bawling and fled home again, alone, right through a big forest and a valley with a big brook which had ferns as tall as houses and adders and pikes and toads and blindworms and lizards, but got home alive all the same and never wanted to taste chocolate again.

It was this summer that his leg was bitten by a horse leech when he went bathing and learned to tie a string around its rear end so that it filled up with blood and let go. Then they opened it with sticks and filled it with sand.

It was a long, warm summer. There was sunshine, thunder and rain. In the evening the birds sang, the mosquitoes buzzed their spinning wheels, the grasshoppers squeaked and squeaked. In the morning the sun shone; bumblebees and wasps knocked against the panes eager to get in and knocked against the panes eager to get out, and the flies walked on the window as on a clear lake. Pussy caught mice and rats and shrews, but also birds and nestlings once in a

while. For it was only an animal and had no share in the
Fall and didn't know the difference between good and evil.

The days were full of rain and they were full of sun. But
each day brought new times, a new world.

Anders and Åse became much older that summer. They
were by themselves a good deal.

Fall came.

Mother was so difficult. She often cried and was often
impatient. Harald was sick. The doctor came and went.
Mother cried. Outside it rained. The days were dark.

One morning Gorinè came to wake them as she used to
lately, now that Mother didn't have the time. Big tears
streamed down her face, sideways along the deep old
wrinkles. Anders and Åse at once grew sad.

She helped them get dressed. Her hard, bony hands hurt
him more than usual.

"Hurry up!" she said.

It was dark in the bedroom, because it had only one window and there were so many grownups standing around,
reaching almost to the ceiling. Kari and Tora were there
too. Everybody was so quiet that Anders and Åse hushed
up at once. Father stood hunched over the cradle, pale and
strange. He held a small round mirror to Harald's mouth.
He turned the mirror, looked at it and straightened up.

"He's dead," he said. And as if she'd been waiting for
these very words, Mother suddenly became old and ugly
and strange and wrinkled in the face, and she moaned and
began to cry. Father said something in a low voice, he and
Mother left the room, and it became a little brighter right
away. Harald lay in his cradle, still and pale and without
moving; something had happened to him. Everybody in the

room cried, and Anders grew even more sad than before. He noticed that he and Åse began to cry at the very same moment. He thought he must remember that in case she came and told him afterward that she had started first.

Someone came and took them away.

They went to the kitchen. The floor was freshly scrubbed, the knots stuck out like knuckles from the boards. Pussy came and rubbed himself against them. Åse pulled his tail, she wanted him. Anders pulled his forelegs, he also wanted him. Pussy poked at Anders' legs with each side of his head in turn, his jaws itched. They petted him awhile, until someone came in and Pussy ran out through the half-open door.

The kitchen was bright and cozy, it felt almost like Sunday. Anders and Åse got into such a merry, joyful mood that they took each other's hands and began to jump and dance on the kitchen floor. Someone hushed them, loudly. It was Gorinè. What did they think they were doing? With Harald having just died and all? Didn't they have a sense of shame!

They became sad and ashamed and stole out of the kitchen.

He stopped by the woodshed with Embret and stood watching him awhile.

"He's dead," he said.

Embret looked up.

"What?"

"He's dead."

He didn't say anymore, turned around and left. It was just that he had to hear once more the words that Father had spoken.

"He's dead."

It sounded so strange. He said it to himself several times.

Afterward there were many days of fun. Something was happening all the time, both indoors and outdoors. The baker woman came, and the butcher, tailor and shoemaker. The tailor, sitting cross-legged on a table in the small room upstairs, was snooty and no fun at all; but the shoemaker, sitting in the servants' quarters, had nails in his mouth and long hairs growing out of his nose, wiry black hair that stood on end and looked like black nails, and a bristling wiry stubble that looked like gray nails. Wearing a shiny brown apron called a lap rug, he sat at a table strewn with hammer and plier, knives and files and awls, leather and nails and cobbler's thread. With a shiny pair of glasses that threw back the sunlight on his nose and a boot between his legs with the sole turned up, he took a nail from his mouth and knocked it into the sole; then he sprang up and put the boot away, walked a few steps up and down looking as though he was making sure of something, and blew a loud fart that sounded like canvas being torn, his face all the while looking like he was thinking about something terribly funny he wasn't allowed to think about; then he sat down, took the boot between his legs and a nail from his mouth and knocked it into the sole. A seamstress, a cook, and a helper came, in the kitchen they were all running loops around one another, and Mother grew more cheerful than before— when two of them ran into each other so that both took a tumble, she couldn't help laughing, though she checked herself at once, but she did laugh. And Embret stood in the woodshed chopping wood—long sticks for the baking oven and short sticks for the kitchen—making the chips fly on the pile. And one day he went down to the pasture and cut a whole load of spruce twigs, carted them up with Brownie and chopped them small down by the woodshed. It came to several tubsful. What it would be used for? It would be strewn in the yard to make a broad path from the door to the road. That's where they would drive off with Harald.

But they wouldn't have bird bushes with sheaves in them, like at Christmas.

Then the carpenter came with the little black coffin. That's where Harald would lie while they drove him out to the churchyard. There they would lower him into a hole in the ground. Anders had seen that hole—he'd gone with Embret to talk to the gravedigger and looked at the gravedigger's fiery-red beard and at the earth he tossed up, a brown earth with stones in it—and the hole was square and brown inside. Anders would have liked to be down there a little while, but not long. Harald wouldn't either, for when he'd been there a little while he was going to heaven, and there God sat waiting for him with cake and waffles.

Anders and Åse were dressed in their fine new clothes. Anders had gotten a dark-blue jacket and dark-blue trousers and they'd been woven from dark-blue yarn and were bought at the store and were prettier than ordinary clothes. Åse wasn't that pretty. But when this made Åse cry, Mother said that Åse was just as pretty but it wasn't true, for she had only an ordinary dress of ordinary material and a bib, because she was so small and spilled on herself when she ate.

Outdoors, Embret brought several tubfuls of evergreens and strewed them in the yard from the door to the road, and in the kitchen they ran back and forth worse than ever. Then a lot of visitors came with horses, they tied the horses to the garden fence one after the other. Anders went with Embret to give them some hay. They munched and munched and dropped the horse manure in little mounds one after another at the back of their tails. Afterward Anders had to go in because they were going to close the coffin; but first everybody had to see Harald for the last time, for now he was starting on a long journey, and first of all they would sing a hymn and listen to the parish clerk.

Harald lay in his coffin, white and still, and didn't look much like the Harald that Anders had known. Anders held Father's hand, Åse held Mother's hand, and Kari and Tora pressed themselves against Mother. They sang a hymn, and the parish clerk with his gray beard stepped forward in his long black coat and glasses and spoke a long piece. Then they sang a hymn. Everyone cried. Gorinè cried and Mother cried, and Kari and Tora and Åse cried as though being whipped. Father's hand trembled, and Anders felt something surge up and started to sob.

Now all the rigs were driven up and placed behind one another in front of the door, and four men carried the coffin out. They were Embret and Anton and two strangers. They placed it on the wagon and drove off. Anders and Åse weren't allowed to come along, they were too small. But they went into the kitchen to Gorinè and got Christmas cake. The church bells were ringing, and Anders and Åse walked out on the play rock behind the house. From there they could see across to the churchyard between the tree tops. They saw the funeral party drive down the road and turn at the bridge toward the churchyard. There were eight horses. That was many. But in the funeral of Ola Nordberg there had been thirty-three horses, Embret had said, and that was many more than eight.

It rained. The church bells were ringing. It was windy, and the rain came in brief showers with breaks in between. The church bells sang in the wind. They said, Come to me! Come to me!, wailing and crying high in the sky.

The funeral party was lost for a while going down the hill by the bridge, then appeared again on the other side of the bridge and crawled slowly up toward the church, like a long black snake. There it stopped and the bells ceased ringing, leaving a long lingering sound in the air; then everything was quiet.

The party entered the churchyard, first a small black group with something black between them, then a big black group.

Everything was quiet and empty.

And then came the singing of the hymn. It came in sudden gusts and was full of rain and wind and mourning. It was far away and nearby. They couldn't hear the words, only the tune which was rocked by the wind. They could hear the parson's voice, it was stronger than everything, he stood there singing and calling up to God.

The wind came in gusts and squalls, it howled and sighed and brought the hymn and the rain with it. Anders and Åse stood and listened on the play rock.

Anders cried and wanted to die. He wanted to be lowered into the grave, and Mother and Father and many, many others would stand around the grave, crying, grieving, singing, and calling up to God.

Åse stood and cried beside him. She pressed the Christmas cake in her hand, chewing and crying. Her eyes were streaming with tears, her cheeks went up and down as she chewed, and her tears streamed and streamed down her cheeks.

Sometimes he would come back again at night. And then he didn't always lie quiet in his cradle. He soared in space or he came walking—once he walked on water. But his face always looked as it had lately—it was as if he listened for something he couldn't hear, or struggled with something he was unable to say. Once he looked at Anders with the same eyes he'd looked at him with when Anders wanted to put a pillow over his face because he cried so terribly. Anders got terribly scared, screamed and woke up, and then he wasn't there anymore.

Little by little he stopped coming. And it turned out as Anders had thought. A better time came. Mother often cried, but she came back to them.

At first she would sometimes call Anders Harald.

The first time, Anders stuck out his tongue at her and got slapped. Then he understood it was wrong and only stuck out his tongue inwardly. Later he didn't understand what she meant, and she had to say the name over again, and then she checked herself. Little by little she learned to say it correctly. But she would still call Anders Høgne sometimes, after the eldest who had died long ago, before Anders was born. There was nothing you could do about it. The grownups were like that.

Harald was gone and wouldn't come back. He lay out in the churchyard. The snow came, it grew cold. Was he cold lying there?

He didn't want to talk to Mother about it and went down to Embret. And then it turned out there was no danger of that. Harald was in heaven, had been there a long time already. He was comfortable where he was. As far as Embret knew, it didn't snow in heaven, but there was supposed to be a good supply of palms and olive branches up there. Olive branches were a kind of plant that only grew in flower pots here, but in the far south and in heaven there was plenty of them, he'd heard, and there they were as tall as houses.

He was comfortable and he was gone. Later Anders didn't think much about him anymore.

"I wish you were dead!" he said.

It was Tora who started, for she pulled his hair and said he was spoiled. Still, Mother gave her only a little smack, while he got two big ones, and a rattling shake.

Afterward she took him into the bedroom, looked at him and told him that he must never say such things. It was a great sin. She cried. And Anders was sorry and cried and promised never to say it again.

He thought about it later. It was really quite odd. Those who were dead were comfortable enough, after all. For they went to heaven and were with God, and God was kind to them all day.

Still, he mustn't tell them that he wished they were dead. It was a sin to say such things aloud. For the grownups didn't want to die. They didn't want to go to heaven. Because first they had to go to the churchyard, and that's where they didn't want to go.

Anders never said it anymore. But he meant it sometimes when Tora pulled his hair with nobody watching, or when Mother called him Harald, refused him jam, candy or cookies, and smacked his fingers when he tried to take a little anyway, or when Father—but when he thought about Father that way, he became scared and quickly thought that then he would lose Father and never see him again and be without a father forever. Father, who had often been so good to him and was so fond of him and only did it for his own good when he spanked him. He felt sorry for himself, and he got a lump in his throat when he pictured Father dead.

Sometimes when Mother called him Harald he stood still for a moment. He thought about Harald. They were in the bedroom, and Mother lay still and was dead. Father cried, and Anders was grown-up and talked to him and then led him out. Afterward they drove her down the road, and all the horses walked so slowly and were sad and hung their heads. The church bells were ringing, and the funeral party crawled like a long black snake up the road to the church. He and Åse stood on the play rock, it rained and blew, and a mournful singing came from the churchyard. And he and Åse stood there alone—.

"Why are you so sad, Anders?" Mother said, stroking his head. It warmed Anders' heart, he got a lump in his throat and was fond of Mother and felt kind and good. He didn't quite remember why he was so sad.

If all the others died and he was the only one left, then he could do anything he wanted. Then he would be free to go to the pantry and eat up all the cookies, climb a chair and take down all the pots of jam and eat all the jam, grab the sugar bowl and eat all the sugar, eat heavy cream and jam and cookies and sugar all day long, never go to bed at night and never get up in the morning, never say his evening prayers when he'd gotten a spanking during the day, and never wash his hands, face or ears.

But Embret could live, because he chopped wood. And Gorinè, because she was kind and had to help him button up his trousers.

Anders had become so fond of the church bells. They said, Come to me! Come to me! It was as if they promised him something. It was as if the sound went right through him and he became new, both smaller and bigger, full of regret, sad and happy, kind and good. When he grew up he would be a parson and let the church bells ring all day.

He was even more fond of the hymn singing. Then he mourned everybody—Mother and Father, Tora and Kari, and all the others. And everybody mourned him. It was as if the whole world cried and mourned and he became much, much better than usual.

Often a long time would go by without a funeral and without church bells and hymn singing. But Gorinè had taught him something. If he took a silver spoon and a long woollen thread, tied the middle of the thread around the handle of the silver spoon, twined the ends around his forefingers, stuck his forefingers in his ears, bent forward and knocked the silver spoon against the edge of the table, then it would sound exactly like the church bells: Ding-dong! Ding-dong! Come to me! Come to me!

In the evenings he often borrowed a silver spoon and a woollen thread and sat there ringing. He became good at ringing and could ring just the same as for a funeral.

The hymn singing and the wind and the rain, he imagined.

Something

IT WAS GETTING DARK. In the kitchen things got bigger than they were, and you couldn't be sure that they stood where they stood. All the shadows melted into one, which stretched from one end of the room to the other; only the window was a light square, with a big cross in the middle and four smaller crosses in the lesser parts. The dusk fell from the ceiling like dust, he could hear it in his ear like a little sound, much finer than a mosquito—ssssssssss! it said. This sound was the dusk.

He sat on the threshold to the side bedroom. He was alone, as he often was at this time of day. It was winter outdoors, with cold and snow.

He was looking at a knot in the door frame. It resembled a man's face. A dark man with big mustaches who was looking at him and laughing, not kindly or pleasantly but angrily, fixing him with a cold stare—and he never stopped laughing, but without a sound. Anders had often sat down here to watch the angry laughing man. He thought: what if he would shut his mouth and stop laughing? But it never happened. Now he sat watching the man again. The man was staring at him with two small angry cracks in the knot, and laughing silently and dangerously with a big black crack in the knot. Anders sat there watching him, but he wasn't scared, for Father and Mother were in the bedroom behind the door.

That was the moment he heard it.

He heard Father's voice, recognized it and turned stiff with fright: "It *is* something! I know it's something! And now I demand…"

Mother cried. Mother said, crying, "It's nothing. It's nothing…"

Father said, "It *is* something. It's no use denying it! It *is* something—and I want to know!"

His voice made a booming noise in there. A crash was heard as he banged the table. Mother cried. A door slammed hard, and then there was only Mother crying.

It had grown darker. An ashen dust fell and fell. The shadows hung like a spider's web. Big black spiders sat in the corners, stretching their long crooked arms after him. They made a whistling noise, softer than a mosquito: sssssssss! The man in the knot, grown bigger now, fixed him with an angry stare and laughed soundlessly with open mouth.

Anders didn't dare to move, blink his eyes or breathe. A door was opened and Gorinè came in. Then he was freed, ran across the floor and cried as he had heard Mother cry. Gorinè stopped to stare at him.

"What is it, Anders?"

He couldn't say what it was, didn't know anymore, only stammered and pointed everywhere.

"It is—*Something*!"

She didn't understand him.

"Stuff and nonsense. There's nothing here!" she said.

Then she went to light the lamp. And at once everything was different—the windowpanes turned blue, and the

shadows snuggled up to the wall and hid behind the cupboard and the woodbox and the clock and under the table.
Outside a harness bell tinkled, it was Embret coming back
from the forest.

It was getting dark. Mother sat by the stove looking after the coffee kettle and telling him fairy tales about Jesus.

People were so nasty, and God the Father got very angry
with them and wanted to punish them. Then Jesus, his only
begotten son, felt sorry for them and came down to earth
to save them. And he was born in Bethlehem in a stable and
placed in a manger....

And he grew up and walked around doing wonders and
eating with publicans and sinners. But the Pharisees got
angry and hanged him on a cross....

And thus God the Father sent his son into the world to
save all men....

"Was it the father in—was it God the Father who wanted
that Jesus should hang on a cross?"

"Yes, he sent him to the earth to die on the cross, so he
could take the punishment for all who sinned, so everyone
could be saved. And now Jesus sits in heaven at the right
hand of God the Father...."

The man on the door frame was looking at him and
laughing, without a sound.

There was a hum, thinner than a mosquito: sssssssss!

It was getting dark. The shadows spread out, everything
was turning into shadows—walls and ceiling and everything. A tiny sound: ssssssss! The window looked like a
big, grayish-white opening in the middle of the wall, with

a big dark cross at the center and four little crosses in the four parts. And the big cross was Jesus dying on the cross, winter and double windows, and Jesus being born in Bethlehem in winter. Later, he remembered, the double windows would be taken down, that was April fourteenth, the first day of summer, the days were brighter then and Jesus would be taken down from the cross, for then it was Easter, with summer around the corner and long-dead flies lying around on the windowsill, legs up and wings down. But it was still winter and dusky twilight, and the darkness fell and fell with a tiny little sound in your ear: sssssssss!

In the middle of the night the house was suddenly full of sounds, of shouting and weeping and many people talking at the same time, dark voices and bright, shrill voices. He awoke and sat up, it was dark; his room was quiet, but from outside came loud cries, the world was in uproar; he heard people calling down the road and saw the light from a swinging lantern that moved farther and farther away. He got out of bed and toddled to the door—the floor was ice-cold. In the kitchen stood Father and Mother and Embret and Gorinè, and a man he didn't know, and everybody's eyes looked scared. They weren't dressed but had thrown something over their shoulders, and Father had the rifle in his hand. He heard them say, "Crazy-Fredrik!" He heard them say Crazy-Fredrik several times. Then Mother picked him up, and the door closed behind him and Mother. She said he mustn't be scared and there was no danger, he should just go to sleep again. She put him to bed and sat with him. When he asked what it was, she said, "Oh, it isn't anything!" He said, "It *is* something! It *is* something!" Then she said, "It isn't anything. It's only Crazy-Fredrik." But he noticed that her voice trembled, and when she patted his forehead her hand trembled. He fell asleep and dreamed the house was full of voices and of strangers carrying big torches, there was a candle in the middle of the table and huge shadows dancing along the walls, and in the middle of everything was Crazy-Fredrik, the half-wit from Bråten, who always drooled into his stubble and talked aloud to himself on the road, but now he wasn't talking to himself, only watching with angry eyes and laughing without a sound.

In the morning they sat at the kitchen table talking about the terrible thing that had happened during the night. About Crazy-Fredrik who'd chased his daughter-in-law out of the house and killed his son with an ax. Crazy-Fredrik, who'd been crazy for so many years that nobody thought he was dangerous—he chopped wood, carried water and went to the store, drooled in his stubble and talked aloud to himself. And now his daughter-in-law was scared out of her wits and sat at Haugom screaming, "Something is after me! Something is after me!" And the Sheriff with three men in tow was out hunting for Crazy-Fredrik. The son had got his head severed from his body with four blows, and the blood had squirted all over the kitchen floor at Bråten and run down to the basement straight into a bowl full of heavy cream.

Gorinè repeated it several times: "Straight into a bowl full of heavy cream!"

Embret said, "I've been thinking for a long time that something was bound to happen. I've seen something in his eyes."

At dusk that same evening the Sheriff, his assistant and

two more men came up the road, leading Crazy-Fredrik between them. His hands were tied behind his back, but otherwise he looked the same. He was drooling a little and smiling noiselessly. There was something—he reminded him of something—he was the man in the knot. That, Anders suddenly knew, he'd seen long ago. He'd always been scared of Crazy-Fredrik, who walked the road with his mouth open, drooling and talking to himself.

At dinner the following day everybody knew much more. Crazy-Fredrik had confessed everything. He'd gotten so mad at his daughter-in-law, she reminded him so terribly of his wife. So he'd grabbed the ax and chased her around the living room—and when his son came in between he knocked him down with the butt of his ax. He'd meant to let him lie there. But, he said to the Sheriff, "...then I felt sorry for him, because he was my son, you know! And so I chopped off his head, I did!"

They were telling the story, turning it this side and that and looking at it from every angle, as they were having their meal—big brown meat patties and big yellow potatoes. And Embret said, "I knew that something was going to happen! Because I've seen something in his eyes!"

The others all nodded and went on eating their big brown meat patties and big yellow potatoes.

Anders sat on the threshold to the bedroom. He kept staring at the man in the knot. He could see something in his eyes. It was there—*Something.*

But then I felt sorry for him, because he was my son, you know! And so I chopped off his head, I did!

Tora was going to the store. It was getting dark; Tora was afraid of the dark but didn't want to admit it, and everybody knew she was and didn't want to admit it. Embret was having his afternoon meal, he laughed and said, "Take care, now, that Something won't come and get you!"

Everybody laughed. Tora was pale, but laughed. Anders was sick to his stomach and felt his face going stiff with fear, he stepped back a little to get away from their eyes and laughed. Then Tora left and Anders sat on his stool by the fireplace, following her with his thoughts all the way. He thought he had to be with her in his thoughts every moment of the way till she got to the store and was safely home again. But he fell asleep on his stool and awoke from Tora coming home again, right through the door and home again, almost the same as before, only a little paler.

"What's wrong with Andrea?" Mother asked. "Why does she go around crying to herself?"

Gorinè looked away and said in a low voice, so nobody else would hear, "Oh, I suppose it's Something."

Afterward they whispered among themselves.

Dusk reminded him of something. When nobody was in the kitchen and the silence fell from the ceiling like dark dust, he was reminded of something—Something—SOMETHING!

Something was in the stillness, in the big cross of the window over there, in the shadows in every corner, in the knot on the door frame yonder.

I have seen *Something* in his eyes!

Jesus on the cross in the window.

The angry voice of God the Father in the bedroom: I know it is *Something!*

But then I felt sorry for him, because he was my son,
you know! And so I chopped off his head, I did!

Stiff with fear, he heard the tiny little sound of Something, sssssssss!

At night when he slept Something would come to him. He was alone. He was sitting somewhere, on a threshold, in a room, in a forest. Dusk was coming on, the darkness fell over him like a thick dust. Something was lying in wait for him. *Something* had a long neck like a snake—the body he couldn't see, for it was nothing but dusk and darkness. He couldn't see the head either, but he knew it was watching him and waiting. It was watching him and smiling, without a sound. It was the knot in the door frame, it was someone drooling in his stubble, it was a faraway hand raising a big black cross in a big gray plain with dusk and darkness all around. And on the cross hung somebody, bleeding and bleeding...

But then I felt sorry for him, because he was my son,
you know! And so I chopped off his head, I did!

Something rolled over, like a big gray troll, something big and gray that was watching him and smiling without a face, with only a big hole for a face...

He screamed and woke up and knew that *Something* had been watching him.

The grownups knew about Something, were scared of it and would rather not talk about it. But once in a while they talked about it, and then they often looked away and grew quiet and strange.

In the daytime he wasn't scared of Something, then it

wasn't anywhere. It lived inside the dusk, in the shadows that came creeping up so quietly and only made a tiny sound in his ear: sssssssss!

It didn't have a face or hands or legs, it just laughed with something empty, a big hole that led to nothing. It lay in wait for him because he was a little boy.

But then I felt sorry for him, because he was my son, you know! And so I chopped off his head, I did!

It was impossible to talk about it.

Once he tried to.

He sat in the chimney corner one afternoon with Tora, Kari and Åse; there was a low fire on the hearth, making the shadows flicker, but it wasn't so dangerous now that they were four. And Tora had been nice lately, so he thought he might talk with her a little and hear what she knew.

So he said, "Tora—have you seen Something?"

Tora looked at him. "Something—what?"

"Have you seen *Something*, Tora?"

Tora stared at him. "*Something*—what do you mean?"

"I mean *Something*—you know, *Something*—don't you understand—haven't you ever seen *Something*?"

Tora looked at him for a moment. Then she turned to the others. "See, now Anders is going crazy again!"

Kari and Åse laughed. Now Anders was going crazy again.

They laughed all three.

He ought to have known. Only women, all of them. He remembered it so well from all the other times—it was no use talking to women.

Best to keep everything to yourself. No use trying to explain.

R

Below the stairs in the hall was a dim nook. It had some boots, umbrellas and rubbers in it, but nothing else. There he could sit, there no one saw him.

There he could sit looking at the wall.

Down in the pasture he had a place just below the gate, between a pine tree and three thick little spruces. It was a fine spot, with grass on the bottom and a wall of spruce twigs on every side. He was the only one who knew about that place. There no one could find him.

He was four years old.

It was a lie that he was five. For it was still summer, at any rate when the weather was nice, and his birthday wasn't till well into the fall, a long way off. And people were four till the day they turned five.

It was Tora who said he was five. But that was because she was angry with him, because he had been sick and had made a long journey and was a man.

The grownups said it, too. But that was because they lied.

The grownups were terrible liars. They lied almost all the time.

Andrea lied, telling Mother she'd been to the cow barn. But she hadn't been to the cow barn, she'd been in the hayloft with Anton. Gorinè lied, telling Andrea to fetch water by herself because she didn't have the time, she was busy tidying up in the bedroom. But she'd tidied up in the bedroom already. Embret lied, telling Father he'd been out in the field looking for rakes. But he'd been to the store to buy tobacco.

And Anton did nothing but lie.

It was stupid to lie because it brought its own punishment, Father said.

The grownups were so stupid.

Anders was only four years old. But he was already much smarter than most grownups.

Sure, the grownups were much bigger than him and therefore older, they had learned more and could tell him many things.

But they were so stupid.

They believed in so many things that weren't true.

Embret believed in the brownie. But the brownie, that was only someone they believed in in the old days.

Gorinè believed in forerunners. But that was superstition, because there was no such thing as a forerunner. But poor thing, she hadn't gone to regular school.

Andrea believed in coffee grounds. She sat at the kitchen table staring out the window and letting Gorinè read her fortune in the coffee grounds. As if anything could be written in coffee grounds.

But maybe Andrea didn't really believe in coffee grounds; she just didn't know for sure whom she wanted. So she must be rather stupid anyway—she who could have Tøsten

Teppen and still would think of somebody like Anton, who was so stupid and disgusting.

The grownups were such awful braggarts. They nearly always bragged.

Andrea stood in the kitchen bragging how she picked up a hayfork and gave Anton a smack on his fingers and said, "You just go home again to Mommy!" But she didn't pick up a hayfork at all and didn't give him a smack on his fingers or say a single word, but just whispered, "Look out! What if somebody should come!"

Embret sat at his mid-morning meal bragging that he'd answered Father so smartly out in the field yesterday. But he didn't say a single word until Father was far away.

And Anton did nothing but brag. He said he grabbed the sacks of grain by the gathering and tossed them onto the load. But Anders had been watching—he tilted a board against the cart and pulled the sacks along the board, and even so he was puffing afterward and wiping the sweat off his red face.

Anders understood, of course. They liked to be praised; but nobody praised them, and so they had to praise themselves. But they were such a poor lot and didn't really have anything to be proud of, and so it came to nothing but lies and brag.

Once in a while they knew they bragged; he could see it in their eyes. But sometimes they seemed to believe it themselves.

"He lies till he believes it himself!" they would say about each other. But they didn't say it to each other's faces. They sat around yessing, pretending to believe each other, toadying, pretending to like each other, playing up to each other, never daring to tell the truth. "Yes, that's so, for sure!" they'd say. But no sooner had someone turned his back than they laughed and said, "He lies till he believes it himself!"

It was stupid to lie. It was pitiful to brag. It was cowardly to sit around toadying and yessing.

Oh! The grownups were so stupid! They were so pitiful and cowardly! They were a bunch of stupid cowards! They were a bunch of bluffers, toadies and sneaks!

It was strange that God would stand for something like that. If Anders were God he'd grab both Anton and Andrea, pull their hair, knock them down and step on them. Gorinè too. Embret too. Tora and Kari and Åse too. Oh, would he grab them!

He would grab them and chase them! He would grab them and whip them with a big whip and knock their heads against a thick wall, kick them in the rear and call them names!

"Say *r* then!" they said.

And Anton said, "Now, Anders! Have they learned to say *r* today in the country you're from, eh?" Then he laughed.

"If you can say *r* I'll give you a lump of sugar!" he said, holding out a lump, like to a dog. Then he laughed till the hairs in his ears wiggled.

Each time Tora and Kari were angry with him they would thumb their noses at him and shout, "Say *r*! Bah! Come on, say *r*!"

And Åse, who was so small and didn't understand anything, would echo them, saying, "Tay *r*! Bah! Come on, tay *r*!"

For Åse was so small and couldn't say *s*.

And then they all laughed. They sneered and laughed and enjoyed themselves.

Anders knew heaps of things he could have answered, things that would have shut them up one and all. But he never dared to answer right away; he was afraid he'd come across a word with *r* in it.

It was so senseless. It was just impossible to understand.

Everybody else could say *r*. Gorinè could say *r,* and Andrea and Tora and Kari—even Åse, who was more than a year less than he. Well, even Anton, who was so stupid and such an awful boaster and liar.

Sometimes when he thought about it he would get quite beside himself and go down to his hide-out to roll on the ground, crying and screaming and biting the grass because it was so senseless. Often he couldn't bring himself to go that far, but went to sit below the stairs and look at the wall.

This whole period smelled of rubbers.

He had become quite good at getting around all words with *r* in them. When he didn't get excited, he could talk a good deal and get around them most of the time. For there were so many ways of saying something. Most ways were dangerous; but nearly always a way could be found that wasn't dangerous.

He never said *herd,* because then everybody could hear it. He said the *cows* and the *calves* and the *bull calf.* He never said *Bliros* or *Dagros* or *Raina* or *Flekkros* or *Rausi* or *Brandros.* But he could say *Skoglin.*

He was fond of Skoglin.

He never said *Brownie,* and never mare. He said *filly.* When he was thirsty, he never asked for a drink of water but always for a glass of something.

He loved certain words. Others he didn't like.

He loved *sunshine.* He didn't like *rain.*

Now and then he would sit down in his own place between the pine tree and the three little spruces and repeat in a low voice some of the words he loved:

Village. Sun. Sky. Clouds. Lake.

Day. Evening. Sleep.

Come and we'll go to sleep.

Come and we'll go to sleep.

Some words it was impossible to get around. When somebody asked him how old he was, he had to say: Four years!

He had wondered a moment if he shouldn't say five years. Because then there was only one *r* and perhaps they wouldn't notice. But he didn't do it. For if they noticed, his shame would be even greater.

If he fell and hurt himself, he didn't call anybody. Because all had *r*'s in them, except *Anton,* and he wouldn't call Anton.

It was best to get along by yourself. If he had to call somebody, he called Åse. Even if he was angry with Åse; for it was when she learned how to say *r* that they started teasing him.

He could call Father and Mother, of course, for they had only *r* at the end, and it wasn't a clear one, and they never made fun of him. But he didn't call them if somebody could hear him.

It was best to get along by yourself. Best to keep quiet.

Anders got used to being quiet. He sat without saying a word, listening to all the stupid things the others said.

While he sat listening like that, he got into the habit of turning around what they said so that it became even more stupid. And at the same time he tried to avoid all words with *r* in them. He would keep quiet, playing with the words and enjoying himself. And he noticed he was becoming better and better at it. He found more and more words. It was so strange—*he* walked ahead calling, and the words followed like a nice herd of cattle.

They said about Embret that he was so good at turning words. But little by little Anders knew in his own mind that *he* was better. Nobody could turn words the way he did. He often thought of that. He played with this thought. In the morning before he got up and in the evening when he'd gone to bed, he would play with the words and with this thought. And he felt strong and clever and happy. He would be so glad that he sang.

But sometimes when he lay thinking how good he was at it, it suddenly occurred to him why he was so good. Then he seemed to fall down from a high peak into a deep black hole. He was condemned to stay down there, abandoned and alone. All the others were up in the sunlight.

High up, deep down. It was so wearisome. Sometimes he felt he was tired. He seemed to be constantly tensing his muscles. He seemed to be stretching and stretching himself and growing tall as a mountain. It was so wearisome. And it was so cold up there, and he was so alone.

He was different from the others. They were so stupid, and he stood on a tall mountain looking down on them.

But they could say *r*, and he sat in a deep black hole envying them.

It was so difficult. And now and then he got a bit mixed up. How was it—did he look down on them because they could say *r*? Did he envy them that they were so stupid? He could tell he was tired.

Mother had told him about Jesus, and about the devil who took him up to a tall mountain to show him all the kingdoms of the earth and their glory. He could see it before him: he'd been up on Berg Hill once and seen the people down on the road—they'd looked like little insects.

And the devil said: "All this I will give you if you fall down and worship me!" But Jesus wouldn't.

Anders felt now and then, however, that he longed to get down to the small insects swarming about down there and able to say *r*.

It was his tongue that didn't want to.

He worked hard at it, trying over and over again. In the morning before he got up he would lie in bed trying, his eyes fixed on the ceiling. But he couldn't do it. Then Mother came and scolded him because he never wanted to get up.

Later in the day he was unable to practice indoors, he wasn't safe anywhere. It wasn't quite safe in the outbuildings either; before he knew it somebody might come. Embret came to the threshing floor one day he was practicing there, gave him a queer look and asked if he was talking to himself.

The best place was his spot down in the pasture, and in the woodshed. In the rest periods and on Sundays he would wander down to the woodshed, as if by chance. He kept an eye on the road through the cracks in the wall, to make sure he wouldn't be surprised by anybody. He often practiced there.

But he couldn't do it. His tongue didn't want to. It felt so numb and strange in his mouth after he'd been trying for a while. Then he could get quite frantic. Crying with rage, he would grab hold of his tongue with both hands, wanting to tear it out of his mouth. But he wasn't able to do that either, it was stuck, too.

If they hadn't teased him he might have been able to do it. In fact, he was quite certain he could have done it then. But they'd teased him and teased him, and now the whole world seemed to be watching him when he practiced— watching him with an unblinking eye. He wasn't sure, but it reminded him of the snake he'd seen. He felt as if a big snake lay staring at him with an unblinking eye. And deep within its eye *it knew everything* and didn't blink, crept closer when he wasn't looking and stared at him again without lowering its eyes or feeling ashamed. Then he became numb, his tongue withered in his mouth and he couldn't do it.

No, he couldn't do it. He told himself in rage and despair, "Say *r*!"—and then he recalled everything, all the teasing, all the taunts, all the pain; everything was staring at him and his tongue withered in his mouth.

Why should he alone be like that? What had he done to God that he should have a harder time of it than everybody else?

One morning Anders woke up from the sun shining on him in bed. It had to be late, he was alone. It was a nice, bright day, the birch leaves glistened in the sun. A little bird sat on a twig near his window, bobbing up and down and peering into his room, its head askew.

Anders lay still looking out. It was so nice, it almost felt like Sunday today, though it was only mid-week. He would take a holiday today. He felt so glad and light as he lay there looking at the little bird.

"Today I'll take a holiday and not say *r*," he said to himself.

What was it? A sound lingered in his ear—he'd said *r*.

He lay still as a mouse for a while, barely able to breathe. It had happened much too suddenly.

Perhaps he'd heard wrong. His heart pounded. He would try once more; but his heart throbbed and throbbed, so he didn't dare to.

Little by little he grew calmer. Now he *would* try—.

At that moment Mother came in. He had to get up.

He had never before been so quick getting dressed. Mother sat looking at him in wonder. He just slipped out the door.

He was lucky. They were eating. He rushed out, clattered down the back stairs and ran down to the woodshed.

He could do it. He tried several times in a row and could do it every time. It wasn't a random thing anymore, he knew what to do with his tongue to make it say *r*.

He felt so glad, he knew he had to thank God. He didn't quite know what to say, and so he said his evening prayer. There were lots of *r*'s in it, so he'd often had nasty thoughts when he prayed. But now all was just fine, now he could say all of them. He said the prayer twice.

He walked slowly up to the house again. He practiced

difficult words with *r* in them as he walked. Shower, herd, Embret and Gorinè, four years and eleven months. He could do it all almost right away. Nothing was difficult today.

He met them on the steps. And, of course, Anton couldn't keep quiet. "Well, Anders! Have they learned to say *r* today in the country you're from, eh?" He laughed till his tufts of hair wiggled.

Anders didn't even bother to answer him, only walked in straight past him.

It was more difficult than he'd thought. He noticed something strange—he felt uneasy about saying *r* now that he could do it. Andrea was in. She said, "Hello, Anders!"

He remembered that, ever since he'd begun trying, it was her he'd thought of most, it was for her he would say *r*. But now he went around all words with *r* in them, as if nothing had changed.

At last there was one word he couldn't get around. He stammered a little, then he said it. He stood waiting, hot and trembling.

But nothing happened. Andrea walked back and forth, she gave him something to eat, and once she patted his hair.

He couldn't understand. He used a couple of more words with *r* in them, saying them as clearly as he could. But she was doing something over by the stove and seemed barely to listen to him.

Anders felt so strange. It was hurting terribly somewhere. Andrea didn't care about him, she didn't even listen to him. Oh well, no matter. When he grew up he'd come riding in a fine carriage and meet Andrea, and she'd be on foot and have to step to the very edge of the road, and he didn't even look at her. No, he stopped the carriage and…

Mother came into the kitchen and started doing something on the counter.

He couldn't wait any longer. "Mother! I can say *r*, Mother!"

"Really, my boy?" Mother said, without turning around. She was busy with her own things and didn't even seem to have heard what he said.

But then she realized. She turned around and looked at him. "What are you saying? You can say *r*? Let me hear!"

And so he had to let her hear. And Andrea came over. "You can say *r*, really?"

And Åse came toddling in from the bedroom and said what she'd heard the grownups say, "You can tay *r*, really?"

Mother took him by the hand. "Come, we'll go see Father. He'll be so glad!"

Father sat at the table in his office turning the pages of something and didn't look especially glad right away. But when he heard what it was, he smiled and patted Anders' hair several times. He seemed to ponder a while. Then he got up, went over to the big cabinet and opened the door. When he turned around he held something in his hand. It was a shiny little ax. He passed his finger along its bit a couple of times, looking at Anders.

"Look here, Anders, I'd meant to keep this stashed away till your birthday. But since you've been so clever today you'll get it right away. But be careful with it, go down to Embret and ask him to teach you how to use it."

How nice it was. And how heavy it felt in his hand. And it was so shiny. It glinted in the sun. It was the finest ax in the whole world.

"Let's go then, Anders," Mother said. "Now you've got

an ax and have turned into a big, grown-up fellow. Remember that!"

Andrea clapped her hands when she saw the ax. "Well, now I think—now you're a big, grown-up fellow, with an ax and all. Come to me!"

And she put her arms around him, lifted him up and hugged him. Anders was terribly ashamed because somebody was watching. His hands felt so weak and funny and he was about to drop the ax, the handle slipped in his hand. But then he clenched his fist around it with all his strength. He couldn't lose the ax.

He walked down to the woodshed with the ax in the crook of his elbow and a bend in his knees, the way Embret walked.

"Big, grown-up fellow!"

He felt like jumping about and rolling in the grass from sheer joy. But—he had to walk like a grown-up fellow now. Slowly, he walked down toward the woodshed.

Anders stood outside the woodshed chopping wood. Embret had made a small chopping block for him. And Embret had taught him how to use the ax and had put out a whole armful of sticks he'd cut himself. It was these Anders was chopping up. He chopped them up fine, cut them in two, and piled them in a nice stack by the wall of the shed.

It felt strange to stand here chopping wood and making yourself useful. That was something quite different from wandering about alone, playing and fooling around—and turning words!

He struck with both hands, so hard that the ax got stuck in the chopping block and the stick of wood jumped far away.

It was so cozy down here with Embret. It smelled of wood,

resin and sawdust. Especially sawdust. Behind him was the sawhorse, in the midst of a huge pile of sawdust. Embret had made that sawdust, all of it. Every time he pulled the saw, a thin stream of sawdust flew out of the cut and came to rest at the foot of the sawhorse. That's how this big pile had been made. It must have taken a long time, at least several hundred years. It had taken Embret all that time to become as good at chopping wood as he was.

Anders was going to become just as good much faster.

But then he would have to keep at it and not stand around idle! He set about it so eagerly that Embret straightened up inside the shed and looked at him for a moment. He was quite astonished.

"What do I see! I really believe, Anders, you chop just as fast as I do. Look at that nice woodpile, now! It's almost as big as mine!"

Anders felt he was growing in his boots. As good as Embret already! And it was Embret himself who said it.

He heard a voice inside him: Nothing but lies and brag! it said.

Every time Anton and the others had bragged at the table, Anders had been saying these words in his mind. He recognized them very well.

But he didn't want to listen to that stupid voice. He thought of what Embret had said, what Mother had said, and what Andrea had said.

Big, grown-up fellow! As good as Embret already. He thought it again and again; and his woodpile over by the wall seemed to grow and get nice and big.

The bell rang for dinner. Embret planted his ax in the chopping block and came lumbering out of the shed.

"Well, Anders, aren't you coming in with me? You could use a real good meal now."

Yes, he was hungry. He was about to turn around and go with Embret.

But—if he remained here and chopped as hard as he could without a break while the others ate and took an afternoon nap, his woodpile would get still much bigger, as big as a house, and Embret would be in for a great surprise and would call the others, and everybody would come and look at his big woodpile. And they would all say—

"I'll come later!" he said.

Then he was alone. He went into the shed to fetch another armful of wood. That way the pile in there became a bit smaller, too.

He chopped as hard as he could.

Actually it was quite tiring. He didn't think the ax was as sharp as it had been. He often had to chop two or three times to cut a little stick of wood in two; and it was so difficult to hit again the same spot he'd hit before, for the stick seemed to lie in a different place, and therefore the ax hit a different place. And many of the sticks were so difficult to split. And the sun felt so awfully hot.

He chopped and he chopped. It wasn't as much fun as it had been at first. Had he gone at it a bit too hard? Or had he been going on a bit too long? He felt it was fagging him out. Something wasn't quite the way it ought to be, somewhere.

It was probably time to quit now. Somehow he felt it was.

But no. The woodpile wasn't big enough. It was tremendously big already and he could chop as fast as Embret already, and soon his pile would be just as big as Embret's. But it wasn't quite big enough, it had to be even bigger, so it became the biggest woodpile in the world, so that Andrea and Gorinè and Anton and all of them would come running, cry like crazy and say...

But he would straighten up and take a little breather anyhow.

He straightened up.

It was as if a cloud covered the sun, the whole world faded and turned gray. And in the same moment he made poo-poo in his pants.

His thoughts were in a whirl. But one thought appeared again and again: This God had done.

This God had done to take revenge.

He was falling and falling. Falling and falling—from a tremendous height, from a tall mountain, down, down, down into a deep black hole.

"Lies and brag! Lies and brag!" He'd heard the voice the whole time. He'd heard it clearly, oh, he'd heard it so clearly! But he hadn't wanted to listen—because he wanted praise.

And now he probably had to go in. He looked about him, but there didn't seem to be any other way. He looked at the woodpile. Poor little woodpile. Then he let the ax slip out of his hand. It fell to the ground.

He started to walk.

He had never noticed that the walk from the woodshed up to the house was so long. It was awfully long. It was because he himself was so small. His legs were so short. Especially now when his pants were so bothersome.

Slowly, he inched his way toward the house.

He climbed the back stairs. His thoughts were busy with

one thing: whether he could get through the kitchen and into the bedroom to Mother without being seen. Oh, if only God would be nice this one time and let him get through unseen…

But they were eating. And they had been talking about him. The moment he came in he heard Anton's voice.

"There he is!"

And Anton looked at him and had such a nice, friendly voice. "Well, Anders, I hear you've been such a clever fellow. If you want to, you can come to the mill with me tonight!"

Embret nodded. "Sure, chopping wood—that he knows already. He chops like a grown man, he does."

Andrea looked at him. "Anders will soon be a big, grown man now, you'll see."

"That's so, for sure!" Gorinè said.

Andrea got up and came over to him. "Now that you've been so clever, you must come and get something to eat with the grownups."

She patted his hair. But then she seemed to become a bit doubtful.

"Or perhaps we should—."

She laughed.

Anders tore himself away and rushed into the bedroom.

The World

THE ROAD RUNS to the world's end. It's like a long snake that reaches around the whole world. It gets lost and pops up again and runs around the entire hamlet and all the way to the world's end.

All who come from far away and have far to go travel the road. All who live close by and lie in wait and listen travel the road.

Mother says, and Gorinè and Andrea say, "Remember the people on the road."

They say, "What will the people on the road think if they see you now!"

They say, "What will the people on the road say if they see you now!"

It's mostly the womenfolk who say such things. Father and Embret don't care very much what people on the road may think.

A tall skinny man comes walking down the road. He's leading a little boy by the hand.

They stand by the kitchen window following him with their eyes and talking in low voices.

Martin Millom. His oldest son is dead. His oldest daughter is dead. That's her boy.

TB.
They lower their voices.

An old woman comes trudging by.

She walks so unevenly. Every now and then she stops and makes angry gestures in the air. Sometimes she lowers her head and butts. At other times she squats at the edge of the road. She sits there in broad daylight making ca-ca, and if somebody comes she just keeps sitting; because she's crazy and is called Kari. Her eyes are planted deep in her head, a black something with a fire inside.

She's been walking like that for many, many years. She goes around believing her husband is in hell. It's him she's talking to on the road. It's the devil himself she's lashing out at with her fists. The grownups shake their heads and feel sorry for her, then repeat something she has said and laugh.

She's allowed to roam around freely in the summer, for she isn't dangerous. In the winter they take her in, so she won't hit the road and freeze to death. In the winter she dirties herself and is worse than a pig.

The sunshine grows a little darker when Crazy-Kari from Moen trudges past.

The sun shines, there's thunder and rain. Once in a while the rainbow stands like a big gateway over the lake and the east hamlet. Once he thought that was where the Garden of Eden lay. That was a long time ago.

People from cotter country walk the road with loads on their backs and pails in their hands. They're on their way to the store with blueberries.

"Thank God a little something still grows in the woods,"
they say.

In the evening people stroll back and forth on the road.
Darkclad men and women in light colors. Dark and light,
dark and light down the road. They stop at the crossroads.
The air rings and echoes with dark laughter and light laughter.

"Now you must come in and go to bed," Mother says.

The sun hasn't set, it's daylight, he's not tired. The air
rings and echoes down the road.

Now you must come in and go to bed.

Through the open window float the murmur of the waterfall, a fragrance of clover, footsteps and voices from the
road, three notes from a bird over and over again. The dry,
fluttering rustle from the aspen down by the woodshed.
And ever and always, the ceaseless murmur of the waterfall. He falls asleep within it.

"The road is for everybody!" the grownups say.

All sorts of oddities travel the road. Folk on wheels—
you can always tell who they are by the horse. They bend
forward over the table, put their faces against the pane and
say: There's Brownie from Garmo! There comes Blackie
from Østmo! And afterward they have something to talk
about for a long time: who sat inside, who was driving,
whether they went fast or slow, where they might be going—to midwife or doctor, to grocer or sheriff. If it was a
post run, whether it was on time or not. On some farms
the post run is always late taking off, for the wife dawdles
and quarrels with her husband till it's past starting time,
and so the horse has to suffer.

If somebody drives past while the grownups are eating, they remain at table longer than usual. There is so much to talk about.

A boy scurries up the road just before noontime. Some time passes, then he scurries down the road again. He isn't much bigger than Anders, but is much bigger anyway because he goes to school, and it's from school he's scurrying and to school he's scurrying back. It's the long break. He's from Tuven and his name is Lars; they are so poor at Tuven that Lars doesn't bring his school lunch but has to run home and suck his mother.

It's strange. Much bigger than Anders and still sucking his mother. It's sure to be a sin. That's why his back is so long and his legs so short.

The wife at Tuven once dropped by the kitchen. She sat crying on a chair. Afterward she ate at the table. Then she was gone.

She looked almost like other women, but she ate in such an ugly way and swallowed such big pieces. And her husband is in jail, because he is a criminal, because he stole half a sack of flour at the store.

"Today there is a funeral!" one of the grownups says at the dinner table.

Then the day becomes big and fine and solemn, almost like Sunday. He and Åse are on the lookout, waiting for the quiet black procession.

The party drives slowly through the yard. Slowly and heavily. Overcast weather and a low sky always hang over a funeral, even if the sun is shining.

Anders has learned to count to twenty. There are hardly ever more horses than that.

Up a bit from the yard the road runs across an open field; there the sexton can see the funeral party from the belfry, and then he begins to ring the bells. There's a taste of Christmas cake and a smell of evergreens. It's so pretty.

If it is a funeral procession from the north hamlet, it doesn't cross the yard, but they can see it from the stairs to the storehouse as it crawls onto the grounds of the parsonage, long and black like a snake. Then the church bells start ringing.

Not all funerals are equally nice. Some are small and end quickly. Others are much bigger and last longer. It's best when it rains and the wind blows. The wind has to blow from the church toward the play rock, and it shouldn't be an even wind but a gusty one, and every gust must bring a little rain. Funerals are nicest in the fall.

Funerals are some of the nicest things on the road.

Near the road sit the servants' quarters. A window with small panes faces the road, and those who are inside can see the head and half the body of every passerby. In the evening it's always full of people in there—they come and go, most of those who walk the road drop in. You can hear the chattering a good way down the road. And if you get close and open the door, you are met by a crash of talk and a cloud of blue tobacco smoke. They sit there wrapped in a blue, sour cloud, spitting, talking and laughing. Many belong to the most famous people in the entire hamlet. Martin Teppen, Per Myra, who is perhaps the strongest man in the whole world; Ole Fallet, Nils on the Slope, Karl Norderud, Ole Hagaen with his stiff, crooked leg, so that they call him Hobblehack; Tørjer Lykkjen, Kerstaffer Nust, Mons Bru, Edvart Saga,

Amund Inngjerdingen and Even Oppi, the shoemaker, whom they call Even Pitchatwine. And many, many more.

They chat and laugh and tell stories. When somebody walks past the window and doesn't come in, they tell stories about him.

Embret sits on the edge of his bed. He smokes in silence. He says a few words only once in a while, but then the others often laugh. He has such a knack for turning his words, Embret does.

In the fall, when it gets dark before supper time, Anders is allowed to go to the servants' quarters to give the call for supper. There's light from the kitchen and it's such a short distance, so he's never scared. For it's so exciting to go in there and see all those men sitting around on the benches and on the edges of the beds, to hear their voices, their laughter and bits of stories.

When he grows up, he'll sit up there in the servants' quarters every evening listening to stories about fist fights and tough guys, and about weird people from faraway hamlets.

But it's dangerous to walk past such windows.

Embret is full of strange sayings.

He says, "He who lies on the floor doesn't take a fall."

He says, "You can never cast a stone so high it won't hit the ground again."

He says, "It's safe to brag when you're far from home."

He says, "Good fortune leads to pride and pride leads to more pride, and so it ends up on the dunghill."

Anders understands very well what he means by it all. He means, "Good fortune makes you stuck-up and foolish, you want to be more of a man than you are—and so you make poo-poo in your pants."

He means, "Be careful and think things over, and you won't have to make a fool of yourself and make poo-poo in your pants. Then they won't sit behind the panes laughing at you."

"Devil up my ass! Devil up my sweet ass!"

He stands out on the stoop. It's getting dark. It's Christmas time. At dusk the known part of the world grows smaller and smaller, and all that's unknown and dangerous draws nearer and lies in wait. He stands on the stoop staring into space, hears the howls far away and the screams much more nearby: "Devil up my ass! Devil up my sweet ass!"

He hears somebody hollering, a hard sound and a long scream, then the thud of somebody falling. Suddenly Gorinè is behind him, saying, "Come Anders, let's go in."

In the corner stands the clock. With a big, bright dial of brass and a long, red-painted stomach. In the middle of the stomach is a hole. There he can see the pendulum move back and forth, back and forth.

There's something—he doesn't quite know—the clock reminds him of something.

It must be the dial.

The dial is of brass, full of strange signs that he understands and doesn't understand.

It reminds him of the year.

He has seen a picture of the year. It's an old man with an hourglass, and the clock on the wall marks twelve, the old man is leaving and a little boy comes in. It's the old and the new year.

But no, that's not the way it is. The year is a big, big wheel—like the mill wheel but much bigger. It stands behind the clouds somewhere. And *Time* passes, pulling it around, much the way the horse goes around by the barn pulling the horse walk to make the threshing machine turn inside the barn. And *Time* is a hoary old man with an hourglass in his hand. Once in a while he is God, with a white beard, but sometimes he is skinny.

Anyway, the clock and the road are somehow part of everything, only he doesn't quite know…He dreams that he knows it every now and then, and can see the connection. But when he wakes up it's gone again, and he can only see a glimpse of the connection, a man who turns his back to him and walks down a dark road.

Later that winter he gets sick and stays in bed. Mother sits with him, and her face grows big and small, big and small. He dreams that he sees the connection, big and terrible, and he's filled with dread and screams till he wakes up. Then it's the middle of the night, it's lonely, and the moon shines into the room through the pane—it looks bright between the clouds and is a horseman riding off in a flapping cape, it's a dial of gleaming brass with strange signs, it points at him with long fingers which come in through the pane and mean to get him. But he sees how cold and terribly lonely it is up there and doesn't want to go. And all this has happened to him once before.

Afterward the moon is always there when he thinks about the clock ticking and the year turning around, and it gets more difficult than before to see the connection. And when he dreams about it, it's terrible, and he wakes up in fear and with a taste of medicine in his mouth, but the connection is gone—it flees down the road like a shadow with an hourglass in its hand.

This happens in the winter, he's a little over five years old.

Sometimes there are long periods when he doesn't dream. Then, again, a time may come when he dreams every night and knows he'll dream every night.

It may start some evening, after a day so joyful and lively that he's dead tired and goes to sleep in his chair in the evening. Asleep and yet awake, slumped uncomfortably in his chair with the sound of voices in his ears, sitting in the warm yellow light of the winter lamp which he senses through his eyelids, he dreams, remembering that he's standing alone in a dark attic, in a white yard, that he's lying alone in a white room with many people, that *Something* is coming toward him, that he's seeing the *Connection*, big and terrible—until he wakes up with a scream. The scream sits in his ears when he awakes and starts up from his chair.

"He's growing!" the grownups say.

The Writing Table

"No!" Father said.

It was in the spring, Anders was between five and six years old.

New things were happening every day, which gave him more than enough to do.

The sheet of ice north of the stoop was getting smaller and smaller day by day. Anders put sticks along the edge of the ice in the evening, and in the morning he measured how much it had shrunk while he slept. There was a little pool of water by the ice sheet every morning, and he guided it down the yard in long streams.

The yard was free of snow, but a long sheet of ice remained where the road to the woodshed went last winter; there he could go skating. But it was quite difficult, because the many horse droppings on the ice made him fall on his face. Large flocks of sparrows came to eat the horse droppings, looking like gray old horse droppings themselves; but they didn't sit still.

It was wet in the yard. Embret had put out boards to walk on. Meeting Pussy there was fun, for it was smaller than you and had to step into the mud. It didn't like it but said nothing, just stepped up on the board again right away and shook its paws one by one before going on.

Down by the hayloft was a hollow in the ground after an old well that had been filled in long ago, before Anders could remember. The ground was wet and sticky and you weren't allowed to play there, but nobody could see you from the house. Afterward your boots said squish, squish.

A new bird had come to the farm. It would sing in the birch tree around the corner and was much more of a bird than crows or sparrows. Anders didn't know it. Every now and then, when he sat in the yard making himself some big things out of clay, it would come hopping along and stare at him, its head cocked. Anders stared back.

It was called starling, the grownups said.

It was called starling. He knew it a little better from then on.

He had to be on the watch for all this and much more—the trees changing from one day to the next, the growing river carrying the first logs, which crashed with a thundering noise into the waterfall, the coltsfoots and the white anemones that were popping up beside the road. And then the puddles all around him, where he could sail with bark boats and an old shoe. No day was alike, and Anders fell asleep in his chair every evening.

Still, he would often forget what he was to watch for and become lost in thought, not knowing where he was. Sometimes he had just made a fine long trench for the water from the ice sheet, opened the dam and placed a log on the stream, ready to follow it closely to see if it went all the way down to the big gray stone called Denmark—but when he came back to his senses, the water had long since run out and the log was gone. Or he would sit on the strip of ice by the woodshed looking at the sparrows eat and make a row, and at Pussy blinking its eyes a little way off. Then, before he knew where he was, his fanny felt cold and wet and unpleasant from the ice that had melted under him.

The thing was that Father and Martin didn't want to be friends.

When Anders grew up he wanted to be like Father. But he still had far to go to get there, and he wasn't always sure he would ever get that far.

Father had a beard like God in the Bible, though he was much younger. He was the strongest man there was, almost as strong as God. Grabbing Anders under the arms, he would lift him all the way to the ceiling.

"That's how tall you'll be some day," Father said.

When Father said so it was true; for Father never lied. He was the only one who never lied.

Father was the smartest man there was. When he walked back and forth in the office with his long pipe in his mouth, he wanted to *think*, and nobody could disturb him. Then he was alone with God, like Moses on the mountain who Mother had told him about. And when he came out of the office, he had the tables of the law.

And now Father had forbidden Anders to spend time with Martin.

It wasn't all that unreasonable, perhaps. Martin had his faults, and if Anders had been a grown man, old, he might not have wanted to spend time with him. But things were quite different. There were so many things you couldn't talk about with the grownups, but you could talk to Martin.

Martin was much more grown-up than Anders. He was three years older and that was quite a lot, yet he was much closer to him than the grownups were.

Martin had light-red hair and many round freckles in his face. That was because he was stronger and braver than others.

Martin had a wet spot under his nose. Not always, but nearly always. Anders had asked him once why he always walked around with a wet spot under his nose. Because it wasn't pretty, Mother had said so, and Anders himself almost never had a wet spot under his nose anymore.

Martin just sniffed. All the regular guys had wet spots under their noses, and when Anders didn't, that was simply because he was a little worm.

This might sound quite right at first. But later, when he'd thought it over, Anders felt less sure; anyway, he still kept dry.

All in all there were many things about Martin that Anders didn't feel quite sure about. Martin didn't always tell the truth, and he was an awful braggart. And Father had said that only scared or stupid people went around bragging.

Martin often looked stupid when he bragged, and Anders felt so ashamed he couldn't utter a word but had to stand still with his eyes on the ground. He felt that Martin was making poo-poo in his pants before his very eyes. But then he'd found a way out. He let on he believed it all. Then he also felt ashamed of himself, and the shame was on both sides. That way it was a little easier.

But it was true that Martin was terribly strong and brave. It was true he dared to do lots of things Anders didn't dare. He dared to call his mother an old biddy right to her face, and he dared to say almost anything, whatever it might be, about nearly everybody. And he knew lots of things: he could do headstands, he could say the Lord's Prayer backward, he could spit between his teeth, he could put three fingers in his mouth and whistle like a hawk, making all the chickens cackle and take cover, and he could wiggle his ears.

When Anders grew up he wanted to be almost like Martin.

But when he really grew up, he wanted to be like Father.

Things were not very easy.

When nobody was in the office Anders would sometimes steal in. He would walk back and forth with a long stick in his mouth, smoking a long-stemmed pipe. He wanted to *think*. But he had to take out the stick once in a while, because he couldn't possibly spit between his teeth with a stick in his mouth. And then he couldn't help remembering what Father had said: No decent people walk around spitting that way.

No, things were not very easy.

And now Father had forbidden him, in so many words, to spend time with Martin. Because Martin was no good, Father said, and besides he had lice.

But that was unfair. Martin wasn't to blame for that, was he? It must be his mother who was to blame for that? And *her* he used to call the most awful names.

Sometimes Father was almost like God in the Bible. For he also was a too strict and unreasonable God, in the Old Testament.

These were the things that made Anders have a difficult time these days and gave him so much to think about.

One day he was indoors he noticed Martin in the yard.

But Mother went out and said something to him, then said some more, and Martin left. Martin's pants looked so droopy in the back as he left. It was very painful. It reminded him of so much that was painful. And Anders understood that he had to talk to Martin.

One day he met him down the road.

"Why don't they let you spend time with me?" Martin asked.

Anders had to come out with some of it. "They say you teach me things."

Martin snorted. "You can tell them from me you could use some, by golly!"

He wanted to know more, and Anders had to come out with some more. But he didn't say anything about the lice, that was impossible. And then, all at once, he felt he had a guilty conscience about so many things—about Father, about himself, Martin, the lice—he couldn't quite keep track of it.

Martin said, "You can tell your father from me that he's a stinker. And you can tell your mother from me that you're a sissy!"

With that he turned around and left.

Anders remained, thinking he ought to have hit him for what he said about Father. But he was so far away. And besides—what he'd said about his being a sissy was true.

He thought for another moment. Then he ran after Martin, caught up with him and hit him.

"Take that one for the 'stinker'!"

Martin gaped, astonished. "Do you want me to show the good Lord your shoe soles?" he said.

Then he did it.

Anders got a nosebleed. Martin helped him wash it off. Then they parted.

Anders still spent time with Martin on the sly. It couldn't be helped, because Martin wanted it, so what was Anders to do? If only Father hadn't mentioned the lice...Anyway, it wasn't only that.

When Martin whistled behind the hayloft, Anders had to get up and obey.

It wasn't as much fun to be with Martin now as it had been. For Martin had become so suspicious, was often cranky and stubborn, and he bragged worse than ever. And Anders' conscience always bothered him about something or other. Oh, he was probably afraid his father might come. And then, perhaps—well, he somehow felt Martin was sort of making poo-poo in his pants so often...

He would often sit lost in thought.

When he grew up he would send for Father and Martin and make a speech for them.

And then he would say, Now shake hands!

And so they shook hands and were always friends afterward.

But once in a while when he had such thoughts, he suddenly felt as though he could see right through them. And then he saw that his thinking was wrong. Martin and Father didn't suit each other and couldn't ever be friends. And Anders understood that, as long as he lived, he would always find himself in between these two, who could never take to each other. It was like having a heavy burden placed upon your shoulders. And he had to carry it alone, he couldn't share it with anybody.

Then came a day when much of this changed.

It was right after dinner. Anders sat in the yard working on some canals. It was quite still in the yard and all quiet in the house. Father and Mother had gone off to a meeting, Embret and Anton were asleep in the servants' quarters, Tora and Kari were at school, and Gorinè and Andrea weren't to be seen. Pussy lolled on a board, too lazy even to purr. Anders was lost in thought and his work came to a dead stop.

Then he heard the signal.

He didn't feel very happy. Actually, he would have liked to be alone today. But that was out of the question now. He got up and headed toward the back of the hayloft.

Martin had been to the smithy with his father today— his whole face was nice and sooty, except under the nose, where he was white and wet.

Martin looked at him. "Can you rhyme?" he asked.

Anders didn't think he could rhyme.

Martin sniffed. "You can't do anything. Say *cakes*!"

Anders didn't understand but said *cakes*.

"Jakes!" Martin said. He looked cocky and unsure. His whole face took on the air that Anders knew so well by now; it seemed about to take off—backward or forward.

So that was how he knew how to rhyme! Anders was terribly ashamed and didn't know what to do, he was so afraid Martin would notice. He smiled, full of admiration. Martin became very happy.

"Say bump!" he said.

"Bump!"

"Rump!" said Martin. "Say lamb!"

"Lamb!" Anders stood looking at the ground.

"Damn!" said Martin. "I can rhyme, can't I?"

"Yes."

"It's more than you can do!"

"Yes!" Anders said, looking away.

It grew quiet. Restless, Martin kept shifting his feet. Then something occurred to him and he pulled a big stick from his pocket.

"You see this? It's a willow flute. Father made it for me 'cause I helped him in the smithy."

And Martin blew the flute, making a long, slightly wheezy sound.

Anders had never heard anything so pretty. He became so glad, he forgot everything else right away.

"Blow once more!" he said. And Martin blew. Anders wasn't allowed to blow, he was much too small. But perhaps Martin would sell him the flute some day, because Martin's father could make another flute, he could make a hundred flutes a day if he cared to. Anders' father couldn't make even one.

Anders wasn't going to let him get away with that. He said, "But my father has got a nice writing table. And your father doesn't."

Martin pricked up his ears. "Writing table, what's that?"

Anders had to explain. "It's a nice big table, and it's black and made from a tree that doesn't grow here and is called oak, and it has three drawers on each side and a big hole in the middle, and when you want to write you have to put your legs into this hole. It takes two men to carry it, and there isn't another table like it anywhere."

The last bit Anders had heard from Embret, and *he* was down in the woodshed chopping wood. Anders could hear the blows from where he stood, they somehow made him more confident that he was telling the truth.

Martin was speechless and unsure of himself for a moment, but then he waved it aside. "I don't believe what you're telling me. There aren't any tables like that. You've been giving me a bag of lies lately."

"I never lie!" Anders said. And as soon as he'd said it he knew he was lying. For he hadn't always told the truth lately, he lied and bragged every now and then. And he knew he'd learned it from Martin. And from Martin he'd also learned to say: I never lie.

Martin wanted to see the table before believing in it. Anders could show it to him, couldn't he? After all, his father was away, jaunting about in his carriage. Or perhaps Anders was scared?

Anders was terribly scared. But he saw Martin's wry smile.

"I'm not scared," he said, "and I'll show you the table right away—if you aren't too scared to come into the house with me."

"Scared?" Martin spat between his teeth. "I'm never scared."

Both remained silent for a while, without looking at each other. They seemed to be lost in thought.

Anders was the first to speak. "Come, let's go then," he said, a bit huskily. He didn't recognize his own voice.

"Okay, if you insist!" Martin said. His voice also sounded a little strange.

Perhaps he wasn't so very keen on it either.

Why did they do it then, if neither of them was keen on it?

But he couldn't think any more about it, for now they had to go.

They went along the back of the barn. Nobody could see them there, but they walked on tiptoe anyway, with arched backs. They turned the corner and came up to the garden fence. There was nobody around. They stole forward, snuggling up to the gray old picket fence. It couldn't give them cover, since they were on the side that faced the yard, but somehow they still felt safer there than in the open.

Now they were at the corner of the house. They hugged the wall and inched their way to the stoop. There they stopped to look around. They were both out of breath, even though they'd gone at a slow, gingerly pace from the very start. Anders pricked up his ears, but the only thing he heard were his own heartbeats. Could Martin hear them too? After stealing a glance at him, Anders felt more at ease, fairly sure Martin hadn't heard anything—he was looking about him in every direction, and if Anders hadn't known better he might have gotten the idea that Martin was a bit scared.

Anders turned and walked toward the stoop. He wanted to get this over with.

The three steps creaked loudly. They'd never groaned like that before. Both stood still again for a moment, without breathing. But not a sound could be heard.

They had to move on. Only the entrance hall remained.

The entrance hall was dangerous. It was big and dark, and to one side was the kitchen. Far up was the door to the office.

Several floor boards creaked awfully, and it was hard to believe that nobody could hear them. But no one came. Then they stood at the door.

It opened without creaking.

There was nobody in the office. Anders drew a sigh of relief, he noticed that his whole body was trembling. He let Martin walk past him through the door.

In the middle of the floor stood the gleaming table, big and black and glossy.

Martin stopped to look at it for a moment—then he turned to Anders and whispered, "Father could lift that thing with one arm."

Anders didn't answer. He was just wondering if they would get out again safely. Oh, if only they got out again safely—then he would never again—never—then he'd say his evening prayers every evening and wash his ears every morning, and he'd give away his knife—or at least not use it Sundays anymore.

Martin paced about the room. He was beginning to look like himself again. He gave a long spit between his teeth, from near the stove almost to the window. And then he caught sight of the long-stemmed pipe over on the pipe rack.

Anders whispered quickly, "Don't touch it!"

But Martin had already grabbed it and was walking around the room, the tip of the pipe between his teeth. Anders felt so small, his stomach so empty and queer. There was no denying it, Martin was brave, braver than anybody else. But if he'd been a little less brave, life would be easier.

Somebody opened and closed a door farther back and Martin dropped the pipe on the floor; the seat of his pants seemed to droop suddenly, and in a twinkling he slipped through the door.

Anders was transfixed. He just stood there, staring at the pipe. It was lying in the middle of the floor. It was probably broken. And now somebody was bound to come in from the living room—.

But nobody came, there wasn't anybody in the living room, it seemed. Anders edged up to the pipe.

He didn't dare pick it up at once, just circled it for a while. But he couldn't see any crack in it. Perhaps it was still whole?

He bent down and picked it up.

It was still whole. And Anders felt how glad he was—he would be nice to everybody from now on.

Then he replaced the pipe and left.

There was nobody in the yard, but he heard a whistle behind the barn. Slowly, Anders walked down there.

Martin was gazing straight ahead of him. He was the same as ever. Without looking at Anders, he said, "My father has a cabinet, it stands in the room behind the smithy. Along the edge it has a carved molding. That cabinet is much nicer than your writing table."

With that he left. He was sullen and crabby.

Anders remained for a moment, pondering.

The last thing Martin said had hurt a little. Not because he minded what Martin said. He didn't care about him. But it was annoying about the carving. For it was true, there were no carvings on the writing table.

Anders started thinking. And when he went up to the house again, he knew what he would do.

Anders had a knife. It was a jackknife, he had gotten it from Embret. It was an awfully nice knife, Embret had said. And part of the nice thing about it was that it was almost impossible to cut yourself with it. It had only one fault: it wouldn't shut properly, because the spring was a bit slack. It had a handle as bright as silver, and on the handle it said

Eskilstuna in big letters. Anders couldn't read, but Embret
had read it to him, and he could see it was written there.

Anders would carve a molding along the edge of the
writing table with his knife. Eskilstuna. Anders was very
good at this. He had carved a border on one of the chopping
boards with the knife and been praised for it; and not many
days ago he'd drawn a nice long edging with red chalk on
the foundation wall outside the office. And then Father had
patted his hair and said, "That's very nice. Do more things
like that, but not on the house."

On the way up to the house Anders clearly pictured how
the carving was going to be. It would look like Hardanger
embroidery, and he would cut it with the knife point along
the edge of the table. Then the writing table would become
much prettier than the cabinet. And Father would call him
into his office, stroke his hair and say—. He didn't quite
know what Father would say but felt warm and happy. He
started running toward the house. There was little time,
they were expected home again soon.

It went so smoothly, there was nothing to it. The knife
point cut lines in the glossy surface and forced its way into
the oak wood. Pretty, gray lines formed at the black table
edge. And the pattern became even prettier than he'd imagined beforehand.

What would Father say when he came home and noticed this carving? He would say: Well, look at that! as he
used to when he was happy about something. And then he
would call, Anders! And Anders would come in from the
entrance hall. Father would look at Anders and say, "Is it
you who have done this, Anders?" "Yes," Anders would
say. And Father would look gently at Anders until Anders'
eyes began to water, then he would say—.

Anders was dreaming.

But the knife was taking its course, and the carving was getting bigger and bigger and prettier and prettier. Then it was finished. Anders blew away some wood dust from the streaks. The pattern was there, fine as a spider's web but clear. And now he could hear the carriage wheels in the yard. He sneaked out into the entrance hall.

Father was in a good humor, he patted Anders' head when he walked past him. Anders felt a lump in his throat.

Father went to his office. Anders remained standing in the entrance hall. His heart was pounding. He had to sit down on the stairs to the second floor for a moment.

A long time passed. Anders had counted to twenty many times.

Then it came.

A crashing noise started up in the office—quite low, but Anders knew the sound well. It came so abruptly, the floor seemed to melt away, he sank and sank…

He suddenly understood what he had done.

It was all due to…

He understood very well what it was due to. But when he looked closer, it turned into a long line of many things, one behind the other as far as eye could see. He couldn't quite make out the last one… It bothered him that he thought he'd gone through all this before—many times before—only he couldn't quite remember—

"Anders!"

It was Father, standing in the doorway.

"Come in here, Anders!"

Mother was also there.

Father looked at him, red in the face.

"Is it you who've done this, Anders?"

"No!" Anders said.

Father banged the table so hard that the inkwell jumped.

"I ask you once more, Is it you?"

"No."

He didn't recognize his own voice.

Mother didn't say anything.

"Go into the hall and think it over!" Father said.

He went into the hall. He sat down on the lowest step of the stairs. He tried to think of something but couldn't.

A few moments passed. Then Mother came out. Not from the office but from the kitchen. She sat down beside him.

"Is it you who've done it, Anders? Tell me."

He burst into tears.

"Yes."

"But why did you do it, Anders?"

He didn't answer.

"Why did you do it?"

He saw a long line of things. But it was so far away, he couldn't get hold of it.

It was no use, no use at all, to try and explain.

"I don't know."

She sat for a while, but he had nothing more to say. She got up and went into the office.

A moment later Father stood in the doorway.

"Come in here, Anders!"

Mother was there.

Father had a very sharp, staring look in his eyes.

"Well. So it was you who did it. *Why* did you do it? Answer!"

She had gone straight in and told him.

"*Why* did you do it, I say! Answer!"

"But—," Mother said.

Father waved her aside.

"You take a walk. Anders and I will manage this."

"But—."

Father stamped the floor. Mother stayed another moment—then she left. She turned around at the door, as if she wanted to say something; but then she left and the door closed behind her.

He was left alone with Father.

"Why did you do it, Anders?"

He looked at Father's face way up there.

It was no use.

"I see. You won't answer?"

He went to fetch the birch from behind the mirror. Took his place and looked at Anders.

"You know, Anders, you've often done things I've told you not to do. But I haven't seen anything really wicked in it. Today is the first time I've seen you doing naughty things out of wickedness.

"Wickedness pure and simple!"

He was getting himself worked up. Puffing himself up.

"You've ruined my writing table out of sheer wickedness. But I'll teach you! I ask you for the last time, Why did you do it?"

Anders looked at him. Father had grown so tall, he almost reached the ceiling.

"Because you are a stinker!" he said.

Father gave a start. But otherwise he almost seemed to be pleased. He stopped puffing himself up.

"So. You've been keeping company with Martin?"

"Yes."

"I see. Unbutton your trousers!"

Anders counted to seven.

Father put him down. "Will you say you're sorry?"

Anders looked at him without a word. Slowly, Father's face was getting red again.

"So. It wasn't enough!"

He hit harder now. Anders didn't scream or cry.

"Will you say you're sorry?"

He looked at the tall, strange man. "No."

It hurt more and more each time. He shivered, his body was seared by red-hot flames. He had to scream but couldn't cry, he seemed to have become dry and cracked inside.

The fifth time he said he was sorry. Father's face was so big. It was strange that he could have such a huge face when he was so far away.

When he got out into the hall, she was there. She took a step toward him.

"Anders!"

He saw a straight line leading up to the door from where he stood, followed it and got past her.

They were talking and laughing in the kitchen. It was the afternoon meal.

She'd gone straight in and told him.

It was so strange—he was so far away. If only he could remember when all this had happened to him before.

He walked down toward the woodshed.

If only he could remember....

There was a smell of resin and sawdust in the woodshed. The sun was shooting curtains of light through the chinks in the wall.

He just stood there looking at the wall.

Alone

H E DIDN'T TELL HER what he thought of her. That would be to let her know something. And she wouldn't get to know anything ever again.

A couple of times she tried to talk to him—very cautiously, she seemed to find it very difficult. But he pretended he didn't understand. Each time was just like that day in the entrance hall, as if he saw a straight line up to the door which he had to follow, without looking either right or left.

He managed to get away both times.

The days were going by. He stayed away from her as best he could. He shunned the office. There was the writing table, and he didn't want to see it ever again; that wasn't why, though, but he knew that, if he met her alone in there, then they would have to talk.

He avoided her every way he could. But that, too, was dangerous.

"You've changed so, Anders!" she said one day.

"Me? What do you mean?" he said, and managed to slip away. But he understood he must be careful, still more careful, so she wouldn't notice anything. Because he just wouldn't, he wouldn't, talk to her. And little by little he realized why. He was afraid he might cry. And that must never happen. He would do anything in the world rather than that.

And so he was still more careful—he watched himself, did his best to act the same as before and made sure he was never alone with her.

Embret had a saying, "Walk quietly and speak softly and sit by the door, then few will notice you and you'll be left alone."

He remembered that.

Some time passed. She no longer noticed anything. Perhaps she'd forgotten it all. He breathed more easily. But he took note of the fact that she no longer noticed anything, and that made him even colder. It was a cold that pierced him to the quick. Summer came, with warm weather, but a teeth-chattering cold would grab him in the middle of a warm summer day.

It wasn't only Mother. Mother was a woman. Every woman was like Mother. They curried favor and buttered you up, and then they went and told on you. Tora was like that. Kari was like that. Andrea was like that. Even Gorinè was like that. They had the same eyes, all of them, women's eyes that weren't to be trusted.

Only one woman wasn't quite a woman, and from her he didn't quite shut himself off, not always anyway. That was Åse. Åse was different from the others. But perhaps it was because she was so small.

Once in a while he went down to the woodshed to talk a little with Embret. But apart from that, he was often alone this spring and a good part of the summer.

Then came the haying season, and Amund along with it.

Amund had gone to confirmation class the year before but was much taller than others the same age. Three of them were helping with the mowing this summer, all three the same age; but Amund was much taller and stronger than the other two, and the best in every way.

Amund had such a remarkably handsome face. He looked just like the Indian in the picture book, brown and skinny, with a sharp, curved nose, high cheekbones and deep-set eyes. Anders stopped to stare at him the first time he saw him, at the morning meal the first haying day.

That was what he wanted to look like when he grew up.

He kept thinking about Amund all day long afterward, wanted to be around only where Amund was and wished to make friends only with him. But nobody must know about it. If they knew, they would laugh, shout and laugh, slap their knees and laugh, thumb noses at him and laugh, laugh, laugh—everybody would laugh, Tora and Kari, Andrea and Gorinè, Mother and Father and Embret, even Åse would thumb her nose at him and laugh—that he could dream of something so absurd, something so impossible as to make friends with Amund and get to be like him when he grew up.

So he kept it a secret. Admired him at a distance, never dared show it, or say it. He would sit by the kitchen window in the brief morning and afternoon rest periods, when the hired hands sat in the yard or lounged about by the wall. He sat watching Amund all the time—following him with his eyes and noting how he walked and stood and sat, how he turned his head and looked back over his shoulder. When Anders grew up he would do all these things, exactly like that.

In the work periods he went along to the fields to watch the hired hands as they walked in a row, mowing in time with one another. Their knees rocked as they walked, their scythes swept in an arc, the grass was cut with a hissing, satisfied sound and settled quietly and softly in the swath. He walked around observing it all. But it was always Amund that he saw, how he swung his scythe and made it cut; it was an art to get the scythe to cut, and it was an art to mow steadily and evenly, leaving the stubble nice and even, without a single blade of grass remaining. Amund knew it all.

He didn't realize till afterward that he always paced his walk to keep abreast of Amund.

It became too difficult to stay in the kitchen when Amund and the others were outside. He, too, started to go out, by chance sort of, and to stand where he could hear what Amund was saying. Anyway, Amund didn't say much, he was rather close and quiet. But very grown-up. Just as grown-up as the old hands. The other two were nothing but children compared to him; once they wanted him to toss pennies and play stickball with them, but Amund merely shrugged his shoulders without a word. He was too grown-up for such things. Anders became quite embarrassed for Peter and Ole, who were so stupid. They knew it too and found nothing better to do than to lean against the wall of the barn afterward, looking shamefaced because they'd been so childish.

During the long afternoon rest period these three didn't sleep, unlike the old hired hands. They sat somewhere in the shade and chatted, on the barn bridge or in front of the storehouse, or chewed on a stalk of grass without talking; or they wandered about, around the buildings and down the field, slowly, as grownups are in the habit of doing in the rest periods.

One day, during the long afternoon rest period, Anders

just couldn't help himself. Amund and the other two wandered in the direction of the potato cellar. Anders hurried out of the kitchen and trailed after them. Not that he joined them; he wandered about by himself and just happened to go the same way.

They followed the downhill path toward the spring in the valley. Anders shuffled after. He kept his distance, but shuffled after them. They didn't talk, the three of them, they probably felt a bit sluggish and lazy in the heat, the way the grownups do. Once in a while one of them would bend down to snatch a sorrel or a flower by the roadside. If it happened to be Amund, Anders also bent down, without thinking, and snatched a blade of grass.

They got down to the valley. It was cooler down there. The place was shaded, and the cold spring surfaced there. They sat down, the three of them. Anders sat down a bit uphill, letting on he didn't even see them. Amund turned his head and glanced up at him, but Anders made like he didn't notice. He was thinking that perhaps Amund would call him, invite him to join them down there. No, he didn't dare think it...Then they could talk about the weather and the hay and the tedding of the hay...And perhaps he would tell them about that nice willow flute Embret had made for him last spring. The one with two notes in it.

They got up and walked slowly uphill again. They hadn't talked to him. He let on he didn't even see them and waited till they were well past him. Then he padded after. He kept his left hand in his pocket like Amund, and waved his right one in the air once in a while the way Amund did when he occasionally swiped at a sorrel.

Then Amund suddenly stopped and looked back. He

looked at *him*. Perhaps he would ask him to come walk with them....

Amund said something to the other two. They also turned to look back. They looked at *him*. Amund smiled— Amund never laughed, it wasn't grown-up to laugh. But the other two laughed. They laughed aloud. And Peter put his left hand in his pocket and waved his right one, aping Amund—no, aping Anders, because he'd aped Amund. Then he slapped his knees and laughed.

They continued up the hill. They didn't talk about it, only continued walking, a bit sluggish, as grownup people are in the heat.

Anders remained down there, alone.

He had known what would come the moment Amund turned around and smiled. In fact, it seemed to him he'd known it beforehand—it was as if he'd gone around expecting exactly this to happen. He knew it from before, he knew it all from before.... He became very busy looking for something on the ground, a flower, snail, earthworm or whatever. He didn't lift his eyes for a moment, he was down there on his own errand and didn't have anything to do with the others, he was completely engrossed in looking at the ground. But with the corner of his eye he could make out what the others were doing, to the tiniest little thing.... He fell behind, all engrossed in looking at the ground. And at the same time he knew quite clearly that it was no use, because they'd understood him. The whole world was laughing at him. He felt only one thing—shame, shame, shame. He felt as if his heart were slowly sinking through his body as Amund and the others stood up there looking back— seeing him stand there a little farther down trying to act like nothing. They went on, lazily, indifferently, with a little smile over their shoulders—while he pretended he was looking for something down among the stubble, his thoughts ever so far away.

It was humiliation itself. Later on he met it often. But it always seemed to have the same face—a stuck-up, handsome face turning lazily to look down at him and quietly smiling. And he always handled himself the same way, whether he wanted to or not—acted like nothing, let on he was on a quite different errand, fell behind and took his time, searching the ground....

They disappeared over the crest of the hill, the three of them. He remained, puttered about a bit, fumbled among the stubble—the grass had been mowed only a short while ago, but the weather had been rainy, and timothy and white clover were starting to push out of the ground again. The new shoots looked so small and green among the thick, grayish-yellow stubble.

He shuffled and puttered about a little, plucked a sorrel, put it in his mouth—but it was much too old already, with a dry, wooden taste. He sat down and didn't stir. He didn't look at anything in particular. He didn't think about anything. He sat like that for a long time. Time had stopped. He got up again and sat down in a different place, but time wouldn't pass.

At long last the storehouse bell rang, marking the end of the rest period. But that didn't set him free. He knew that right now the hired hands were waking up in the servants' quarters, and now Embret, Nils and Martin were getting up and stretching, lighting their pipes and shuffling to the kitchen to have coffee. It always took some time getting started again at the end of the after-dinner nap. Amund and Peter and Ole followed them in. Then came the coffee drinking, and afterward they had to sharpen their scythes on the grindstone by the north wall of the barn. And when they were through with that, they had to haft the scythes again. Only then did they walk out to the field. They were mowing in the east field today and he was sitting on the west hill, so he could come forth when he was sure they had left the yard.

He sat on the slope looking down toward the spring, toward the little brook running down the hollow from the spring. It was always so green and lush down there. The difference was even bigger now, when the surrounding hills were rather gray and bare after the mowing. Cowslips grew down there, and tall meadowsweet with yellowish-white flowers that smelled so nice, and many other flowers he didn't know the names of. There were always swarms of bumblebees buzzing about. Here up the hill there were no bumblebees anymore. A couple of wagtails walked about among the stubble bobbing their tails; they put their beaks down among the grass stubs, raised their heads again and looked about them in little starts, while their tails bobbed up and down. Then they put their beaks down among the stubs again. Everything about them happened in little starts like that, as if they suddenly happened to think of something, then suddenly thought of something else. They probably found worms and insects down among the grass roots. Anders took a peek, and before long he noticed a little insect scurrying about down there, a tiny one with a shield on its back. It looked a bit like one of those gold-cows that came so often to sit on your hand and flew to where your sweetheart was. There were many kinds of crawling things down among the grass roots, and he could have sat there looking at them a good, long time. Then he heard the sound of the grindstone. There were six scythes to sharpen, and each scythe had to be sharpened on both sides. He tried to keep count but had to give up, because it came to much more than twelve—he knew why, too, because they would often go over the first side of the scythe once more and then give it another little scratch on the other.

At last it grew quiet up there. He thought: Now they're putting the spike of the scythe into the handle—now they're winding the strap around it—now they're putting in one wedge, now the other—now they're tapping it, no, not yet— oh yes, there he heard the little pops. And then—then they try them against the barn wall to make sure the scythes aren't too far forward—now they're correcting them—now they're putting them over their shoulders and walking off, six men, one behind the other.

He didn't dare get up and go home yet. He continued to sit there, watching the wagtails. One of them jerked its head, then jerked its whole body; and then it suddenly took to its wings, as if it happened to think of something that couldn't wait. No doubt it flew home, to its nest and its young. The other still walked about a bit, put its beak down among the grass roots, looked around with a little jerk, noticed suddenly the other one was gone—there it, too, darted off.

He got up and shuffled slowly up the hill. Hesitated and pondered a bit longer with every step as he got closer and closer to the crest of the hill. Now he could see the roof of the barn, now the little window in the barn wall, now the roof of the stable, now the window in the stable wall—and there was the grindstone. Nobody was around.

He felt his heartbeat in his throat. Then it slowly sank again as he quietly followed the path up to the buildings.

It seemed a long, long time since he'd walked down this way. He felt he'd grown old since then.

The days were going by. He thought only about one thing: he mustn't meet Amund anymore. Mustn't. Or—since that couldn't be avoided, since he was forced to sit at the table once in a while—he must at least watch out he wasn't alone when he met him. If Embret was there, or Åse, it didn't matter very much, then he simply acted like he didn't see him.

He watched out. He thought of nothing else but watching out.

He managed it, day after day. But when the haying was over, the haying porridge had been eaten, and Amund and the other two said goodbye and left, he felt so relieved it was almost like being empty inside—he felt as if he'd been weighed down to the earth by a huge stone and suddenly it was lifted off him.

And he noticed he was very tired.

Strangely, he didn't think Amund less of a man now than before. He saw him on the road now and then, noticed his light, lackadaisical walk, his skinny, stuck-up face.

Only, now it did him no good to see him anymore, or to think about him. He would think and think about him, but he never again thought of making friends with him—he never even thought of talking to him again, and he became tired and exhausted when he thought about him.

When the summer was over and the fall had come, he noticed that something had happened to him. Nothing was like before. He himself least of all. Sometimes he didn't recognize himself, he thought he'd come to a strange place.

It seemed to him it had been warm and safe and snug where he'd been before. It was colder and often quite lonely where he was now. He longed to go back sometimes. But he felt there was a locked door behind him, and he knew quite well that he could never again get back to where he had been.

He was six years old.

THE HAMLET

Embret

A LONG FALL and a long winter. It rained, and then the snow came.

The winter was cold and clear with good skating ice, it was mild with a heavy sky and sticky snow. Harness bells tinkled on the road, the runners squeaked against the snow, the drivers yelled and laughed with hoarfrost in their beards.

It was all familiar from before.

Every day he learned something new. But then he'd learned it, knew it, and had always known it.

He learned that *a* plus *b* spells *ab*. Then he was educated, because in Russia they didn't know it. Later he could read long words and had always known how to. Only when he stopped to think did he remember that at one time he didn't even know how to read.

In the fall, Christmas was waiting somewhere far ahead; but time had stopped, it was always the same distance off. Afterward, Christmas was over long ago.

In the spring a man drowned in the lake, it was a big thing and had never happened before. Oh yes, it had—when Embret worked at Rud a man had drowned in the lake; so that, too, had happened before and wasn't such a big thing anymore.

The days were getting long, the air was full of sharp

knives, and there were many more shiny windowpanes than before in the houses of the hamlet.

The church bells rang, it was a funeral. A tall, skinny man walked next to the coffin. Gorinè and Andrea stood by the kitchen window talking in low voices.

Martin Millom. Now his second daughter was going to her grave.

TB.

An old woman came trudging past. Then it was spring again. She walked unevenly—now she trotted along, now she stopped to shake her fists in the air, now she squatted at the edge of the road.

She was talking to herself, "Aha, Marius! Aha, I can see you well enough! Ha-ha-ha! Now you're burning!"

Her eyes, black with a fire in them, smoldered deep inside her head.

Father was often away, he had so much to do in the bank and at meetings. When he came home, everybody was glad that he was home again. When he left it was sad, but it became safer.

One day Mother stroked his hair.

"You've become so good, Anders, I almost don't recognize you," she said. He was terribly ashamed that she stroked his hair and ran off to hide.

It was this winter and spring that he noticed something about Embret.

Embret was angry with Father. Anders hadn't known it before. But one day he knew, and noticed that he'd always known.

When Embret was eating and Father walked through the kitchen, Embret would sometimes clear his throat. Not as long as Father was there, but often the moment he closed the door behind him.

He did it because he was angry with Father.

When Embret was working in the barn or out in the fields and Father came to watch, Embret always put forth more effort and would often break something. And when Father had left, Embret would sometimes fling a word after him, spoken in a low voice so nobody could hear him. Or his throat made a snarling sound, like the throat of a dangerous dog.

Father was big and strong. When the others were tackling a heavy job, Father would often come and give a hand. And then there was a glint in his eyes and a glint in his red beard, and it worked out fine.

"My, is he strong!" Anton said.

But Embret was strong, too, and he was older. And he'd done many things that Father hadn't done. On the chest under his bed in the servants' quarters was written E. E., for Embret Elstad, because he was from a large farm in the north village called Elstad. But he told his father, "Do you imagine I'll go here and work for you till my back is bent!" he said. "Do you imagine I'll stick around this worthless farm like a slave for the rest of my life!" he said. And so he took off. He'd been a hired man at Rud, and he'd worked on the timber booms at Fetsund a whole summer and on the Smålenene Railroad a whole winter, and once he'd taken his knife in one hand and his tobacco tin in the other and cleared a whole dance floor.

And Embret was dangerous. He would say a couple of

words to some fellow, making the others laugh, and the one he'd talked to became a laughingstock for everybody.

Nils on the Slope, who was around every work season, did a handspring once to tease Embret. For Nils on the Slope was so spry and limber, though he was past sixty.

"Sure, you get pretty limber from sitting in the privy every work period year in and year out," Embret said. And there was Nils, with everybody laughing at him; for Nils had quite a knack for dodging work.

Embret could be so awful to Gorinè. He would sit at the kitchen table and sort of talk aimlessly and say, "Mouse droppings and old wives' twaddle smell bad and taste even worse."

Then it was Gorinè he meant, even though she wasn't a wife but an old maid.

He would say, "The good Lord ain't like a poor soul, reckons old wives' noise no more than a caterwaul."

He would say, "God saw that all was very good. And so he created an angry woman!"

Gorinè stood over by the stove lifting pots and pans and putting them away with a bang. Embret looked at the wall and said, "The strength wanes and the temper waxes!"

Then he got up and left.

Gorinè remained by the stove, banging pots and pot covers. She removed the cover from one pot and slammed it on another, then slammed it back again. Then she grabbed the pot and put it on the stove with a crash, lifted it off again and put it on the floor with a crash. Then she began to do the dishes, dropped a bowl on the floor, picked it up again and dropped a cup on the floor. Then she cried a bit, wiped her eyes with the corner of her apron and felt a little better.

Meanwhile Embret stood in the woodshed, chopping away to make the chips fly and ready to fight off everybody.

"Get out of my way, boy! I've got other things to do than talk nonsense with you!" he said.

And if Father came by at that moment, he chopped so hard that the ax handle snapped.

Embret was often crabby and contrary. He would drop what he was holding and flare up in anger for nothing. He would pull and tear and wrestle the earth as if it had done him some wrong. He would rant and roar for nothing at all. "To go and work till my back is bent on this worthless farm!" he'd say. "To go and slave the rest of my life on this worthless farm!"

That was because he was angry with Father.

Some day, maybe, Embret would fly at Father. Or—some day Father might hear Embret say something and fly at Embret.

It was awful to think about. They were like two dark thunderclouds that were far apart but edging closer and closer and threatening each other. One day they would run into each other with a flash and a roar. It was terrible to think about everything that would happen then.

Anders often thought about it. Even in broad daylight, with the sun as bright as could be, he would get so scared that he ran into the house to hide in the corner.

"Dear me, what's the matter with you?" Gorinè said.

The summer went by and fall came. He started school, and that was new. Suddenly he was with lots of boys the same age and didn't have to look up or down but could look straight ahead.

School was so new that when he'd been there for awhile, it was as if he'd been there always. It was a world to itself.

But in the old part of the world Embret and Father were poised like two thunderclouds. He thought and thought about it and prayed in his evening prayer that God must watch Embret, who was so awful and angry and dangerous and wanted to fly at Father.

It was some day in the fall. They were busy with the potatoes. Embret was working on a heap of potatoes in the cellar vault. Anders was watching him.

The potatoes had a lot of dirt on them, it had rained when they were dug up. Embret was moving them, picking out those that were damaged and brushing the dirt off the others so they would dry. Nobody knew about things like that the way Embret did.

Then Father came and stood in the doorway, watching.

Embret didn't look up. He just brushed the dirt off the potatoes more quickly, tossed them more quickly, and chucked the damaged ones farther away.

Father stood for a moment. Then he said, softly, "Perhaps you could go and take care of the grain in the south loft, Embret—"

And then, even more softly, "—which I asked you to do…"

Now the two thunderclouds were right next to each other. Now, in a little while—now…

Embret didn't answer. He tossed and tossed potatoes.

Father just stood there.

Then Embret said, without looking up, "All right."

Father turned his back and walked a few steps. Then he stopped and looked down the field.

Anders could breathe again. It was over.

Embret pitched some potatoes terribly hard, so they hit the wall and got smashed. He snarled between his teeth, "…which I asked you to do—damn idiot—go to hell—crazy fool…"

He straightened up, looked around for Father and let out a fart in sheer disdain. His throat growled. Then he bent down again to pitch potatoes.

Father had stopped outside. He didn't budge. He just stood there looking at the potato field. He hadn't heard anything.

Father slowly turned his head and looked at Embret. Calmly, with calm eyes.

He had heard everything.

He stood for a moment. Then he left.

He knew everything.

Embret hadn't noticed anything. He muttered something to himself and pitched potatoes for another few moments. Little by little he pitched them more slowly. He straightened up and looked around, and saw that he was alone. Then he rubbed the dirt off his hands, wiped them on his trousers, stood for a moment and went up into the barn.

Remaining behind were two heaps of potatoes, a big heap he was through with and a small heap he hadn't had the time to do. From the little window in the back wall came a bit of gray light; the grayish-white potatoes and the grayish-white floor gave off a faint glimmer of light.

Anders stood for a moment eyeing the two heaps of potatoes. Then he made his way out. Outside the turf was green, the trees yellow and the sky overcast and gray, just the same as before.

Nothing happened, after all! he said to himself afterward, when he couldn't help thinking about it.

Thank goodness, nothing happened.

Father just stood there, watching, then he left.

Nothing happened. It hadn't been necessary to be so scared. Two thunderclouds—there hadn't been any thunderclouds at all.

Nothing happened, after all.

The worst thing was…

He knew that something was the worst, but he couldn't remember what it was.

As he walked around these days without thinking about anything, he would sometimes suddenly catch himself thinking about *it*. He was standing in the dimly lighted cellar vault again, Father had left, Embret had just left….

The worst? What was it that made cold shivers run down his spine?

It escaped him every time.

And came back. Escaped and came back, and escaped— couldn't be captured.

The worst were those calm eyes.

They knew everything. They'd known everything the whole time. That was the worst.

No! It was that they looked so calm. So terribly calm.

They weren't merry, anything but merry. But they were even less angry.

They felt sorry.

They were calm and sad and felt sorry. Perhaps that was the worst.

The worst thing was Embret. To see him stand there, be the smaller one and not put up with it and become still smaller because of it! What was he saying to the wall? The strength wanes and the temper waxes? To see him stand there and become so small, throwing potatoes at the wall!

He couldn't bear thinking about it.

To see him stand there making poo-poo in his pants. Before Father's very eyes.

That was the worst of all.

No. The worst of all was this—that there was nothing to be afraid of. Nothing at all. Embret was angry with Father because of something…one thing or another. But it wasn't anything to worry about, Father didn't get angry, Father was only watching. Nor was there anything to get angry about. Two thunderclouds?—it wasn't even worth taking seriously.

He couldn't understand why just that was so unbearable. He only knew that this—the fact that there was nothing to be afraid of even—was the worst of all.

Sometimes he would dream he was standing in the cellar vault, and Embret was there, Father was there, and he himself was right in between. It was terrible to be there, because the thunder was awful and the lightning struck him. The door was nearby, and outside there was green grass and lovely weather, but he couldn't get out because the light-

ning had struck him, paralyzed him and cleft him in three—
Father, Embret and himself.

That was the worst—to stand there and be paralyzed
and cleft in three.

He noticed it later that fall and wondered. Embret had
gotten closer to him.

He knew it from that day in the cellar vault.

Strange, wasn't it?

Father was as far away as ever. Perhaps even further away.
It was strange. He who'd been so big and strong and wise
and had been right in every way—and who knew everything.

Embret had become almost like Tora, or Kari, or Åse. Or
like himself. Once in a while he almost thought about him
the way he did about Pussy.

He'd become fond of Embret.

He would sometimes lie and weep for Embret's sake:
Why must you be so small and pitiful and stupid?

At night he would lie and weep over him for hours. It
was so strange.

He would go around watching Embret. He followed him
with his eyes, followed him with his thoughts.

Embret wasn't always the way he should be, not at all.
He was often irritable and stupid, often foul-mouthed, and
he often bragged. Nor was he very big or strong.

He could get frantic over Embret—fall into despair, into
a quivering rage. He sometimes had to go hide and bawl,
that's how angry he was with Embret.

Why couldn't Embret be bigger and stronger and wiser
than everybody else? He hated him because he wasn't. He

was in despair because he wasn't. He would lie chewing his blanket at night from wretchedness.

But once in a while Embret was wise and calm and confident. Then he would tell him so many things, then he knew so much.

Later that fall, Anders spent more and more time with Embret.

"You've made a little cotter for yourself, haven't you, Embret," said the other grownups.

They said it to make fun of him. To make a cotter was to go to the john and do ca-ca.

Anders didn't care about that. He followed Embret down to the woodshed, to the hayloft, to the fields. He would watch him, listen to him, ask questions of him.

"He straggles like a tail behind his ass!" Anton said.

He didn't care what Anton said. Now Anton had used his tricks to win Andrea, who by rights belonged to Tøsten Teppen. But the new girl was called Emma, had brown eyes and yellow hair and was much prettier.

Embret often sulked, and then it was hard to get him to talk. But Anders could easily tell that he liked his being there.

Gorinè

To say that EMBRET was mean to Gorinè and nothing more, would be untrue. For Gorinè could be just as mean to Embret.

At mealtimes it was usually Embret who was the worst. But at other times it might be Gorinè. She would run down to the woodshed to fetch firewood only to stand around fussing and fuming, until Embret took his ax and left. But then she would follow him across the field. Embret walked ahead and Gorinè after. It was like seeing a man leading a cow, said Nils on the Slope. Sometimes they circled the field. You could hear the sound of her voice without a break. Once in a while you could hear the words she said too—although Embret did what he could to steer people away when she was in this mood.

"To throw oneself away—for that it'll always be soon enough!" she would say.

"I wouldn't want you even if they threw you after me," she would say.

"I would really have to be hard up to look your way!" she would say.

Embret walked ahead, she after. "Yeah, yeah," he said. "No, no," he said.

The rest of the day he was snappish like an angry dog.

"Get away, boy! I don't have time to talk nonsense with you!" he said.

"Well," Father said. He and Embret came out of the office together .

"Well, Embret. I think it's too bad to lose you, you know that yourself…But since you really want to…Maybe you could think about it for a day or so?"

Embret said, "I have thought about it. It's definite this time."

He put on his greenish-black hat and was already on his way out. But then he turned, took off his hat and came in again.

"You know, maybe I ought to give notice for Gorinè while I'm at it…"

"Oh, really…," Father said.

Gorinè was sort of stirring something in a pot over by the stove.

"So, that's what it has come to?"

Gorinè cried.

"Yes, we're agreed on it."

"Let me congratulate you, then," Father said. "Of course, we hate to lose you, but…when that's the way it is…let me congratulate you, then…all the best to you both!"

Mother came in and said, "What, is it really true?"

Then she congratulated them.

Gorinè cried. Father and Mother remained for a moment and then left.

Embret stayed another moment, then he put on his hat and left.

And now it was once more Michaelmas and only two weeks left before the winter nights.

For several days Embret and Gorinè were so strange. Sort of bashful with each other. They never talked.

Then one day Gorinè was away for a while. She went to Brenna to see her mother, they said.

Sitting at the kitchen table the following day, Embret looked at the wall and said, "A mean woman is like an old mill, something is always wrong."

He said, "Nobody can be safe from fleas and from old gossips."

He said, "It must be trying to be angry when nobody is scared."

For Gorinè was making such an awful racket with her pots over by the stove.

He said, "The east wind and women's quarrels begin with a blast and end with a downpour."

With that he got up and left. Gorinè was crying over by the stove, and banging the pot covers on and off.

The next day Father and Embret came out of the office. Father said, "Well, you know—in a way I think it's too bad… But in another way I think it's nice too, you know, because then we can keep you both."

"Hmm, yeah. Oh well," said Embret. Then he put on his hat and left.

Gorinè wasn't in.

That was nothing new, the grownups said.

It had always been like that with Embret, said Nils on the Slope.

In everything, he said.

What was the matter with Embret and Gorinè?

Oh! That was an old story! the grownups said when he asked.

That was a long story! they said. And then they laughed.

It had always been like that with Gorinè, Mother said.

In everything, she said.

What was it?

He was too small to understand it yet, Mother said.

"Love, of course!" said Emma, the new girl, laughing.

"Pooh! You don't even know that!" Tora said. "You don't even know that Gorinè and Embret were sweethearts once, do you! A long time ago, before almost anybody was born. And when there is a change in the weather it breaks out again," Andrea said.

"Pooh! You don't know anything!" Tora said.

One day Gorinè had followed Embret all around the field. Finally Embret didn't see any other way out, he jumped over the fence into the pasture. Afterward he was so angry he went to bed.

Anton and Nils on the Slope were on the threshing floor. They had been ordered to finish up after the threshing— cast and clean the grain, sack it, sweep and tidy up. But Embret was in bed and Father was at the bank. So they sat there and talked.

It was Nils on the Slope who talked most, for he was the

same age as Embret and had known him throughout the years.

"It was Embret's temper that was so out of the ordinary. And then the fact that he thought he was made for something great."

Anton snickered, "Fffffff!"

"He told the others the summer he read for confirmation, 'You can stay here, crawling on all fours and grubbing away at the earth,' he said. 'I'm getting out,' he said. 'I'm going to see the whole world before I die, I am!' he said.

"And, sure enough, they said he managed to get both to Lillestrøm and Moss."

"Fffffff!" Anton snickered.

"He left Elstad. He fell out with his father, as the eldest son usually does. His father didn't want to hand over the farm, and so Embret told him: 'You just sit here on your rotten farm,' he said, 'until both you and the farm are covered with moss,' he said. 'I'm leaving,' he said. 'I'm going to see the whole world before I die, I am!' he said."

They sat casting grain, the two of them. They sat each on a half-bushel container, which they had turned upside down. They had each a heap of grain in front of them. They sat with their backs to each other but cast in the same direction—Nils on the Slope was left-handed, they called him Nils the Poke when he was out of hearing. Now someone crossed the yard and they cast for a while. Then Nils started telling his story again.

"Well, and so he came here. At that time the father of the old lady was still alive—well, she was only a little girl then and her father was poorly, so Embret was a sort of steward.

"Gorinè was around in those days. But as for getting engaged, there was nothing doing this time around, they said—"

"This was before the Master came to the farm, wasn't it?" Anton said.

"This was before the Master came to the farm, sure. He was an agronomist at Hoff then. No, when *he* came, there was no need for a steward then, you know."

"Ffffffffff!" Anton snickered.

Nils turned around. "But look, there's Anders, I believe. Go in and bring us something to drink, Anders, will you?"

They were both laughing at something when Anders came back. Nils went on.

"And so he left and was gone a whole year. It was then he got so awfully far—both to Lillestrøm and Moss—"

"Ffffffffff!" Anton snickered.

"Then his father died and Embret went home again. But his younger brother told him he thought it would look mighty strange if Embret took over the farm now—'since I've been toiling and moiling for the old man all this time,' he said. Two years that was. Embret was boiling with rage, for it was he, you know, who had toiled and moiled all those other years. So he said, 'Just take the farm, you louse, and go to hell,' he said. That way Embret lost his fine big farm. For Elstad, you know, is really a good little farm. Me oh my, how angry he was when he had time to think it over—"

"Ffffffffffff!" Anton snickered.

"Then he came to Rud. And there, you know, Gorinè managed to pull off an engagement. But Gorinè's mother, you see, was a farmer's daughter and had married a cotter boy—Tørjer Brenna. She did it out of anger, to tease her father, they said; but the moment she'd done it she got so angry she nearly killed her husband. All he could do was to run away to America; but by then he'd managed to get her with child, a little girl.

"The old lady had only one thought in her head—and that was that her daughter must marry a farm. And no sooner had Gorinè become engaged to Embret than she had to go to Embret and break it off.

"Embret went into a blistering rage.

"'Then stay up there in heaven with your mother, and go to hell!' he said. They repeat that saying after him even today—you know, they call it heaven up there at Brenna with her mother, because it sits so high up and because her mother wants to be so refined—"

Anton blew his nose and snickered.

"The very same day Embret learned that his brother had died, so now he could have his farm back. But no. 'Now it doesn't matter!' he said. 'If I'm not good enough without a farm, I'm damned if I'll have any farm,' he said, and so he let his nephew take the farm.

"He grew even angrier afterward, they said, when he'd had time to think it over.

"And so he came here again—to get rid of Gorinè, they said.

"But Gorinè followed him. Well, a few years passed before she did, to be sure, but still.

"And so, well, you've seen how it is—once in a while Embret is angry, once in a while Gorinè is angry—in fact, it happens exactly at every new moon, oh yes, you can set the calendar by Ol' Gorinè—"

Anton snickered. But now someone crossed the yard and they began casting again.

They cast in time and without talking anymore. It was Father coming home.

Nils on the Slope was always so sly when he told a story. He had a thick gray stubble, his chin looked like a pin cushion full of pins, and when he laughed the pins glittered and the skin around his mouth twitched and twitched. Anton sat and listened, snickered and asked for more, and pretended he knew more than he did.

Anton always pretended he knew more than he did. That was how he'd managed to get Andrea, Embret said. He walked around pretending he knew something about Tøsten Teppen, and finally Andrea went to ask some questions and learned that Tøsten had a kid in some other place. For Tøsten had been far away, he'd been with the timber booms at Fetsund a whole summer.

Tøsten felt so sad that he went to America.

Embret said, "She's a fool. Kids in some other place? Boy, that's done in a wink, oh yes! If I'd been less lucky, I could've had the entire pasture here full of kids!"

But in the evenings and on Sunday, Andrea would sometimes beat Anton, Embret said.

"Anders can come with you and help you carry," Mother said.

Gorinè was going up to Brenna to see her mother.

"Mind you bow nicely and behave properly," Mother said. "Don't forget that Gorinè's mother is terribly strict about such things."

They had enough to carry, both he and Gorinè.

Gorinè didn't say much.

"I keep thinking about Mother," was all she said. She said it several times.

Anders had never been at Brenna before. But he'd often

seen the cottage, sitting as it did at the very edge of Vesleberget Hill. Brenna was the uppermost cottage in cotter country. And he'd often seen the old housemaid who stayed with Gorinè's mother; she was clad in black, was named Maren and was always busy knitting.

The cottage looked small from the outside and was dark inside. The panes had green glass in them—it was like looking at the world through the bottom of a bottle.

Tørjer Brenna probably did just that every now and then, before he ran away to America, Embret had said.

At the table sat Maren, busy with her knitting. Over by the wall stood a big loom with something black in it, and on the floor stood a yarn reel and a black spinning wheel. Maren spun and knitted socks and wove homespun all year, they said.

Anders bowed.

How was Mother? Gorinè wanted to know.

Oh, she was fine.

Gorinè went to the innermost corner of the room. A bed stood in the half-light in there. In the bed sat her mother. Her face seemed to shine—no doubt because she was so sallow.

"Is it you, Gorinè?" she said. "Is it my Gorinè?"

Gorinè bent over her. "Yes, it's me!" she said.

"Yes, it's your Gorinè!" she cried. Her mother heard her this time. She nodded and nodded.

"My Gorinè, sure."

"And this is Anders!" Gorinè shouted. But her mother didn't hear. Gorinè shouted, "Mother! This is Anders!"

Then she heard and looked at Anders, and Anders had to step forward and make a bow. In the past he always became so bashful that his back went stiff, but now he'd learned. Gorinè took her mother's arm and raised it, so that Anders could shake hands with her. Anders shook hands and bowed. It was like touching a bunch of dry, withered carrots. Anders dropped the hand at once, and it fell on the sheepskin blanket. Gorinè's mother didn't notice, she looked at him, nodded and said, "Oh, it's Anders! Oh, it's Anders!"

She was the oldest person Anders had seen. Now, close up, her whole face was crisscrossed by wrinkles. She was yellow like sheepskin. She chewed whenever she didn't talk, but had nothing to chew on.

Suddenly she raised her head, and her face turned so sharp that Anders gave a start. But it wasn't him she stared at, it was Gorinè. She shouted, in a harsher voice than before, "You must never marry beneath you, Gorinè!"

"Oh no, Mother!" Gorinè said.

Her mother didn't hear. "Do you hear me, Gorinè? You must never marry beneath you!"

"Oh no, Mother! Oh no, Mother!" Gorinè shouted. The three hairs on her wart trembled.

Then Gorinè was going to unpack the things.

"Why don't you go out and play a bit, Anders!" she said.

Anders was glad to go out, because the straw mattress gave off such a sour smell, and it seemed to him the place was full of bats.

A big spotted cat appeared from under the stove and followed him out. It was very cuddly and they became good friends. Behind the storehouse they found an old hen that had embedded itself in the dirt. It was probably the hen that Embret had talked about. It was the same age as Gorinè's mother, Embret said, and hadn't laid an egg in five years.

This one certainly had the looks of it, for it had no tail and almost no comb and looked even more stupid than hens usually do. And then Gorinè came and invited him in for coffee. They had coffee and square waffles. That was the best thing Anders knew, and he got it only in the cottages up here in cotter country. The waffles had butter on them, which he recognized, it was from home. The coffee wasn't good—it tasted like burnt barley and Maren had put syrup in it—but the waffles were so good that he drank three cups. He had clean forgotten the old lady over in the bed. Suddenly she shouted from her corner, "Who is that lad sitting there?"

Gorinè jumped up from her chair and over to the bed and shouted, "That, Mother, is Anders! That is Anders!" And then she rushed back again to the table and whispered to Anders, "Come over here, Anders, and say hello again, will you!"

And in an even lower voice she whispered, "Mother is so forgetful! She's almost ninety, Mother is!"

Anders went over to the bed, bowed and took her hand. She looked at him with runny eyes and said, "Oh, it's Anders! Oh, it's Anders!"

That way Anders didn't get any more waffles.

Afterward they had to go.

He bowed in the doorway and heard the mother ask, "Maren, who was the lad that was here?" And Maren answered, "It was little Anders, from where Gorinè is."

On the way home Gorinè was very quiet. She looked at the ground for quite a while. Then she said, "You know, Anders, Mother is from a big farm and she can't ever forget it."

She walked a bit. Then she said, and Anders could hear she talked more to herself than to him, "I'm so worried about my mother. I'm wondering if Maren is good to her. And then I'm so worried that she'll die. I keep thinking about it every hour of the day. I dreamed about it last night—that's why I had to drop by today—."

She walked a bit again.

"No, I guess Embret and I won't be able to get together as long as Mother is alive!"

She walked a bit.

"Poor Mother!" she said, crying so bitterly you'd think her mother had died already.

Christmas

DEEP, DEEP DOWN lay the memory of Christmas. Like a well where he could fetch water in periods of drought.

Ugh, it was fall. A gust of wind from the north made the leaves fly.

The grownups began talking about the winter nights.

"Fall is early this year," they said, "snow on Sognkjølen Ridge three weeks before the winter nights!"

The winter nights, that was the fourteenth of October. The day winter began.

He saw a picture before him: an old man on the road closing a gate. He was closing it to summer. He was extremely tall, his head rose up into the gray winter sky; he stood on a frozen road that was hard as iron, and the first thin snowflakes were flying around him. It was winter itself standing there with a white beard.

From then on all roads led toward Christmas.

On those dark, wet days at the end of September and the beginning of October, he thought more and more often of Christmas. He saw it like a remote light deep inside the darkest end of the year, a shining pane beside the road, far away, on some dark and quiet winter evening.

It was so cozy and safe at Christmas time. People were so kind and friendly. They all stuck together, nobody was alone. All people were good to everybody.

Every time something dark and painful happened, he thought about Christmas. It was like being on a swing. He rocked himself away from all that was painful and difficult.

Ah, yes, at Christmas, at Christmas...

Deep, deep down lay the memory of Christmas. Wrapped in layer upon layer of winter darkness, falling snow and bygone days.

One Christmas behind another, lights behind lights, cozy darkness and twinkling lights.

Low clouds sweeping across the hills. Fluttering snow-flakes flying about in the darkness.

Sounds emerging from the darkness. Church bells ring-ing at twilight and during snowfall. Sleigh bells and hoof-beats, creaking snow, whinnying horses, loud shouts from the road on pitch-dark evenings, the ice booming and crack-ing out on the lake.

One day Embret came to him and said, "Today is the winter nights. Come along, we'll go and take down the gate in the roadway!"

And he explained, "It's an old reckoning that by this time of year all grazing out in the fields is over. Now there won't be cattle outdoors anymore and all the gates must be open."

Embret lifted the gate off its hinges. He picked it up, carried it away and put it beside the fence.

The sky was overcast all around. It was a gray winter sky. The road was hard-frozen, the wheel tracks were like iron. Anders remembered—last year too he'd gone with Embret to remove the gate.

The ground was frozen and there was ice on the lake. One morning Embret stopped on the stoop, sniffed the air and said, "The snow's coming!" And as if he'd been calling the wind and the weather, there the snowflakes came sailing by.

Everywhere white snow. Three horses and three men were bringing home long loads, wood for Christmas. They unloaded and drove off again, then came back once more.

It was seven weeks before Christmas.

The weather was often cold and dank, and time hung heavy. Then it rained and the snow went away, but that wasn't much better—there was nothing but dirt everywhere, and the cold rain seeped through everything.

The women were running faster and faster around each other, and were fussing and fuming more than usual. Embret stood by the woodshed picking up heavy sections of wood, placing them on the sawhorse and sawing away. The sawdust spurted in a thin stream from under the saw blade, fanning out to a thin yellow disk in the air, shooting up in an arc and then sinking and quietly settling on the snow under the sawhorse. The thin stream spurted and spurted. It was so monotonous that it was impossible to keep looking at it. Five minutes lasted for ever. Embret would stand like that all day. Wherever you went on the farm you heard the even fretting of his saw. He would stand like that day after day. He had stood like that last year and the year before, and the year before that. This was Christmas.

Afterward he stood inside the shed and chopped, and wherever you went on the farm you heard the cracking of his ax. When somebody came to fetch firewood, he would fret and fume because they were breaking into the Christmas pile. Two huge stacks of wood in front, the height of a man from wall to wall, and farther back a pile all the way to the ceiling—that was the Christmas wood. Then it would last till Twelfth-tide. But the women, with their roasting and baking, came and made a *hole in the pile.* Embret growled and put the dampest wood in front. He and the women were enemies from the very moment he started his Christmas chopping. He and Gorinè were mean to each other. Sometimes they would quarrel with raised voices when Embret came in for dinner.

This was Christmas. He hadn't remembered it till now, but this was Christmas all right.

Closer and closer. Early darkness, sleet and cold. Three weeks left, a fortnight left. Christmas had come real close, casting a shadow on each day from morning till night.

He walked around thinking of what he wanted for Christmas. He wanted a new pair of ash skis, with bindings that didn't slip. He wanted a new pair of skates made of fine steel, so he could race faster than Ole and Erik. He wanted a harmonica like the one Hans Teppen had got, it had so many nice sounds and dances in it.

Tora wanted a pair of brown boots with long legs, the same the doctor's daughter had. Kari wanted a fur cap of gray, curly fur, just like Anna Berg's cap. Åse had gotten a picture book for her birthday—afterward she just wanted a stuffed fox.

It was a shame to say straight out what you wanted. But you could hint at it. They walked around hinting at it and hinting at it, looking at one another and being ashamed; but it wasn't possible not to do it either.

Had Mother and Father understood that he wanted new skis? Or did he have to say it more clearly?

Tora and Kari had no sense of decency. But Åse was the worst, she talked about nothing but stuffed foxes.

This was Christmas.

One day at dusk Mother went into Father's office. She was going there to talk about money for Christmas gifts, that they could tell from her face. She closed the door behind her. They played quiet games and moved closer to the door. Soon they were sitting on the threshold, all four of them.

Now they heard Mother's voice, now Father's. Father was angry, as so often where money was concerned, Mother talked softly and tried to explain. Now she mentioned Tora.

Perhaps he didn't have any money. Then there would probably be cheating on the Christmas presents this year, too. Like last year. Perhaps he would get a woolen sweater this year too, or something else that he had to have anyway. Other places they got interesting Christmas presents. Mother said they didn't have so many children there; but that wasn't true, they often had many more children other places.

When he grew up he would always have lots of money and always give interesting Christmas presents.

He didn't want to hear any more. He got up and went out. The weather was raw, with a biting north wind and thin, rushing snowflakes. From the woodshed came the eternal fretting of Embret's saw.

Last year it was even worse. Then Father and Mother quarreled loudly about the money for Christmas presents, and Father banged the table in his office. Never mind the Christmas presents, but it was all paltry and mean. Oh, if only he were grown-up and rich and had the power to do everything!

This was Christmas.

One day at dusk Mother sat down and told them about the Christ child in Bethlehem, and about the shepherds in the field who went to the stable where the Christ child lay on a bundle of hay.

It was dark inside, but the window stood out as a grayish glimmer around a cross, with four smaller crosses in the lesser parts. It wasn't dangerous, only pleasant, now that they were many. There was a fire on the hearth. The clock, which was often so lofty and strict and said shame on you, shame on you, was nice and said yes yes, yes yes. It was peaceful in the kitchen. The table was barely visible and the flaps were lowered, it looked like a nice quiet bear on its way to the stable to say hello to Jesus.

Next morning the butcher came.

The moment he came through the door, tall and bearded, with his club and the muzzle strap over his shoulder and the butcher boy hard on his heels, it wasn't *now* any longer, it was last year and the year before and the year before that.

The butcher put away his club by the door, as in previous years. He placed the muzzle strap in a coil in front of the club, it looked like a fat, black snake which had coiled up. The butcher and the butcher boy sat down on the bench by the wall, as always before. The fronts of their work blouses were black and shiny with blood and old animal fat. They moved up to the table to have coffee and a bite to eat. They never stopped talking while they ate. About butchering on other farms, about big sows, angry boars, and dangerous bulls. They chewed and ate and bragged. Huge slices of bread disappeared in their jaws, huge gulps of coffee. Back out came all their brag. About the big bull at Hoff, with a skull so thick that the first bullet got stuck in the frontal bone. About the angry boar at Opsett, whose pen nobody dared enter. But the butcher just climbed into the pen, and the boar came at him with wide-open jaws, huge tusks jutting out on both sides of its chops; the butcher, well, he just threw the muzzle strap behind the tusks and gave a pull.

The butcher boy chewed and swallowed huge bites. You could follow them on their way down his gullet, it was like a horse drinking. His large Adam's apple was going up and down. He grinned with his wide mouth every time the butcher told something smart about a sow.

Anders stood watching them from the middle of the kitchen floor. He thought: if only something would happen differently, only a single little thing.

But everything happened exactly as in all the previous years. He always knew what would come next and was unable to move. And then it came.

Now the butcher laughed, his jaws opening in a big long grin and his thick gray beard dividing in two, with a wide opening across it, a black opening down to something black.

He laughed loud and long, and his laughter was from the previous time. Everything was from before, it had simply been hanging in the air somewhere, waiting for this day.

There!

They were through with their meal, had brought up their belches and finished their acrid pipes; now they got up, now they went to the door, now the butcher bent down to pick up the muzzle strap, took the club and put it over his shoulder. The butcher boy took the leather bag with the knives. Then they walked out. Gorinè went with them. A raw creeping winter fog covered the entire world. He could feel his stomach tighten, right beneath his chest, and something trying to come up.

It grew so quiet in the kitchen, everyone stood stock-still, staring straight ahead with empty faces.

Now it would probably begin—no, not yet—it flashed through his mind that it wasn't too late yet, God could still do a miracle if he wanted to, he could strike the butcher and the butcher boy; and he himself could still run into the bedroom and lie down on the bed and stick his fingers in his ears, then perhaps he wouldn't hear anything—. *Now*—there the scream started, now they put the muzzle strap on it inside the pen, now they pulled it across the floor of the cow barn, past all the cows—he'd never seen it but suddenly he saw it quite clearly—*now*, now they were outside the cow barn, the scream was getting louder, a piercing shriek that split the world in two, going on and on and on, like a knife thrusting home, then twisting and turning: wouldn't they ever manage to put on that mask! You had to think of something to do, run away and never come back again—there! a dull crack, like the sound of a stick against a skin rug, a thud, the pig collapsing in the snow. The scream is gone, it's completely quiet, but the sound lingers everywhere, in the walls, in the air, in the faces inside the room—they're still standing motionless, all of them, with taut faces. The moment he regains his usual self, he finds himself in the middle of the floor, arms outstretched and crooked at the elbows, his fingers stiff and splayed. Everyone draws a sigh of relief and starts moving around, and he himself walks over to the kitchen window. Down by the cow barn he sees something lying on its side, with two men and a woman bent over it—it's the pig that used to walk around in its pen, grunting and touching everything with its snout. It's the blood pail Gorinè is stirring down there.

They rolled it onto a sledge and hauled it off to the washhouse. A patch of blood and a trampled spot remained in the snow. Gray steam from the boiling water in the caldron came pouring out of the open door of the washhouse; it poured and poured, mingling with the air and making the fog thicker and heavier. Inside, the pig was scalded and shaved and cut up, and now they looked at the clock to see how fast they'd worked, so they would have something to brag about at their next stop. Then they took the stomach and the entrails and threw them onto the snow, in the field below the washhouse. The crows came flapping heavily through the snow-laden air, hoarse from the fog.

Caw! Caw! It was the cry of the fog and the winter day. A sharp smell of fog and warm entrails spread in all directions, along with the darkness. This was *Christmas*, this year like last year.

The dusk grew deeper, the fog heavier; the butchers were

gone but the smell was there and the crows were there—three moving blackish-gray spots in the snow, hawking and squabbling, tugging and pulling.

Caw! Caw!

In the evening a fire blazed on the hearth, the sooty big pot sat on the yellow flames, and there was a smell of fresh meat, for now Mother was going to make headcheese.

The big kitchen was so bright and warm and cozy, with a festive air—a little bit of Christmas already.

The thought of the scream wanted to come out, the thought of the entrails, the crows, but something pushed it aside. No point in thinking about that now. A whole year till next time. A whole long year. And now *Christmas* would come.

The pot smelled incredibly good. A lovely light came from the hearth, just like in the fairy-tale book. Mother was sweet and talkative in her big apron, she walked back and forth between the table and the pot preparing the head-cheese, cutting and packing and sewing. Everybody could have a taste. Afterward the headcheese was to stay pressed till Christmas Eve.

The fresh meat tasted even better than it smelled. Much better than the finished headcheese—*that* was just cold and gray and fat.

He couldn't understand why they weren't allowed to eat it all at once.

And then Christmas was real close, breathing at him. For now he and Embret were going to the pasture to look for a Christmas tree.

It had snowed during the night. Embret didn't ski but stomped along in tall boots. Anders followed.

They left the road and walked over to a tree they thought was rather nice. They walked around it, because you had to see it from all sides. Embret went first, his boots made big holes in the snow. Anders followed, putting his legs in the holes. Embret went up to the trunk and tapped it with his ax, making the snow fall down, and Embret's back turned white. They walked in a circle around the tree. But it wasn't nice enough.

They walked around one tree after another this way. One circle after another lay behind them in the snow. No tree was nice enough. A branch was always missing somewhere, or the tree was too chubby or too scraggy. They ended up by having to go back and take one they'd walked away from. It was the same last year—no real Christmas tree.

They got to the yard and put the Christmas tree in front of the stoop. Gorinè came out to look at it, was cross and didn't think it was nice.

She said the same thing last year. Womenfolk—they would stand on the stoop and hardly set foot in the snow, but what you did was never good enough.

Embret looked at Gorinè and said, "I think you should take all the trimmings and hang them on yourself. You would never find a Christmas tree to match it in these woods!"

Then Gorinè went in. Embret walked down to the woodshed and chopped so hard that the chips went flying, and it was impossible to get a word out of him.

And then he awoke, and it was the morning of Christmas Eve.

This day was the worst of all days. He couldn't understand how he had ever been able to forget it, for all the nasty things that happened reminded him of nasty things that had happened before.

Everything in the house was topsy-turvy. The women rushed around the rooms squealing, overturning everything that stood in their way. No food to be had even, only abuse and nasty cracks. Things had been pulled away from the walls and stood in the middle of the floor, water and soapsuds and floor cloths were all over—the whole incredible mess that women made every time they were going to clean. All the hiding places had been torn up and rummaged through, the Christmas presents he'd hidden behind the corner cabinet had been thrown on the floor, right into the dirty water, by Emma, and Åse's doll house, which he'd whittled on in the woodshed during so many afternoon rest periods, had been trampled and destroyed.

He took the little birch-bark box he'd made for Emma, and that Embret had helped him with, threw it on the floor and trampled on it.

"There's your Christmas present, you slut!" he said.

Might as well forget about Christmas Eve altogether. He knew what he would get himself—there were a couple of things he didn't know, besides that cap he would have needed anyway and that blue wool sweater he quite certainly would have needed.

Everything was just lies and fraud.

Strange—suddenly the kitchen was clean, things were back at the wall again, the floor had been sprinkled with fresh juniper and everything smelled clean and fresh; it was Christmas.

Embret was good enough to help him with the doll house and the birch-bark box.

Late in the afternoon something happened to him. Or—well, actually it was nothing.

They were fetching wood from the shed for Christmas. Soon they would be through. It was beginning to grow dark. Over by the barn Embret was putting up the bird bushes with the yellow sheaves in them.

He was about to go in with an armful of wood. Then, suddenly, it was as if somebody blew a friendly breath on his face. He stopped on the back stoop and looked south. A blue cloud came drifting up the dark hill. It drifted slowly up the low, ice-gray sky. Beneath the cloud, the white hamlet was turning blue. Sighs arose from the snow, whispers came from the birch by the garden fence. He perceived a fragrance of wet snow, it reminded him of spring. He dropped the wood and bent down to touch the snow—it had turned sticky.

It was the coming of Christmas. Standing there on the stoop, he felt much smaller and much bigger than usual.

Only a few moments, then it was over. Another breath of wind fiddled briefly with the birch tree branches—he understood it was the coming of an ordinary thaw.

He bent down and picked up the wood.

They said it was the nicest Christmas tree he and Embret had ever found. They said so every year. But when all the candles had been lighted and Mother had tied up the ugly branch with a piece of string, perhaps it was almost true.

Father read the Christmas gospel. He read it quite fast and stumbled over the words a few times, which the schoolmistress had said they shouldn't do when they read.

Then he closed the book and looked much more cheerful, and now they would go around the Christmas tree. They joined hands and went, singing "Silent Night," and there was a smell of burned evergreens and lighted candles, and a glitter of gold threads and baskets made of glazed paper with goodies in them.

At the second verse Gorinè joined in. She sang loudly but a bit off key. She kept on one side of the tune for a while and it went quite well, but then she seemed to change her mind, made a jump and got to the other side of the tune. She jumped back and forth like this several times, just like the old lady last summer who got so scared of a bike that she ran back and forth across the road until the man jumped off the bike, swearing terribly.

At the third verse Emma joined in, and she sang so loudly and nicely, even more nicely than Tora, that he forgot to think about Gorinè's jumping around.

Embret only moved his lips as he went, he didn't sing. But when they'd gone around the tree several times and had sung all the songs, Embret and Gorinè and Emma and Father and Mother had such a strange expression on their faces and such a faraway look in their eyes, and they were gazing directly at the candles as they went.

Then they took their seats again, and Father went to pick up the Christmas presents under the Christmas tree. Embret, Gorinè and Emma sat on the sofa and couldn't figure out what to do with their hands, and he and Tora and Kari and Åse sat around on chairs, trying to pretend they were thinking of something else.

Afterward you went around to thank everybody and said "You're welcome" when the others came to thank you.

Everybody's face was a bit stiff, because they were all bashful, and they laughed a lot and were pleased. When it was
over and he could sit down on his chair again, he noticed he
must have hoped for something all the same, since he felt a
bit disappointed. But that cap was quite all right. Inwardly,
he was singing "Silent night, holy night," and it helped
nicely.

Embret, Gorinè and Emma sat over on the sofa, they'd
been around to thank everybody and couldn't quite figure
out what to do with their hands. They looked straight in
front of them, holding on to what they had gotten. Embret
held on to his new mittens, folding his hands around them
as if praying. Gorinè and Emma held firmly on to their
dress materials, not knowing where they should put them.
They looked stiff, sitting there on the sofa. Emma was very
homesick and cried a bit when nobody was watching. She
was angry about the ugly dress material. They sat like this
last year too, but then it was Andrea. He glanced at Gorinè
and Embret, and suddenly he thought: now they had all
grown a year older. It was odd, quite different than on your
birthday. For then it was only him, and then it was only
fun.

He looked at Embret. Embret's eyes were so far away, as
though on a journey, and his mouth was silent and not at
all glad.

He looked at Father and Mother. They sat quite still, looking straight ahead of them. They were far away, thinking
of something.

It had become so quiet. But then Åse began to cry. She
cried because she hadn't gotten a stuffed fox. And suddenly
they were all here in the room again, they were all glad and

seemed relieved, they laughed and talked and comforted Åse. Everything was all right, and even Åse became happy again.

The candles were slowly burning out, and when the flames reached the pine needles they had to be put out one after another. Emma had already shaken hands and gone up to her room. Gorinè and Embret got up to go. They peered at the tree, where only a few candles were still burning. They looked old and tired, as if they'd grown several years older in a couple of hours.

Suddenly it was really Christmas. A long Christmas table all laid, falling snow, sleigh bells and hoofbeats along the road, merry people who suddenly came driving up to the house in wide sleighs with steaming horses, the sounds of accordion and fiddle, and dancing in the parlor that made the house quake.

Not a single day was like another, but they had something in common which set them apart from the rest of the year—girls' laughter and shouting everywhere, the ice booming and cracking out on the lake, all sorts of sounds coming from far away, as though from the Bible or the fairy tales. And then every evening an ugly howl once in a while, it too coming from far away and yet being dangerous and nearby and *now*.

It was the drunk man going for a walk. He always went for a walk at Christmas time.

Then the drunk man came one evening.

The house was empty, as empty as it could be only at Christmas. Everybody was away except Emma and him.

The weather was bad, with drifting snow and a wind that shook the walls. A howl had come from down the road. The house was very big and empty.

"I think we'll go and put you to bed now!" Emma said. There are mummers and drunk people around, and they come to get boys like you if they find they're still up."

She was restless, her eyes fluttered. Anders got scared and didn't want to go to bed.

She promised him cake if he would go to bed. She kept glancing at the window every moment—as if she could see something there, where the evening lay pitch-dark against the panes. He understood she was lying and keeping something from him, got more scared and didn't want to go to bed.

"You're a naughty boy!" Emma said. "And now I'll put you to bed whether you want to or not!"

She tried to catch him, but he darted aside.

Then they both stopped short. The front door sprang open. Unsteady footsteps were heard in the entrance hall. The door crashed open and a strange man staggered in.

Emma hurried over to him and said something very fast, in a soft voice. The man straightened up and looked about him. He moved his head in an odd way, very slowly.

"Anders? Which Anders?" he snuffled.

"Ssh! Ssh!" Emma whispered, leading him over to the bench. He sat down heavily and collapsed, as if dropping off into a light sleep at once. Emma stood over him, whispering something.

Suddenly he seemed to awaken, got up, staggered but managed to stand.

"Go home and to bed, you say?" he said. "Anders, you say? Which Anders?"

Emma rushed over to Anders. "Now you must go to bed, Anders!"

Anders screamed, "No! No!"

He was deadly afraid to be here, but even more afraid of being alone.

Now the man caught sight of him.

"So you are Anders, eh? No, my boy. You won't—go to bed. No plucky lads are going to bed. We'll—take Emma—and put her—to bed, won't we! You come here—and I'll lift you up—to the ceiling!"

He staggered up, got hold of Anders, caught him under the arms and lifted him all the way to the ceiling, so that he bumped his head against the rafter. Then he lowered his arms, held Anders straight out in front of him, looked at him and laughed.

"Are you scared, lad?"

"No!" Anders whispered. Hanging in the air, he looked straight into the stranger's eyes.

Those eyes were different from all other eyes. There was a light inside them, it came from further in and deeper down than anything he'd ever seen before either in animals or people. He saw that this man was mad and capable of anything.

"Are you scared?" the man said again.

"No!" Anders whispered.

The man tottered and suddenly dropped him; Anders fell but landed on his feet and quickly withdrew to the corner again.

The man lay stretched out on the bench. Emma cried. The man got up and struck the bench. "Beer! Beer! Beer!" He struck the bench each time. Emma hurried out and brought some beer. He spilled and drank, dropped the glass on the floor, then collapsed on the bench.

He was asleep. Asleep and snoring.

Emma stood looking at him. Suddenly she plunked to the floor and lay all of a heap, crying.

From outside came the howling of the wind.

Nobody found out about it. Emma came to his room early next morning, talked to him and petted him, and asked him to keep mum. But that was not why he kept mum.

It was something he'd seen in the man's eyes. He couldn't utter a word to anybody about it. For if he kept completely mum about it, then perhaps it would stay where it was, deep inside the man's eyes; but if he told somebody, then perhaps it would be let loose…

He'd seen *Something* in his eyes. Something deep inside the dark, a madness, a dangerous light that twinkled far away on a dark road—he'd seen *Christmas*.

One day it was all over a long time ago. He was standing on the stoop one gray morning in late winter. Christmas was way behind him, Easter was way ahead. Gray weather behind him and gray weather ahead, raw and angry weather, a sharp, biting wind and cold days, low spirits and a long bleak winter.

Suddenly he recalled Christmas. He saw it behind him— last Christmas, one Christmas behind another, one light behind another deep inside the darkest end of the year. A cozy darkness and twinkling lights. Sleigh bells and hoofbeats on the roads, laughter and dancing that made the house quake.

He looked around him. Gray late-winter roads, damp, empty trees covered with frost, a dark barn door without sheaves for the birds, a winter sky as gray as ice.

Ah, Christmas, Christmas...

The World

A RAINY DAY. He sits indoors, watching the drops as they stream down the windowpane.

How often has he sat by the window like this in rainy weather, watching the drops run down and down? He doesn't know.

It's time running away from him.

Outside is the yard. He knows each stone and every blade of grass out there.

Back of him is the clock in the corner. It's there to let the time pass. It hawks a bit now and then, as if wanting to say something. But all it says is—alack! And then again: Alack!

Åse sits at the other window.

"What are you doing, Åse?"

"Counting the drops."

"Are you bored?"

"Yes."

"Why are you sitting there then?"

"Everything else is even more boring."

Mother comes in with some woman.

"So it's Anders, is it!"

Her umbrella is dripping.

"How old are you, eh?"

Countless people have asked him that. It reminds him

of the wallpaper pattern when he was sick in bed and followed the pattern with his eyes, and he had to follow one
and the same pattern till it was part of his sickness.

"How old are you?" Women's voices, men's voices, over
and over again…

"Eight years."

An old woman comes trudging up the road. It's spring
again. Sometimes she stops, sometimes she squats. Talking
to herself and shaking her fists in the air.

"Aha, Marius, I can see you well enough! Now you're
getting a good scorching! Ha-ha-ha!"

The same year after year.

He thinks back in wonder to the old days, before repeti-
tion entered the world.

A tall, thin man comes walking down the road, leading a
little boy by the hand. They're talking around the kitchen
table. Suddenly they lower their voices.

It was the man from Millom. Five funerals in five years.
Ugh, that TB.

They stretch their necks, following him with their eyes.

One day the kitchen is full of people. Familiar people
and one stranger. Nils on the Slope, Martin Teppen with
his fiery-red beard, and Anton who's always there in the
work seasons. The stranger's name is Lars.

It's plowing time.

They stand on the manure heap behind the cow barn,
loading and talking and laughing. They are out in the fields
spreading manure, laughing and hollering. Martin Teppen

harrows the soil with his angry black horse. Tugging at the reins, he yells, "Hey, get going! Hey, get going, you old jade!"

They stomp in for meals with a thundering noise. They scrape their boots against the floor and thrust their huge fists at the pork and potatoes. They talk and laugh. Martin Teppen has a black hole between his teeth when he laughs.

They talk about Crazy-Kari. She went crazy when her husband died. She thought he was in hell.

One day she sat staring at the flames in the fireplace.

"Hey, I just saw the noggin of my Marius, sure did!" she said.

Then she put her hand into the embers and kept it there for quite a while.

"I only wanted to know how my Marius was doing," she said.

Then they understood she was crazy.

They laugh around the table. Martin Teppen laughs with a black hole between his teeth. Anton snickers, Ffffff! The man named Lars lets out a booming guffaw, Ho-ho-ho! Everything is the way it always used to be. Only Lars is new.

They tell stories about Kari and Mari. Kari at Moen was crazy and Mari from Holen was crazy.

Kari would weep and mourn. Mari would laugh and be merry.

Kari heard that Mari was crazy, and Mari heard that Kari was crazy.

Kari started weeping and wailing. "Me oh my, me oh my! That poor devil at Holen is crazy!" she said.

Mari started crowing with laughter. "Thank God I have

my wits anyhow! That poor devil at Moen is crazy!" she said.

They laugh around the table. Martin laughs with a black hole between his teeth. Anton snickers, Ffffff! Nils laughs sharply and coldly, Hee-hee-hee! Lars gives a booming laugh, Ho-ho-ho!

One day it's peaceful in the kitchen again. No one talking, thundering or laughing. The sound lingers in the quiet, empty room.

The bird cherry is in bloom, a bitter smell of almonds fills the days.

The cuckoo crows. Cuckoo! Cuckoo! Gorinè says:

East cuckoo is cheer cuckoo
West cuckoo is best cuckoo
South cuckoo is sow cuckoo
North cuckoo is corse cuckoo.

But he can't remember where he heard it first.

If he can get underneath a cuckoo tree, he'll be able to wish for anything he wants.

He knows very well what he's going to wish for—the kind of harmonica Hans Teppen had. It was so full of sound, you'd almost think someone sat crying inside.

But he'll never get underneath a cuckoo tree, the cuckoo always crows far away from him.

People from cotter country walk the road with bundles in their hands. It's strawberries, they're taking them to the store. "Thank God a bit of something still grows in the woods," they say.

Nils on the Slope sits in the kitchen, tall and thin, his chin like a pin cushion full of pins, a streak of tobacco juice at either corner of his mouth. His hat is on the floor beside his chair. He slips into Father's office and stays there awhile. When he comes out again he's happy, he thanks him again and again. He says in a tearful voice, "I knew you'd find a way out, all right!"

"Move up and get a bite to eat, Nils," Father says, turning to Gorinè. "See to it that Nils gets something to eat, Gorinè."

Then the haying season will be here again soon, and Nils has dropped by to beg a place.

The mowers fill the kitchen. They are the same as in the plowing season except that Lars is gone, Ole Hagaen has taken his place. He has a stiff and slightly bent leg, so he limps a bit when walking the swath and mowing. His face is darker than anyone else's and his grayish-black stubble is so long that it's almost a beard. But it never gets to be a real beard, and the others ask him what he does to keep it just that long. Then he laughs, Haw-haw-haw-haw!

They talk and laugh. They tell stories. About Kari and her Marius. About Kari and Mari. They laugh around the table. Martin Teppen laughs with a black hole between his teeth, Anton snickers, Ffffff! Ole chortles, Haw-haw-haw-haw!

Everything is like before.

They walk their swaths out in the field. If Father is home he walks first. If Father is away Embret walks first. If Father isn't home they usually talk about him as they stand in the shade over by the road taking a rest.

Nils on the Slope says, "Oh yes, the rich are comfy. Sitting in their carriages and roaming around the village, while the poor man must wear his ass out for them!"

"Hmm! I guess it's time to get back to work!" Embret says.

Then Nils puts away his scythe, shuffles slowly onto the road, up to the buildings and into the privy.

He's often sick to his stomach like that in the middle of the work period, Nils is.

Another time somebody may come driving by. He usually stops the horse to have a chat.

"You've got a fine, dandy help with the mowing, I see," he says, with a slight sneer in the corner of his eye.

For the mowers are getting on in years, every man among them. Father can't say no when they come and ask him.

Nils has a quick tongue. "Oh yes, he knows his way around, the boss does. Old people are cheap—but the swing of the scythe is the last thing you lose."

People from cotter country walk the road with big pails and birch-bark bags. They're on their way to the store with blueberries. They stop to wipe the sweat off their faces.

"Thank God a few berries still grow in the woods!" they say.

The sun is low. It's evening.

"Come, Anders!" Emma says. "Come! We're going down for a swim!"

The hired hands, their scythes over their shoulders, are returning from the field in the low, golden sunlight. Long blue shadows stretch across the field from their legs.

Emma and Anders and the little girls go down to the lake.

The sandy beach is at the lower end of the pasture. A couple of sunken logs have been pulled ashore, there is a fresh smell of water, wet timber and rushes. Big, black long-horned beetles, timber bulls, scurry along the logs.

They undress and bathe. Emma big and white, Tora and Kari and Åse small and white. Emma swims, her long yellow hair streaming far behind her.

Afterward, getting dressed on the log beside Emma, he takes in the fragrance of her wet hair. Someplace nearby is a patch of wild clover, he can't see it but catches its smell now at dewfall, it's as if the air were full of strawberries. Emma has yellow hair and brown eyes, it's so pretty. He looks and he looks.

The path back up again is nice and green. He feels fresh and clean under his clothes all the way home. He runs ahead of the others—he doesn't want the hired hands to see he's so small that he goes bathing with the girls.

They're sitting in the yard, they've had their supper and are peaceful.

Nils on the Slope looks at Anders' wet hair. "Ah, yes, guess I'll have to go down to the lake some evening soon. I usually wash for the porridge feast after the haying."

Ole Hagaen has heard it's supposed to be dangerous to bathe in lake water. You can catch many kinds of sickness from it.

People say about Ole Hagaen when he's out of hearing that he has never had water on his body since he was baptized. And scarcely even then, Embret believes, because some people say he was baptized at home with black coffee.

He sits out on the stoop. It's evening. He's watching a still white cloud on the blue ridge to the south, far, far away. The cloud is blue underneath, on top it's white.

Nothing is going on. He just sits there and is happy. A bird strikes up a tune. Embret and Martin Teppen sit over by the barn bridge, talking leisurely about something that's not urgent. Brownie and its newborn foal are in the meadow.

The cloud, white and blue and faraway, rests on the rim of the hill. It's summer, it lasts for ever.

Fall. The wind surges through ripe, golden grain. The barley spikes nod and nod. Now they're mowing the grain, the hired hands from the haying season are back. A woman walks behind each of them, gathering up—Gorinè and Emma and Maria Teppen and Gina Moen. It's the end of August, a clear fall day. Birds fly about. Flocks of thrushes. Will the graylags soon be flying south?

The evening is long and dark blue. Voices and laughter from the road. Who, nobody can tell.

Martin Teppen comes to plow with his angry black mare. He tugs at the reins. "Hey, get going! Hey, get going, you old jade!"

They sit at the table, reaching out for potatoes and pork and sauce.

Kari and her Marius…

He laughs with wide-open mouth, a black hole between his teeth.

Rain days and nights. Grayish-black crows in the trees. Damp, cold and muddy. Dripping-wet people come in and eat, sit for a moment at the fireside to warm up, then step out into the rain and the grayish dark once more.

Nothing to pass the time with. He sits on a stool by the fireside, he sits on the threshold to the bedroom, he sits at the window staring out at the yard wet with rain. A sopping-wet horse with a cart passes by on the road. Far off is the forest, a gray shadow in the gray weather. Everything is gray shadows. A furious impatience seizes him. The clock stands in the corner, sighing and letting the time pass.

Alack!

The grownups' faces have an arrested, patient air about them. They look like the clock in the corner which lets the seconds slip by: Alack! and then again, wizened and patient: Alack!

They walk in a circle, then another circle. Spring and summer, fall and winter. They say the same things with weary voices: "It ain't that easy, for sure!"—"Guess I'll have to go see to the horse."—"Oh, dear!"—"Poor thing, a blessing she could pass on, yes indeed!"—"What's for dinner today, Gorinè, eh? Pork and rice soup?"

People on the road. A scrip or a birch-bark bag on their backs. They're on their way to the woods, it's fall. "A wet fall, sure is. A wet fall!"

The same over again, the same.

He feels old already.

A woman visiting.

"Anders, is it? Well, how old are you today?"

...the same old pattern in the wall paper, a pain in his chest—now you must lie still....

"Nine years."

Going After Pike

BEFORE HE AWOKE, while still gliding up through the bright uppermost layers of sleep and feeling the daylight on his eyelids, no longer sleeping nor yet awake, he knew it was Sunday.

He knew it, just so. It was as natural as knowing it was sunshine or rain. But that it was Sunday he knew from the evening before, and therefore he slept better the night before Sunday than any other night.

Sunday had a place quite apart.

There were so many things. The church bells rang, they had eggs for breakfast, he got a clean shirt that smelled pleasantly of linen and laundry, he wore nice clothes, there was nothing to do, everybody had the day off and was quiet and slow and peaceful—and a bit more solemn than usual. The sun shone more brightly than usual, the gray weather was brighter, the raindrops clearer, the wind friendlier, the birds more cheerful, all the animals happier than usual. There was nothing strange in that—it was Sunday, after all.

Time was a long, long road. The year was a wide, wide circle. The road ran in circles, around and around, but higher bit by bit—the circles were not circles, they were spirals; each year you'd go a little higher and see a little farther; each year you passed through new places, good and bad places; each year you could look straight down to where you'd stood the year before. This way you went on and on with the time, uphill and downhill, but still—you rose and rose and could see farther and farther around. In the end you would reach the top and see *everything*, the whole world, all that was and had been. All, all…

But along this road which ran on and on and on, the Sundays were a little higher than the other days. You could stand on top of one Sunday and look across to the next— backward and forward. Some Sundays were higher than others, you could see them a long, long time.

He was gliding up through the bright uppermost layers of sleep and knew: Today is Sunday!

He rose and rose, as if from the bottom of a deep lake. He soared up through a dense darkness, through a lighter darkness, reaching the uppermost, dimly luminous layers where plants swayed and colors came alive behind closed eyes. Shadows of green fish slipped in and out among the green rushes—he was a pike, rising and rising among swaying stalks. He was a swaying stalk rising toward the light of day. He approached the surface, only a membrane separated him from it, thin as his eyelids. And all along he knew, with a joy that kept rising from the very bottom of sleep: Today is Sunday! Then he felt the light on his eyelids, opened his eyes and was awake.

It was radiantly bright, Sunday-bright, but no real sunshine. A strange, clear white light, as if the air were full of silver.

He still remained in bed a few moments. It was so pleasant to be lying in bed on Sundays, to feel good all over your skin, take it easy and know it was Sunday. It was pleasant to stay in bed on weekdays, too. But that was only week-days, after all.

And it was pleasant to get up and feel the air on your body, get splashed with water and jump around a bit and know it was Sunday—a summer Sunday in June.

He stayed in bed one more moment. Then he got up.

The weather was hazy and calm. The sun was nowhere to be seen, but it wasn't far off. The air, the grass, and the leaves had a sheen of silver, and in *that* there was a touch of the sun. It was nine o'clock. The church bells started peal-ing with a silver sound in the silvery-white air. They rang slowly and calmly: Sun-day, Sun-day, Sun-day. Then they ceased, and the sounds lingered in the air like the streaks in the wake after a boat in calm waters.

The kitchen floor had been scrubbed white, the brown knots stuck out like knuckles from the worn boards. Yester-day the fireplace was cleaned and washed for the summer—there it stood, chalk-white and coal-black, with a green ju-niper twig in the innermost corner. There was a smell of coffee and butter and fresh bread. The coffeepot, scrubbed to a polish and sparkling, sat in the middle of the black stove. In front of the stove stood Gorinè, she too scrubbed clean and sparkling, her face crisscrossed by wrinkles and nearly as brown as the coffeepot. On the other side of the stove the cat was giving suck to a kitten. With her narrow, friendly green eyes, she saw everything.

The egg was fresh. The bread was fresh. The butter had been churned yesterday, it was coated with dew. Anders ate till he couldn't swallow any more. Then he took one more slice.

And there was Hans, knocking at the kitchen window. He and Anders were to take the cows to the woods. The cows had always to be taken to the woods. Because they were so stupid that if you just let them out through the gate and into the woods, they would wander about near the fence all day and not find a blade of grass to eat; but if you took them a little too far, or they got a little too high up while grazing, then they would remember the summer dairy from last year, go to the dairy and not come back in the evening, so that Anne had to go and bring them down again at the dead of night. Poor Anne. Thank God you weren't a dairymaid. But the cows were that stupid. They were much, much more stupid than horses. Embret said they were more stupid than women. Embret said, "It's all as bad as can be, but maybe we should thank God it ain't worse. Maybe we should thank God he didn't make women of us on top of everything." Embret said that womenfolk were the worst of the seven plagues you could read about in the seven books of the Sibyl. Embret had never been married, he'd had his fill just watching them at a distance. Women were the root of all evil and the cause of all suffering; they had the devil and his dam inside them, had neither wits nor a sense of shame, and just went around rolling their eyes and putting on airs, with one thought in their heads—*one* thought— and what that was, well, it was easy to guess.

Embret said that the cows were more stupid than women.

Anders dashed out. For when Hans and he had taken the cows to the woods, they were going down to the lake to shoot pike. Hans had borrowed his father's shotgun and two cartridges. Hans was from Teppen and was already four-teen, next year he was to read for confirmation. His brother,

Tøsten, was in Canada and was making a lot of money. Tøsten had given his father a fine, expensive shotgun so he could shoot grouse and stop shooting moose illegally, unless he wanted to go to jail again. But afterward Martin Teppen shot both grouse and moose illegally, and it probably wouldn't be long before he had to go to jail again. So said Embret anyway—when Hans was out of hearing.

The shotgun was waiting in the servants' quarters and in the cabinet were two cartridges, and as soon as they'd chased the cows to the woods they were going down to shoot pike. Now, in the early summer, nice, big pike often stood inshore, because the water was warmer there and because it swarmed with small fry.

The grass in the yard was gray with dew. White mist covered the whole world. Some distance away the trees looked greenish-blue, farther away they looked blue, and still farther away everything was all-white, radiantly white with a silvery luster.

Hans scooped salt and meal into the feed bag, flung the strap over his shoulder and untied the cows. Anders stood outside with the stick, watching out. Each cow got a handful of oats. Afterward they walked nicely up the road and along the trail to the gate, and through the gate into the woods. Brandros and Raina sniffed briefly at the young clover, but an ever so little rap on their shanks with the stick reminded them of the salt in Hans's bag.

The fog had gotten stuck in the woodland, it floated like wet cotton between the spruces, making each tree seem more alone than usual; a bit farther on everything merged into gray. The weather was nice and strange. The naked rocky slopes of the summer-dairy road were wet and slippery, the cows tripped and skidded and looked back with their big eyes, dark-blue and devoid of thought, which almost gave the impression of being thoughtful. Afterward they walked quietly up the narrow road, knock-kneed and sharp-backed, one behind the other. The woodland was closing in around them, they were walking up through the gap. Hans went ahead with the feed bag, then all the cows at an even jog, then Anders with the stick. Nobody said anything. Everything was deathly still. The spruces along the road were covered with wet beard lichens. No sound had ever been heard here.

A grouse whizzed out of a juniper thicket and crashed its way through the evergreens. There was a scattering of drops. Hans gave a start, Anders gave a start. The cows walked as if nothing had happened. The cows always walked as if nothing had happened, except when they saw a dog.

Hans stepped aside, letting the cows pass him, and joined Anders ambling in the rear. The cows wagged their tails, chasing away flies as they went. The flies would take a little turn before settling again, and the cows wagged their tails once more.

"Strange."

Hans often thought lots of things were strange.

He thought it must be strange to be a cow, for somehow its arm and hand hung down from its rear end. Look at Kolle, now—there she struck out with her arm, so to speak, and smacked a fly with the tassel of her tail. Well, the tassel sort of became her hand then, of course. Had Anders wondered how *that* would be—to walk around with one arm, attached to his rear end?

Anders had never wondered about it. Actually, he'd never

pictured himself as a cow. Occasionally he had pictured himself as a cat, a horse, a cock, and a chicken hawk. But never a cow. He didn't think he could picture himself as a cow.

It struck Hans that neither had *he* pictured himself as a cow. It didn't seem possible to do.

Then they had come far enough. Hans walked over to the bell cow, put his hand into the feed bag and gave out. The cows walked past him one after another and got a handful of oats each. Then Hans and Anders turned to go down again. But oats tasted good—the cows kept standing in one flock, casting a long glance behind them. Mmmmmm! they said.

Hans stopped and looked up at them for a while, puzzled. Strange…

"I wonder what such a cow is thinking when she looks at you like that. Have you thought about that?"

Anders hadn't thought about it. But she was probably thinking about oats.

Yeah. Sure. That didn't seem unreasonable.

Then they walked down the summer-dairy road again, from stone to stone, side to side. A bit of water trickled between the stones today, it had rained during the night. They came to the edge of the steep slope, from where they could look out over the lake. Up here the sun shone all at once, the mist was gone, as though it had been gathered up by the mountain or absorbed by the heather and the evergreens. But the entire hamlet below them looked as if wrapped in thin, thin cotton. The church steeple stuck out, and the Rambøl farms on the other side of the lake stuck out—they were so high up. The other farms you could just glimpse under the thin straight jet of smoke rising upward from the chimneys. A horse whinnied down there, a cock crowed. They walked on.

They were both thinking about the shotgun, but neither said anything. Hans speeded up and coasted down the smooth rocks, making his heel plates shriek and strike sparks and give off a whiff of scorching. Anders coasted after. They were at the gate in a trice. They walked sedately across the field. There they could be seen.

There was nobody in the servants' quarters. As always there was a sharp smell of tobacco and leather, sweat and dust, straw and boot grease. The shotgun stood in the corner, long and lovely, with two dark-blue barrels. Hans went straight for the cabinet, dug up the cartridges and sat down to load.

Then they left. Hans led the way. He carried the shotgun as a loaded gun should be carried—the butt under his arm and the barrel pointed at the ground two paces ahead.

They cut diagonally across the south meadow—they weren't supposed to, but nobody saw them. They waded through lush grass. The dew glistened in the grass ahead of them, their tracks were dark in the grass behind them. They went through the gate and walked on toward the lake between the knolls of the pasture. They couldn't make out the lake, it was hidden by the fog. At the upper edge of the fog there were flashes of sunlight.

Among the mounds nobody could see them, here Anders could carry the gun for a moment. He just had to make sure he held it correctly—the butt under his arm and the barrel pointed at the ground two paces ahead of him. Then they would never have an accident. This was the way Hans's father always walked, both with rifle and shotgun, and this was the way Tøsten walked when he visited from Canada. He had bought the shotgun in Canada and used it there. It was the best gun in all of Canada. In Canada there were many kinds of animals which didn't exist here—they had a moose that was much bigger than our moose, and they had a lynx that was much bigger than our lynx, and a bear that was much bigger and more dangerous than our bear, and it was gray and almost impossible to kill and was called grizzly bear. Tøsten had hunted all these animals and especially—especially grizzly bear, Hans said, in a slightly faltering voice. Especially grizzly bear. And it was so hard to kill that if you didn't hit it straight in the heart it wasn't bothered but pushed on. And this gun, like as not, had been right there when he went after grizzly bear, more than once.

Anders was of the opinion that Tøsten wouldn't go after grizzly bear with a shotgun. But Hans wasn't so sure of that. With a shotgun like this—for it fired so tremendously far and straight and had just the right spread—with this gun you could be fairly sure that one of the pellets hit the bear smack in the heart.

The gun felt heavy, a grown-up thing to carry. The path was narrow and wet, the stones were slippery, and tall, wet heather leaned over the path from both sides, at each step sprinkling a shower of drops so you had to take care they didn't hit the gun. Down where the knolls ceased, Hans took it over once more. They were approaching the lake now and could be seen.

A brook wound its way like a silvery streak out toward the lake. The entire beach area was swamped during the spring flood—sometimes in the fall as well. And if there was a really big flood, the long headland beyond the brook turned into an islet—the water overflowed the narrow tongue of land at the innermost end. When Anders grew up and became rich, he was going to buy that islet—because then it would be an islet, for then he would dig a canal to have a constant flow of water, a moat like in the book *Engelbrekt Engelbrektsson*—and on the islet he would build a house, a large house, or perhaps only a stone tower, and he would make a dock for the boats. But now he had to put off working out the rest, for now they would soon be at the brook.

They waded through tall, stiff sedge grass and rushes. Ssssh! said the rushes as they walked.

They reached the brook. Down here it flowed calmly. Farther up was a current, there they had built a mill and made water wheels in the old days. Many years ago now, far, far away.

They crept forward like cats, arching their backs and treading carefully. They sneaked along the brook. The mossy ground sagged beneath them. Water, wet and cold, seeped into their boots.

The rushes reached out into the brook—it was wide at this point. Here whitefish and perch came to spawn, here small fry came to eat roe, and here the green, dangerous pike came to eat both spawners and small fry. When it had eaten its fill it would stay here, half asleep, and warm itself in the shallows, often for hours on end, as if thinking things over—green along the back, with stiff yellow eyes, a long greedy mouth, and an ugly, angry underhung jaw. Pike could be seen anywhere around here—there look!

Both gave a start, both saw a gray shadow among the rushes. But it had noticed them, and darted down and away before there was time to aim and fire.

"Hell and damnation!" Hans cursed like his father; he gave Anders a hard, excited look. The gun trembled in his hands.

"Did ya see how big she was? At least *that* long!" He pointed at the gun barrel. "Yeah, *that* long, at least!" He pointed still farther.

Anders hadn't thought it was quite that long. Actually, to him, it hadn't seemed very long. But then, he had just seen a glimpse of it, and besides he had been farther back. The longer he thought of it, the longer it became.

They walked on, step by step. The mossy ground sighed and sagged under them. There was a faint rustle among the rushes. They reached the outlet of the brook and followed the lake shore. The rushes extended into the lake like a cracked, many-layered wall. Bits of mist still seemed to be caught among the stalks. Over the lake it had lifted a little. A few wisps of silvery-white mist floated above the un-ruffled surface of the lake. Farther out the fog still lingered, white and even. The water was stirred by a few small waves, long, slowly approaching lines of tiny swells from a boat which could no longer be seen or heard. Otherwise not a ripple, not a sound. The water was like gray silk.

"Ssh!"

Hans suddenly raised his gun, took aim for a fraction of a second—the shadow of something hovered in the water, among the stalks of the rushes—then the shot rang out, coarsely and resonantly, barking like a big, angry dog of iron at the vast silvery stillness. The rushes said "swisssshhh," four or five stalks snapped, a small patch of water boiled for an instant, as if a tiny school of small fry had flapped their fins at the surface—the shadow from below had vanished, it gave a long leap and was gone. Hans flung the other shot after it, without taking aim, and there again came the boom, an angry sound, like a big blow that cleft the world in two. The rushes said "swisssshhh" once again,and then came the echo back from the hills, first one, then one more many times over, as if the gun had a swarm of friends up in the woods who'd heard the baying and came rushing up to get in on the action. Then everything was quiet again, no pike came to the surface, the puff of smoke hovering there was all. Both barrels reeked with smoke, giving off a sharp smell—pungent, scorched, nauseating, as when a stone is knocked against another stone, and something more, something unclean, suggestive of an underground fart.

"Did ya see her?"

Hans was so excited he could only whisper.

Yes, Anders had seen her. It was a long, thick shadow—this time there was no doubt, this time it was one of the big ones. And now it was gone.

They stood awhile and gazed across the lake, as if expecting it to come leaping ashore again. And they didn't even have any cartridges left.

It didn't come. The surface of the lake was smooth as a mirror. Even the tiny swells were gone now. The boat, whichever it was, must have landed long ago. The little wisps out on the lake stood out more clearly now, having broken away from the thin white mist high up, and they might have started drifting ever so little.

Then there was no point in staying any longer. As they turned their backs to the lake, they noticed they stood in water to way up on their boots.

They waded inshore to firm ground. They were really

quite contented. They hadn't caught any pike, but they had *almost* caught a huge pike.

And there some fellow, dressed in his Sunday best, came lumbering down toward them from one of the cottages up by the road—slowly and sedately, Sunday fashion. Shortly afterward two more came, just as slowly and sedately, from two of the other cottages. Hans and Anders recognized all three from far off—they were Amund Inngjerdingen, Erik Bråten and Ol'-Hans Grina. Nobody came from the two nearest farms, Haugen and Nordby—they must have heard the shots there too, were just as curious, no doubt, and probably had their faces pressed flat against the windowpanes; but they were yeoman farmers, and that carried the penalty that they couldn't admit they were as curious as they were. It would probably take at least ten to fifteen minutes before some fellow came lumbering down from Haugen and Nordby .

Amund got there first, his pipe between his teeth and a knife and a roll of tobacco in his hands. He carved, filled his pipe, lit up and began sucking and pulling, lit up again and started puffing—meanwhile ambling on. He was wearing black homespun trousers, a black double-breasted vest and a white shirt, was freshly shaven and had a big cut on his right jaw. Before coming up to them, he had long since understood all there was to understand.

So those were the guys out shooting.

Pike, oh yes.

Really, was it that big!

The other two came ambling up. They were in their Sunday best and shirt sleeves, like Amund, and had understood what there was to understand, like Amund. But a little chat on Sunday morning couldn't hurt anybody. They fiddled a bit with the shotgun.

A fine gun, they said.

A truly fine gun.

And Hans and Anders, who had always known it was a fine gun, now knew it was a truly fine gun.

Somewhat farther up there was a log, dragged ashore several years ago and never picked up when the area was cleared. Now there was next to nothing to pick up anyway, it was half buried in sand, splintered and half rotten. They walked up to it and sat down.

Sure enough, the water fooled you. You had to aim as far below the fish as the depth the fish stood at. Everything seemed to bend a little in the water—a stick seemed to break where it touched the water, but if you pulled it out again it was just as whole. Oh yes.

The cat from Inngjerdingen, a small, ginger-colored one that looked like a little tiger, was finding its way among the knolls; it was sniffing after mice and birds. It meowed when it saw people—its jaws were itching. It came up, clung to their legs and poked its jaws against their calves. Erik Bråten reached down a huge claw of a hand—a hand the size of a shovel, with a thumb like a bull's horn, nails like the bowl of a spoon, wrinkles and deep furrows ingrained with dirt for life, scars and big hollows, and a finger chopped off at the upper joint.

One finger was chewed off in a fight at a Christmas frolic; Sjønne Skuggen lost one eye but went around bragging that Erik's finger had such a bad, sour taste, just like the meat of an old ram. They had fought over Mari Bråten, that was the funniest thing of all. Erik reached down with his weird troll-like hand and scratched the cat's jaws. The cat purred and rubbed up against him. He stroked its back—it was like seeing a pine-tree root stroke a nice little squirrel.

The three men had begun to chat. Hans and Anders sat and listened. They were only little boys and had to keep quiet and listen. Hans held firmly onto the gun. A bit of smoke was still oozing from the barrel, a hot, sickening odor, a whiff of ghosts and darkness in broad daylight.

The sun came out. Suddenly the sky was clear and blue. A light breeze arose. Out on the lake the last remnants of the mist were scattered and routed like a white army of goblins—the white wisps dissolved to threads in the air and were gone, as if an invisible hand wound them up into the invisible. They flitted along the surface of the water like frightened ghosts that couldn't stand the daylight.

How far away it was, the dread of the night breath from the churchyard. There sat Amund Inngjerdingen, big and strong and calm, his hands floppy between his knees—the same who, frightened by goblins, came running down from the summer dairy one fall evening, fell all of a heap at the door of his cabin and didn't dare take to the woods anymore that fall. What had he seen? he wondered. Nothing. Nothing at all. He looked so calm sitting there. The sun was shining. It was Sunday. And right now, this very second, the two pikes were roaming the waters of the lake, free, unhurt and happy. And the small fry—but he'd better not think about the small fry.

The church bells began ringing a second time. It was half past ten, and there went the parson. The lake was clear as a mirror, the day was full of light and fragrance. Up the road the churchgoers walked by twos and threes—old women clad in black, with white kerchiefs on their heads. They gathered like a flock of black goblins in front of the church door, it sucked them in as if an invisible hand pulled them through the black doorway. Out on the lake was a lone rowboat, its oarlocks creaking, its wake lying like a fine, multiple snowplow behind it. It moved slowly, was in no hurry. There it hit the shore, and the plow stretched from shore to shore like a huge fan.

The three men were talking.

"Go to church?" Amund said. "No—

"I wash twice a year and go to church twice a year. I wash for Christmas and the porridge feast after haying, and I go to church Christmas day and Easter Sunday. That'll have to do for a laboring man."

Erik slowly knocked out his pipe. The smoke from the other two, blue and thin, swirled higher and higher in the air, and the strong, sharp smell of tobacco mingled with the fragrance of grass and heather, of evergreens and resin, of old timber, dry pine needles and anthills, of sand and fresh water and swamp yarrow. The ginger-colored cat was staring at a butterfly. A crow winged its way heavily across the lake: Caw, caw! A fish jumped far out. The waves from the boat had reached the shore nearby and whispered about something among the rushes.

"You know, big pikes," Amund Inngjerdingen began slowly, "they make me think of…"

The church bells had ceased ringing. Everything was quiet now—all but Amund's voice, which was in no hurry.

From Haugen and from Nordby two men, dressed in their Sunday best, came strolling toward them.

Sunday in August

ANDERS LAY FLAT ON HIS STOMACH in the middle of the garden lawn reading geography. It was a Sunday fairly late in August. He was going to school the following day—the first day after the vacation.

He could feel the sun on the back of his head—the old apple tree which used to cast a shadow here had been cut down long ago. Now the lawn was nice and flat and green, with flower beds around the edges. You weren't allowed to walk on it. But in the middle of the lawn lay Anders reading geography.

He was reading about Italy. It came so easy today, he sort of grabbed one paragraph after another with his eyes and moved them into his head, to stay there. It was fun. And he was happy because it was so much fun.

He was happy because of so many things. Because of the dinner, which had been so good—he could still feel the taste of the perch. Because Father and Mother had gone away. He felt he was happy about that. He was so happy he could barely lie still, he had to kick up his heels at least, for that alone. He was fond of his parents and glad to have them at home. But he was especially glad to have them when they went away. Then the whole world became larger, he owned it more and noticed many more things, and the hours became more full of—well, of everything.

There had to be more things he was happy about, but he couldn't remember them all. He was happy.

And now he wanted to put the book aside awhile and turn over on his back to look up at the sky.

Way up, a cloud sailed across the sky. It was white and remote. It looked like a rider on a horse. It looked like an old woman on a broomstick. It looked like an army on the march. It looked like a young woman sitting on a mountain—the princess in the blue mountain. It looked like an entire country with bays and peninsulas and tall mountains—east of the sun and west of the moon.

It was perfectly still. So still that he could hear every little sound—the bumblebees buzzing and droning, the thin sound of the teeny-weenie gnats as they whizzed past his ear, and the sound of the summer-Sunday breeze as it rose a little, fiddled a bit with the grass, breathed on him and lay down again. With each breath came a fragrance of many flowers, a smell of dust and heat, and now and then a quiet sound of voices far away.

From the cow barn came—with long, but not too long intervals—the sound of the cock crowing. It sounded as if he said, All's well! And a moment later, The sun is shining! After each crow his throat made a little click, as if he pulled the mechanism in again. He seemed to say, The sun is shining—click! And right afterward one of the hens said, Cluck, cluck! Alack, alack! Fine, fine, fine, fine! And then came Brrrrrrrr!

There were two kinds of brrrrrrr! One was when one of

the hens taking a dirt bath by the sunlit wall would get up and shake its feathers; the other was when the flock of sparrows took off from the hens' feeding tray like a gray cloud.

Anders lay with his back to all this; but he knew what it was, all of it, the sounds were so familiar.

He caught the fragrance of ripe red currants in the last breath of wind and thought that, when he was through with Italy, he'd go and eat a few currants. The idea came to him a bit lazily—he was allowed to eat red currants when his parents were home, too. His teeth were set on edge when he'd eaten just a few of them; and when he ate a few more and a few more, as he was quite sure to do once he started, he would get a stomach ache. When he was through with Italy, he would go and eat some red currants, but only a few.

The sentences moved from the book into his head and stayed there. Italy was a country that looked like a boot, with cities named Rome and Genoa and Venice, and with sunshine and wine and the humming of bumblebees, with chickens and quiet, Sunday and summer.

He was almost through with Italy and could already feel the taste of currants in his mouth when he noticed that it had become very quiet down by the cow barn. Completely quiet, as if a cold shadow had come, closing the beaks of one and all. He looked up—sure, there it came sailing, high, high up, with slow, hovering wing beats. Now it was straight over the cow barn—it flapped a backward stroke again, scouted, circled a moment but didn't seem to find anything; everything that could fly or flutter had crept into hiding—into the hen house, underneath the floor of the hayloft, onto the threshing floor, into the hay.

The hawk still circled twice back and forth over the cow barn. It cast a cold shadow on the entire day.

Then it gave up. It made a couple of long strokes with its wings and sailed on. There, high up, it gave out its hawk's cry—a contemptuous warning to the little animals down in the bushes and in the field, a single whistling note, like the sound of a biting, ice-cold wind. A greedy, lonely and cheerless note.

"Whoo!"

Once more: "Whoo-oo!"

Then it was gone.

A few moments passed—then the cozy old sounds crept out of their hiding places again. There the cock gave his warning, All's well—click! There came the hens, Cluck, cluck! And there—brr!—the flock of sparrows in the chicken feed.

But what was that? Someone whistled sharply, piercingly. Jumping up, Anders saw the freckled, laughing face of Ole on the other side of the garden fence.

The same moment the sun felt warm again. For Ole was the happiest thing in the world. He was always happy, or nearly always; if he grieved, he did it as hard as ten others—hard, but fast; he seemed to rip and tear his way through his grief ten times as fast in order to get out at the other end and be happy again.

Ole had thick ginger hair, so wiry that it spurned the comb, it merely bristled straight out from his head. A couple of other boys had tried to call him the hedgehog, but the name failed to get a rise out of him and didn't stick; Ole was too happy and kind. Ole had light-blue eyes that were set far apart and turned into two narrow light-blue slits when he laughed; then his mouth became a mile long, said the other boys—his bright broad teeth gleamed and twinkled, and his dimples became two hollows far inside his face. He had a nose too, but there wasn't really much you could say about that, it was so small and pointed straight up and a bit askew. And then there were the freckles. No person in the whole world had as many freckles as Ole; he had them both summer and winter. He was also equally friendly all the year round. Now he stood behind the fence, beaming and laughing.

"Father has lent us his boat!" he whispered breathlessly. "We'll row over to pick up Gunder, Erik and Per! And then we'll cross the lake to that large bird-cherry tree at Landneset Point! It's still full of berries, so big, almost like cherries! Let me have a handful of currants, will ya!"

They ran down through the pasture to the landing place. Ole had the oarlocks in his hand, the oars were hidden in a clever place between some juniper bushes. The water level had dropped, the boat sat way up on the shore, and they both had to take hold at the same time, give a sudden push and shout, "Ahoy!" and "Hey, now all heave ho, ahoy!" and "Hey, now make her move, ahoy!" and "Hey, and there she glides, ahoy!" Then it glided out, scraped the sandy bottom and was afloat; the bilge water from yesterday's rain splashed faintly against the lower boards, and they took the wooden scoop and bailed the boat. Everything had to be done thoughtfully and thoroughly, for they could see that Gunder, Erik and Per stood on the headland across the brook and waited for them, following them with their eyes.

They sat in the boat, all five of them. It was a nice big boat, a drive boat—Ole's father was a log driving foreman.

The boat was black, tarred, heavy, and hard to row. It had room for two pairs of oars, and the oars were huge and heavy. They were using only one pair now, Ole and Anders each rowed with one oar—they were entitled to it, because Ole owned the boat. The oars were heavy and the boat moved heavily, the mirror-like surface seemed to be made of tar and not of water. They braced themselves against one of the ribs and pulled at the oars, aimed at a tree ashore and pulled for all they were worth to be the winner. Their backs ached. Anders thought that now it must soon be the others' turn to row a little—he could simply tell Ole, "Now it's time for the others to take a spell," toss the oar aside and straighten his back. Or he could say—but now he had to pull even harder, for Ole had won and the boat was beginning to turn.

The boat glided through the water, heavy and slow. Water rippled against the sides and dripped from the oars, and nice rings formed on the surface, a fine intricate pattern with each stroke of the oars. His back and shoulders ached, now the others surely had to...

There the boat ground ashore. He couldn't have managed five more strokes. He looked at Ole and saw that he felt exactly the same. They stepped ashore and didn't let on, secretly catching their breaths and letting the others haul up the boat.

The big bird-cherry tree stood right by the lake and was like an entire grove. The trunk was so thick they couldn't reach around it, but one of the lower branches drooped toward the ground and they could swing themselves onto it and walk up into the tree like on a bridge. It was the largest bird-cherry tree in seven parishes, and its berries couldn't be matched anywhere.

There were no fights for territory up there. The large tree had room for all of them. They lost sight of each other almost immediately, and only now and then did two of them suddenly meet again, like a couple of savages suddenly facing each other in the jungle. Then they made wide loops around each other, as they knew the savages did—they stared at each other while cautiously sneaking off on a curve, in different directions. This was the way Friday stole his way between creepers and bushes on Robinson's island. This was the way it had to be done.

Otherwise they only heard one another. When Anders, standing in a fork, took a rest to eat the clusters of berries he'd gathered, he could hear padding and puttering right and left, above him and below him. It was the other four climbing, bending the branches and letting them spring back again. Or was it someone else perhaps? Could it be a strange tribe? The large bird-cherry tree was like an entire green world, a huge castle with countless paths and secret passages, with little bowers, all covered by foliage on every side, where you could sit completely hidden, invisible to all. What if a strange tribe had hidden here!

There was a bitter smell of almonds everywhere—from the leaves and the berries. The berries were big and black, shiny and oily, and they melted in your mouth but constricted your throat. You could feel your throat opening get smaller and smaller for a long time and your tongue get dry and thick, but if you just went on eating and eating and didn't give up, it grew worse and worse only up to a point, and then it stayed the same. Afterward your throat was so shrunk that you could barely breathe.

They gathered at the trunk, in the very middle of the tree. They came one after another, at brief intervals. They weren't able to swallow any more. Gunder came last. He climbed more than he ate, therefore he went on a bit longer. They could barely make him out. He was busy at the very top and farthest out, the thin branches tossed under him; he flung himself from one branch to another like a squirrel, placed his foot in a fork, grabbed the top branch like a handle and extended his body horizontally to catch a cluster of shiny-black berries dangling at the outermost tip, dizzyingly high above the ground. He didn't reach it and began to rock, once—the branch bounced back but not quite far enough—once more, a bit more vigorously—he reached the cluster, while the branch he stood on creaked ominously. Everybody drew a sigh of relief. Then he came down to the others, light and thin, slightly wild-eyed from all the climbing.

The spot where they had gathered looked like a huge nest, a sort of cave in the middle of the tree, a natural gathering place. Several branches met here, then went their separate ways, and all these branches intertwined before spreading out again, forming a little house here high above the ground—a house with a green, rainproof roof of foliage, green walls, and lots of black branches to sit on. Lots of people had come to sit here. They themselves had perched here many times, several years in a row by now, at least two or three, and many had been here before them. In a hollow between two branches a tobacco pipe had been left behind, it was there last year too. Who in the world had crept up here to smoke? What if he felt nauseous, let go his hold and fell down! None of the five had ever smoked.

There they sat with branches and foliage on every side, seeing neither the sky above them nor the earth below them, or the hamlet on any side. Just like Robinson—though, did Robinson really sit like this?

They thought of remote islands, shipwrecks in the tropics, savage people and wild animals, pirate islands and pistols with silver mountings, chests full of gold, silver and precious stones, tortoises and footprints in the sand. Anders looked about him for dangerous animals and snakes. When he turned his head again, he noticed that Ole was looking stealthily about him for snakes and dangerous animals...

Startled, Anders jumped and was about to lose his grip on the branch he was holding on to. Something had come tumbling at an angle through the air and had hit him straight in the face. It fell into his lap. It was a bumblebee that had strayed into the tree and become dizzy and sick. It lay on its back, wriggling its legs. Perhaps it couldn't stand the air in here, the bitter smell of almonds. Perhaps that smell was poisonous to bumblebees.

They gathered to look at it. The bumblebee stretched, curled up, stretched again. It seemed to have difficulty breathing. It acted the same when it had been inside a house for a long time, several of them had seen that.

It had to be saved. They didn't dare drop it, then it would simply get killed bumping against the branches. They would have to climb up with it, into the air, and see what happened.

They let Gunder have it. He placed it on a leaf, held it carefully in his hand and climbed upward. All the others after him, staring in suspense at the leaf. Gunder set his course for the lookout branch, the big topmost branch of the bird-cherry tree; it ran upward at a slant, up through the roof of foliage and into the open air, and was itself almost free of leaves. The others stayed behind at the lower end of the branch, while Gunder continued climbing. It was like looking at an angle through a skylight, and Gunder seemed to be climbing a black pole through the skylight. They saw the blue sky and a small white cloud and Gunder, light and small, climbing and climbing the branch, which swayed and swayed…

"She's moving!" Gunder called over his shoulder and down his back to the others. He'd barely said it when a little black spot shot up from the leaf he held in his hand, sailed off at an angle into the open air and was gone.

"There she goes!" Excited, Gunder pointed at it disappearing.

Their breaths came short and fast—they were eager and proud. They looked at each other, a little bashful over this. It was probably quite childish.

Gunder took his time climbing down again. They were quietly waiting for him, the lookout branch couldn't carry more than one. He talked a blue streak.

"She started to wiggle her behind. Then she moved her legs a bit. Then she turned over and *stood up*, sort of passed her front legs over her forehead—then she was gone! She flew straight toward Lauvberget Rock!"

Suddenly Gunder fell silent, looked at the others, dropped his eyes and stared in the direction of Lauvberget. Then he said in a low voice, "Wonder if Albert—he said he might drop by here this afternoon…"

The others looked at him, then averted their eyes again. It grew suddenly very quiet up there. Everyone sat as if expecting some sign.

Then they heard his signal. The brief whistle note. He was standing underneath the tree, hidden from sight.

Without a word, they scrambled to the ground. As if he had a rope around their necks and dragged them down.

He stood in the shade near the trunk waiting for them. When they'd all gotten down, he didn't move for another moment or two while reviewing them. And they didn't move while being reviewed.

Then he gave a short laugh. "Ha!" he said—a single brief crack of laughter.

That he laughed didn't mean that he was happy. It only meant he let some matter drop—that he didn't bother to call them to account for being late. Besides, he laughed at them because they were so childish—because they climbed the bird-cherry tree and ate bird cherries, just like little kids. They all understood this and came closer—relieved that it was nothing worse, weighed down because they had behaved so childishly.

He looked them over once more, as though counting them. He was a head taller than they. He was also two years older, but still in the same grade. He hadn't been in the neighborhood more than a year, and his previous schooling seemed to have been only so-so.

He turned around without a word and walked down to the lake. They followed him.

It had been like this since the first day he came to school—his parents had moved from the north hamlet to a cotter's plot here below Lauvberget a year ago. He took control right away. He was older and taller than they. But that didn't seem to be it. He was stronger—well, he was bound to be; he had never needed to show it.

He was foreign. Dark, thin and bony, with brown skin

and black hair. People said his father came of Gypsy stock. Others said his family was Swedish. Anyway, his father was an outsider, had come tramping this way long ago and settled on a cotter's plot in the north hamlet, had gone away again but came back. He was an artisan and could do anything— tinplate coffeepots, forge scythes and horseshoes and all kinds of locks, fix wall clocks and pocket watches, everything. The doctor used him to repair his most delicate instruments. And besides he was shoemaker, tailor and vet, even a real doctor if necessary. He could work the twig to find water and could see lost things. He was penniless. He and his wife and Albert went around dressed in rags.

His father spoke a foreign tongue, whatever it was—anyway, it didn't seem to be Swedish. Albert himself spoke somewhat differently from the local people. He had gone along with his father on several of his trips, it appeared.

He was foreign and the son of a foreigner.

He was poor in school. Never knew his lessons, never gave a correct answer. But it often looked as if he answered wrong for sheer spite. It wasn't with him as with the others. The others, too, could be poor and would answer wrong, or stand there tongue-tied and looking pretty crappy, and then, when the break came, they would boast and brag and say they'd done it just for fun. And those who listened were nice and let on they believed it, then looked away in embarrassment.

It was different with Albert. He never boasted about answering wrong for spite. But they felt he did. And the teacher felt the same. One day when Albert started by being tongue-tied and then gave an answer quite off the mark, the teacher stepped down and slapped his face. "I'll teach you to make fun of me!" he said.

Albert merely stood still until the teacher had returned to the lectern. Then he said, "You aren't allowed to strike!"

The teacher rushed at him once more: "What do you presume to tell me!"

"You aren't allowed to strike!" Albert said again, standing stiff and looking at the teacher without batting an eye, quite calm, only a little paler than usual. The teacher was very red. Everybody expected him to strike once more. He did strike, but at the desk. He struck and hammered the desk several times, making the books and the inkstand dance, and said that if Albert dared...

But he didn't hit him anymore.

"And you'd better spare me from hearing that sort of thing in the future! That much I'll tell you!" he said as he walked up to the lectern again. "Sit down." Albert sat down. It was extremely quiet in the classroom. Everybody knew who'd won. They could see the teacher knew too.

Albert was bored. He kicked a stone into the lake, slapped a willow herb to the ground with a stick, yawned furiously, stared in all directions; but there was nothing amusing to do anywhere, only childish pranks. He simply snorted at the humble suggestions of Gunder and Ole.

They stood in a huddle, silent, a little way behind him. When Albert was bored he was dangerous.

Suddenly he seemed to brighten up. He turned around to them.

"We'll row out to Geitholmen. We'll chop a hole in the boat. Then we'll have to stay there till people get anxious and begin to drag the lake and comb the area for us."

At first nobody said anything. Everybody looked at Ole.

After all, this mostly concerned him, who had borrowed his father's boat.

Ole swallowed for a moment. Then he said, "I had to promise to be back with the boat this afternoon."

Albert looked at him, screwing up his eyes. "You shut up! Or I might snip off your balls!"

Then he laughed his single crack of laughter, "Ha!"

Ole didn't say anything.

Albert stepped into the boat. The others after him. Ole last. He thought it over for a second, but then he came. They understood he thought he had to be where the boat was. And then he probably was thinking, like the others, that they didn't have an ax on board, so they wouldn't be able to chop a hole in the boat anyway. But better not tell Albert about that, because then he might take it into his head to load up the boat with rocks and row it out and roll it till it filled with water and sank—or something else, perhaps worse, which they couldn't even imagine.

They looked at each other and noticed they were thinking the same thing. Nobody said anything.

Albert stood in the bow, brooding. Perhaps he was beginning to get bored with this new enterprise before it had started.

The others stood in the middle of the boat—a little bent, as though weighed down by something. It was long since they'd spent any time with Albert now, and they felt more clearly that he was a burden to them. Suddenly they remembered: every time he'd gone away they'd breathed a sigh of relief, as if they were getting a holiday. No, no, that wasn't true, they did look up to him, after all. They would go through fire for him. Only, things were so difficult sometimes.

They weren't straight with him. They kept him in the dark about many things they talked about among themselves—but alone with him they each blurted out many things they didn't tell the others. And then he might forget to be contemptuous, or to give out his dangerous, cheerless crack of laughter. It had happened. Then they could walk through fire for him.

And then suddenly, when they were several, he was as usual. Vicious and dangerous.

They puzzled over him a good deal.

They couldn't understand him.

"Ole and Anders, you two can row!" Albert said. He himself sat in the front of the boat. The others were astern. Ole and Anders started rowing.

The oars were heavy. Heavier than the last time. His aching back felt worse now. Anders said to himself, Now it'll be fun, now that Albert has come—now it'll be fun, now that Albert has come—now it'll be fun, now that…He thought this over and over, until he noticed he was thinking, If only I were safely home again—if only I were safely home again…

It was a long way to Geitholmen; the "goat island" lay far out, floating at the upper edge of the lake. Far, far out. Anders suddenly noticed that he was furiously angry with Ole because he'd thought up all this and had whistled for him outside the fence. His back was aching, the oarlocks were creaking, the oars dripping—aching, creaking, dripping…that damned Ole…aching, creaking, dripping …that damned…

The boat scraped the bottom, they'd arrived. The whole

flock of goats stood at the shore and received them. They always did whoever came. And people would come quite often, Geitholmen was much used for outings. The goats would be there to receive them every time—they were unhappy on the islet, there weren't enough rocks for them there. One could often hear them from far away as they stood bleating at the shore for hours on end. Perhaps they longed to be with people.

There were many goats, at least twenty-five to thirty. Black, gray and white goats. But no billy goat. Perhaps that was the reason they were bleating at the shore. Scattered among the grown-up goats were also some half-grown kids. Kids were nicer and funnier than any other animals, even nicer than puppies. They were so incredibly playful, jumped and danced and put their heads askew, and stood up on their hind legs to sort of dance in a circle around their own teeny-weeny horns. They had small cheerful faces, almost like a kitten or a tiny little girl. There were quite a few kids on the islet, and they jumped and danced and played at fighting from sheer joy when they saw people. One kid, which was sparkling-white all over, was especially pretty and merry. It danced more than the others and came bounding right down to the boat, its head awry. It would have been great fun to run up and play with it—but that sort of thing was out of the question now that Albert was there. He would only laugh, "Ha!" and say they were a bunch of little stinkers and that he'd probably have to snip off their balls.

Albert went ashore. He seemed to have forgotten they were to chop a hole in the boat. They relaxed, feeling an uncertain sense of relief.

They roamed around the islet—tossed flat stones seaward to see how often they would skip on the surface, looked for nests and eggs but found none, rolled a large, round stone down the steep rock, making it hit the lake with a big splash. It was rather fun, but then it was over. They wondered if they should go bathing, somebody mentioned it, but it was dropped—Albert wasn't interested; he got the shivers in the water. Thin people easily got the shivers in the water. He knew how to swim, and he knew something the rest of them didn't: he could swim under water with open eyes. But he wasn't fond of bathing. So it was dropped.

They roamed around a bit, trying to think of something to do. But it wasn't easy. And it got worse the more they realized how bored Albert was. He was bored, bored, *bored, b-o-r-e-d.* He didn't say a word. He couldn't bring himself to say a word to anybody. He turned away to avoid seeing them. He was so fed up with them that there were no words for it. He was so bored that his face swelled up and turned grimy.

They were all getting anxious and restless. They began to scurry hither and thither, trying to come up with something that would cheer him up. Erik whispered and said they could light a fire on the beach. Sheer nonsense—there wasn't a dry stick of wood on the entire islet. Ole mentioned in his distress that they could play at Indians. Albert didn't even have to laugh, the others simply snorted at something so utterly childish.

And now they had walked around the whole islet and stood by the boat again. Albert turned away and yawned. His whole face drooped, he had black spots under his eyes from sheer consuming boredom.

How it began? It was impossible to say how it began. Who uttered that one sentence? Gunder claimed, the only time they talked about it afterward, that it wasn't him. White in the face, he screamed it wasn't him. But it *was* him. It was none other than him. But anyway, it didn't matter, for it wasn't with that sentence it began, not at all. It really began while they were still on the other side of the islet, on the side that faced Lauvberget. The sound that separated the islet from Lauvberget Rock wasn't very wide. They could probably swim it, if they wanted to. It was Erik who said it. So it was Erik who started it, in a way. Erik was sure he could swim across and thought it was odd that the goats didn't swim ashore, considering how unhappy they were on the islet. Then Ole said that goats were afraid of water, he knew because his father had kept goats. Goats couldn't stand water. Goats couldn't even stand rain. Goats didn't know how to swim. If they fell into the water they would walk ashore on the bottom, Ole said. His father had seen it once.

So it was Ole who started it, really.

If only the boat had been on the other side, facing Lauvberget, then it would never have happened. But the boat was on the far side, hidden to all. Nobody could see the boat from any of the farmsteads. No one could see them, whatever they did. So, really, it was the boat that was to blame.

And in some way it was the baby goat itself that was to blame. When they got back to where the boat was, it had jumped on board. It stood on one of the floorboards, with its four legs close together, putting its head askew and nodding and nodding. The other goats had followed the boys along the beach for a while. Afterward they had scattered. Now most of them were gathered on the slope, their eyes fixed on the boat. Perhaps the kid knew it and was showing off a bit to the grownups. Perhaps goats weren't much better than people that way.

It was then Gunder said that sentence—for it *was* Gunder who said it, no yelling or denial could help that.

"So, you want to get into the water and walk ashore on the bottom, do you?" Gunder said.

Suddenly Albert wasn't bored anymore. He brightened up. He smiled. Yes, Albert laughed, and he almost gave a real laugh—two brief cracks of laughter, "Ha! Ha!"

He gave the pretty, silky-white, cheerful kid a sort of probing glance. Then he said, "We'll row out with it and drop it in the water!"

They all stopped. Their eyes were one big stare.

"No, but—," Ole and Anders said the same moment.

Albert snorted. "It'll walk ashore on the bottom, after all! We'll only row out a short distance. It has to learn—so it'll know how to when it grows up!"

And he laughed again, "Ha!"

They had never seen Albert so cheerful.

Nobody said another word. Nobody looked at any of the others either.

"Anders, Gunder and Per, the three of you can step into the boat," Albert said. "You, Gunder, can drop it in. But row far enough out to force its head under. Or we won't have any fun."

No one said no. No one probably thought of saying no. No one dared think anything that dangerous. And besides— it was Albert, after all, who…and Albert surely wouldn't take it into his head to…and it would be amusing to see, too…what the kid would dream up….

He felt strangely titillated. His heart throbbed and throbbed. A strangely sweet taste in his mouth.

They got into the boat without scaring the kid too much. It wanted to jump ashore, of course, but they blocked its way. It peeked over the gunwale but quickly pulled its head back—water, nothing but water everywhere! They giggled in suspense. Anyway, things went easier than they'd thought. It believed they wanted to play. When they pushed the boat out, it tilted its body a little and was about to fall— it looked funny as it staggered, its legs close together. But it quickly recovered its balance, nodded its head and bleated cheerfully.

Albert said in a gentle, slow-spoken voice, "We'll teach you how to bleat all right!"

The bottom of the lake sloped gradually. They backed the boat out a couple of strokes, but the water probably wasn't deep enough yet to force its head under. The kid had gotten a bit restless, it skipped to the extreme end of the boat. It took its stand there, its forelegs planted near the gunwale, its eyes staring. But it didn't dare jump in.

Gunder grabbed it under the neck and hind legs and heaved it overboard. To be on the safe side, he dropped it with the head facing offshore. But, sure enough—it turned around as soon as it hit the water and walked ashore on the bottom. The water just barely covered its hindquarters and barely wet its little beard. When it got close enough to the shore to have its whole head above water, it nodded at each step it took, nodded and nodded like a white-haired old woman. It looked terribly funny, they all laughed, howled and laughed, till Albert said, "Ssh!," cocking his ear toward the Lauvberget shore.

They thought this was the end of it. Anders and Per had made a couple of strokes with their oars, just enough to keep pace with the kid. The boat struck bottom the very moment the kid stepped on dry land and gave itself a shake. It shook itself so hard that water squirted all over, and Albert and Erik had to jump back a step. It didn't bleat anymore.

It wanted to go on, to higher ground. But there was Albert. He grabbed it under the neck and hind legs and heaved it into the boat again.

"You'll have to row a bit farther out, to force its head under, poor thing," he said.

"It doesn't bleat anymore," Gunder said in a muffled voice.

Albert merely glanced at him. He'd suddenly become so handsome, Albert had. There was color in his cheeks, and his eyes had become so bright. He wasn't bored any longer.

"You just shut up!" he merely remarked, looking at Gunder. "Or you know what I'll do."

Per and Anders backed the boat out. Two strokes of the oars, then one more, less vigorous.

"Farther out!"

They gave one more stroke.

It was exciting. It was like itching—you had to scratch till it hurt, till you were scratching nothing but red meat—and still you itched and itched...

This time it went under all the way. It disappeared. They all held their breaths for a second. But—there were the little horns again, rising above the surface. The horns nodded and nodded. It was unbearably funny. They didn't dare laugh aloud. They whispered to each other, "Look, he's nodding!"

and giggled convulsively. Anders had to let go of the oar to clutch his stomach and giggle. The oar started sliding, and he forgot to giggle as he struggled to save it. Look! Now its whole head was above the surface. The kid nodded and nodded all the way ashore, as if agreeing with something. It may have taken slightly shorter steps than the first time, or the fact that it had quite a bit farther to go may have made a difference. Anyway, there was one change. The first time—Anders had noticed this quite clearly—it saw the boat and it saw *him* while toddling ashore as he rowed alongside, having to be careful not to brush it with the oar. Now, too, he was right beside it, moving his oar carefully, and its eyes were open just like then—those light-blue, milky-looking big eyes with their vivid yellow irises and vivid black pupils, circled by pink rims. But it didn't see the boat, it didn't see him, it didn't see anything. It seemed to walk quite absentmindedly, looking only inward. It kept its mouth shut and didn't bleat. It walked straight at the shore, nodding and nodding. The water poured from its little beard, the water poured from its hairy belly, it was beginning to look a bit bedraggled—it obviously wasn't made to be exposed to too much water.

Albert stood waiting on the shore. He bent forward and called it in a gentle voice, "There, sweet little nannie, come now! There, sweet little nannie."

Perhaps it could have gotten away from him, if it had had the sense to. Yes, sure it could, quite sure—if only it had made one leap sideways and then jumped—there it walked straight into Albert's arms. It didn't seem to see or understand anything anymore.

"That's a sweet little nannie!" Albert said, stroking it.

He carried it to the boat. It didn't resist.

"*No, no, no!*"

It was Ole who screamed. Ole had suddenly become quite beside himself, he was screaming like crazy, "*No, no, no!*" His face white in between all his freckles, he rushed at Albert and tried to tear the kid away from him. He was frantic, using his clenched fists without seeing where his blows would fall, the tears spurting from his eyes. "*No, no, no!*" he cried, as if no other words existed. He hit Albert's face with several of his blows. He went on striking—kicking and striking.

Albert was taken aback for a moment, he almost lost his footing; one of the blows hit his nose and he started bleeding. The next moment he was in control again, and just as calm. Cool and unruffled, he gave Ole a kick that sent him sprawling. He made a half turn and tossed the kid into the boat.

"Row out!" he said, without raising his voice. Then he turned to Ole, who had scrambled to his feet again.

"It was your idea, after all! It was you who said they walked on the bottom! It was you, all right!"

"No, no, no!" Ole wept bitterly, the tears gushing from his eyes. He no longer saw Albert, only the boat and the kid in the boat; he ran after them, starting to wade into the water.

Albert set off after him, got hold of Ole's shoulder and pulled him ashore again.

"Fool! It was your idea, after all!" He said it quite calmly, in a friendly, slightly patronizing manner.

Ole didn't answer. He just bent over and clutched his stomach with both hands. He vomited. He dragged himself up a few steps and vomited again.

Albert stood watching him with a face full of weary, friendly contempt.

"Looks like it won't even be necessary to snip off your balls," Albert said. He spoke the way you do to a little baby. Then he turned to the boat. "What are you gaping at? Get moving, quick!"

Suddenly Gunder started bawling. "I don't want to anymore! I don't want to!" He sobbed and cried. And as if it were contagious, Per too began to bawl, from sheer fright. Erik stood ashore, pale and terror-stricken.

Albert stood still for a moment—but only a moment. Then he jumped into the boat. "Well, Anders, now it's up to you and me. The others are all a bunch of old women. Row out!"

Anders sat at the oars. For a second he felt as if he were somewhere else. He was here too, of course—he saw the boat, Albert, the kid—but still, it wasn't this that he saw. He saw two paths, he knew he could choose, he dimly realized he was making a choice this very moment, not only for now but for many times to come, for always…he had to choose…for always…

Afterward he recalled something strange: he saw Albert lying dead. He clearly saw his open, glazed eyes, he saw them *under water,* recalling all the while that Albert knew quite well how to swim with open eyes under water. He heard a voice inside him, No, no, no!

"…You and me, Anders," Albert said. The words reached him through a fog. He was far out on the ice…

Suddenly he realized he was turning his head toward the shore, toward Ole. He heard a voice, "Coward! Coward! Coward!"

The voice came from far away. But it was his own voice and he wondered, feebly and remotely and coolly, why it was so far away. The next moment his whole body was quiv-

ering with rage and he cried, "Coward! Ole! You coward!
You—you—you coward!"

"Ssh!" Albert said sharply. "Row out, you fool!"

Anders backed out. Albert took the kid…Albert said,
"Row back again, quick!" Albert jumped ashore to receive
it.

The kid gave a definite impression of walking uphill, nodding and talking to itself. Nodding and talking…it wasn't
possible to hear what it was saying…it was so far away. On
the beach stood Albert. "There, sweet little nannie!" Ole
lay on his stomach up near the nethermost trees. Erik stood
farther down, stiff and motionless. Gunder sat hunched up
in the boat all in tears, Per sat stiffly erect and with an un-
natural, stiff smile on his face. Apart from this, there was
nothing but backing out and rowing ashore again…Every-
thing was far, far away. All these things had always been
and would always be. This was the world, this and nothing
else, over and over again, and each time a little sweet pain—
it had reached the quick long ago—and a little sweet nau-
sea in his stomach, and something that was trying to force
its way up his throat but was pushed back, swallowed and
swallowed again. Over and over…Sweet little nannie, come
now…

Was it the fourth time, was it the fifth? It had lasted
infinitely long, for days, years.

It didn't come up again.

It ought to have been there already.

It didn't come.

Albert stood in the stern with the gaff, on the watch and
commanding, "Back the oars! There, back the oars now!
The left oar! More with the left—no, no, the right! Stop!"

He thrust the gaff down, got hold of something, heaved and pulled, lost his hold and fell over in the boat, got up again, bent forward, regained his hold, used the gunwale as a fulcrum, pressed his body against the gaff handle and weighed it down. The head and front part of the kid emerged from the water, its eyes were stiff and glazed—then it slipped off the pike pole and sank again and the handle struck the other gunwale with a smack, but Albert avoided a fall this time, warding it off with his hands and resting on all fours for a moment.

"It's dead!" he said.

Nobody answered. It was so quiet. Not a breath of wind, not a sound. The goats formed a semi-circle on the islet, way up where the bushes and the brushwood started. They didn't move or let out a sound, they just stared. The entire islet was a big, staring, silent thing. The sun was a blood-red ember in the west, a menacing, staring eye. The whole sky was a huge staring eye.

"We'll leave it there," Albert said. He suddenly turned to Anders. "Row back!"

He jumped ashore, ran up the path through the underbrush over to the other side. He came back again at once.

"There aren't any boats on the lake. We'll take off at once."

He turned landward. "Come, Ole, we're leaving."

Ole got up. Looking wretched, with a grimy, swollen face. His eyes were nearly closed up. He walked straight into the boat, right past Anders, and sat down aft. Gunder had to take the other oar.

"Put me ashore at the bird-cherry tree!" Albert said. He had sat down beside Ole.

They were seated. The goats were gathered at the beach in one solid flock. They didn't move. They didn't follow them along the shore. They didn't bleat.

The lake was still and smooth. The sky was clear. The wake stayed behind them like a many-ribbed fan, a flawless shiny construction.

When the boat ground to a halt at the point below the big bird-cherry tree, Albert got up without a word and went ashore. But up there, in the shade of the tree, he turned around.

"You'd better not say anything about this. You don't want to be sent to reform school, do you?"

He smiled. A flash of white teeth appeared in the brown face within the shade.

He stood watching them awhile. They sat mute in the boat, the five of them. He seemed to be waiting for something. Then he gave up, whatever it might have been. He put his hands in his pockets, shrugged his shoulders indifferently, turned around and walked off. He vanished in the shadow of the huge tree.

They waited till he was completely gone. Nobody said a word. The whole world was as still as if it were dead. In the west the sky loomed red, as from a huge fire.

Gunder and Anders backed out the boat. They turned it and began to row. Gunder had to stop now and then, Anders wasn't quite up to managing the oar.

They reached the headland. Gunder shipped his oar, Gunder, Erik and Per climbed ashore.

They shoved the boat off. Ole took a couple of stumbling steps forward, found his place beside Anders and grabbed the oar.

There were only a few strokes to go now. Perhaps no more than twenty, twenty-five...He began to count. Now there was one less, now two, now three...

There were ninety-five strokes.

He scrambled ashore. He felt as if he'd been sitting in this boat as long as he could remember.

He straightened up, looked at his hands, looked at Ole but averted his eyes at once.

Ole tidied the boat, slowly and thoroughly—removed the oars and carried them to their proper place, removed the oarlocks. He dawdled. He didn't give Anders a single glance.

At long last he was through. And now they were supposed to go their separate ways. But Anders wasn't surprised when Ole as a matter of course took the same path as he—up through the pasture. They walked side by side, without saying a word. Anders was thinking, It was he who started it—he didn't have to come and whistle for me.

They had gotten roughly to the middle of the pasture, where the road passed through a small dip so they could see neither the lake nor the buildings at Anders' home. There Ole stopped and carefully put the oarlocks down by the side of the road.

Anders waited till Ole was ready.

Then they rushed at each other.

They didn't have much practice in fighting, either of them. For some reason or other there had never been much fighting between them. They knew little about averting or parrying blows, and it didn't take long before they were both bleeding heavily. But they didn't stop on account of that. They didn't say a word, only fixed each other's eyes and struck out. Now one of them was on the ground, now the

other. Their clothes got ripped and blood-stained. At one
time they were both so out of breath that they collapsed
and sat on the ground a little while. Then they got up at the
same moment and started over again. Once Ole struck
Anders a blow in the stomach, making Anders feel sick—
he curled up and puked. Meanwhile Ole just stood there.
But when Anders straightened up again, he saw that Ole
was laughing, and sick or not, he couldn't take it and rushed
at him again.

When they started, they didn't know how to fight. They
knew quite a lot by the time they stopped. And all along
they were perfectly silent. They stopped because they'd
gotten so tired that their blows didn't have the slightest
force anymore—they had no breath left, they couldn't stand
up, they fell every time they missed. The fight ended without peace, they both found themselves sitting in the heather,
one on each side of the road. If Anders hadn't known it was
Ole sitting there on the other side, he wouldn't have recognized him. A moment later Ole got to his feet, picked up
the oarlocks and left. He staggered and stumbled. Anders
had seen a drunk man walk that way—it was at Christmas
once, many years ago.

He too scrambled to his feet and went home. He staggered and stumbled. He got through the gate. He heard
that Father and Mother had come home and sat on the stoop.
He sneaked in the back entrance. There was nobody in the
kitchen, and he made his way unseen into the hall and up
the stairs.

They were talking and laughing down there.

It seemed to him he'd been to the world's end—as if he'd
seen everything there was to see, taken part in everything

there was to take part in. He'd seen everything, taken part in everything, knew more than he'd thought he'd ever get to know—and knew that he could tell nothing of all this to any living soul. He felt utterly alone, as if he stood alone at the world's end.

They were talking and laughing down there. He thought of his parents, and they appeared to him like two remote, innocent children.

They never talked with Albert afterward. In the next few days, when they all lived in fear, they avoided him. And he avoided them—if he looked at them once in a while in the break, it was with an alien glance, infinitely indifferent. As if he was so finished with them that he'd forgotten them the very moment he looked at them. He looked straight through them, and beyond. They couldn't stand that look, they would sneak off or think up the most pitiful things. Gunder made himself sick for a week. And when the week had passed, everything was over. Nothing had come out—the man at Lauvberget just went around mumbling a story about a stolen baby goat. And Albert was gone. He disappeared a few days after that Sunday at Geitholmen. He took off with his parents, nobody knew for certain where—to Kristiania perhaps, or to some plant. His father had been a construction worker at one time.

He hadn't said a word to any of them before he left. They were nothing but thin air to him. It gnawed at them. But now he was gone. It was a relief. Oh, what a relief it was. It was pitiful and mean to feel so relieved. They looked past each other for some time.

They never talked about it.

To the Woods, to Møltemoen

IT WASN'T NIGHT ANY LONGER. It wasn't daylight yet. He lay there unable to sleep.

There was something—he rocked up and down in bed, humming to himself.

I'm going to the woods, to Møltemoen, to fetch the cows and butter and cheese—I'm going to the woods, to Møltemoen, to the woods—f-a-r, f-a-r off in the woods....

It was quiet everywhere. No one up. Everybody was asleep. He put on some clothes and stole out.

The sun was below the hill, the day still unborn. Somewhere a bird was singing.

No other sound in the whole world.

He stood a few moments on the dew-covered doorstep looking eastward. The sky was turning red. Then the first sunbeam came, a puff of wind passed over the grass and the flowers, and suddenly there were long blue shadows in the yard and on the road, on all the green meadows gray with dew.

I'm going to the woods, to Møltemoen....

Grete and the others and Grete and I!

The shadows stretched so long and blue.

Embret sniffed the air. "We'll have nice clear weather today!"

At first they followed the parish road.

It was an old thoroughfare, built for the goats. It wound hither and thither, over knolls and hills, around to all the farms.

Gradually Embret's voice grew louder.

They went through the yard at Rolstad, where every other person was born a lunatic in the old days. With a change of weather you could hear them howling in the yard toward evening. They foretold the weather for the entire hamlet.

They crossed Svartbekken brook. A girl had drowned herself there in the old days. As a matter of fact, it was the sweetheart of the man who settled at Møltemoen. She threw herself head first into a deep pool. There was the pool, right below the bridge.

Embret told stories on the road. He did it for Grete. He brushed her with his eyes every once in a while.

"Mighty talkative today, ain't he, Embret I mean!" Gorinè grumbled ill-humoredly. She walked last.

An overgrown byroad took off from the public road, winding its way between muddy hills up toward the woods. This was the road to cotter country. It ran as far as Skuggen, the uppermost cotter's plot at Kleiva. Afterward there was only the summer-dairy trail. You could drive up to Møltemoen only on the snow, in the summer you had to use packsaddle or carry everything in baskets on your back. Kerstaffer Møltemoen even carried his wife to the village in a basket, when she died all of a sudden in the middle of the haying season.

"'I ain't gettin' a pack horse for anything so small, for sure,' he said.

"Tough fellows those at Møltemoen in the old days. They did come from a murderer, you know. Old Kerstaffer killed his master—that was when his sweetheart had drowned herself in the pool. And so he had to work the woods. He built a house at Møltemoen. There he was left in peace. He got himself a wife, got himself children, cleared the place and lived quite well. But he never went to the village.

"'I get scared of the dark in a crowd!' Kerstaffer said."

Grete marveled at all the things Embret knew.

Now and then, when Embret was silent, Hans would whistle at the birds along the road and get them to answer him. Then Grete had to look at him.

Anders thought, When they reached the forest and took a rest, he would do a headstand and crow like a cock. Hans didn't know how to do that.

"Mighty talkative today, ain't he…," Gorinè could be heard muttering in the rear.

It was the time between the work seasons. People were home everywhere in cotter country—they came out on their stoops, men in their shirt sleeves, wives in their night jackets. A night jacket with red and white stripes was the usual day-time wear in the little shacks up here. The wives were all unkempt, with straw in their hair. These were quiet days, with little need for grooming yourself.

Where did they come from? Where were they going? Everybody asked about that. They gave the answer. Then they went on.

They were passing the house at Skuggen. At this hour,

before noon, it picked up a streak of sunlight. The husband stood on the stoop squinting at the sun. He wanted to know what was going on.

"Come along and you'll see," Grete said.

Oh no. Did they imagine he had time to go roaming around in the woods, like a tramp?

Oh well, nobody was likely to miss him anywhere.

He'd come down from the stoop and was making conversation, but only with Grete. There was a gleam in his eyes. There was a gleam in Grete's eyes, too. The others stood a little way off and didn't pay attention.

When he'd found out where they were going, he walked beside them up the hillside and into the woods. He mumbled something, perhaps they didn't know the road, he might as well…When they were halfway up he slowed down a bit, stopped, looked back, then ahead. "Well, perhaps I'd better start on my way down again…"

Nobody answered anything, and little by little he began shuffling downhill. You could tell from his back that he felt very forlorn.

"Say hello to everybody!" Grete said, in a low voice.

Nobody said anything for a while.

There was something special about Grete.

After she came into the house, the menfolk didn't leave the kitchen anymore to go up to the servants' quarters as soon as they'd eaten. They would talk—talk with *her*. And they didn't talk calmly as usual—they all got worked up, almost like they were angry, as they sat there slapping their thighs and roaring with laughter. They seemed to be watching each other, exchanged hostile glances and broke into hot, huffy laughter, as if they could just as well have banged the table or jumped at each other's throats. At times it was almost like being at a party. Or a dance. When merriment runs high and many have had a drop too much, and fist fights and murder are lurking at the door.

Grete behaved as if she were at a dance. When she turned her head to give a snappy reply over her shoulder to some joker or other, she swung her body like a dancer. Sometimes the smart guy, who'd just been chuckling over his own remark, became serious all of a sudden, while all the others slapped their thighs and laughed. Then you could see fist fights and murder in the lone man's eyes…But sometimes, too, she would simply laugh, swing her body and look back over her shoulder. That was mainly when Halvor had said something.

Now and then the fellows would try grabbing her when she brought their plates or walked past them at the table. But they could have spared their efforts, for then she gave a smacking blow, even if it was Halvor himself. And afterward she would laugh, so that her dimples looked like two bullet holes in her cheeks and her teeth gleamed. She was fair and buxom, and her hair looked like a sun around her head; she blushed for nothing, and then her blue eyes turned so dark you felt you were looking down into a well.

Anders sat on the side lines, watching it all. The others didn't give him a thought and didn't hold back because of him, he was just a little boy, after all.

That these big, grown fellows weren't ashamed to lose their heads like that over a girl! That they weren't ashamed to show it, at least. But they grinned and laughed and showed off, they had no shame. Anders sat at the kitchen table watching, not knowing where to turn his eyes. He was ashamed for them all.

Many probably didn't even know themselves what a state they were in. Somehow Anders felt most ashamed for those who didn't even know it themselves.

But the worst of all was that he felt so awfully ashamed for Grete.

She could try not to egg them on at least. She could try not to poke fun at everything they said. She could try not to walk around the kitchen floor as if she were dancing, when others were watching her. She could try not to turn her head and laugh when she answered them.

At least she gave them a real smack when they made a grab for her, that was something. Only, she ought to hit much harder and many times—she ought to beat them till they sagged to their knees, whimpering with fright, because they'd made a grab for her. *He* would beat them—beat them—just wait till he grew up...

What if he were to get up. What if he cried, Stop, or...They would just laugh, laugh and holler, slap their knees and laugh, laugh, laugh—his ears felt burning hot.

He watched in silence. Sat at the kitchen table without saying a word, just laughed when the others laughed. He felt his smile like a stiff slave's grin on his face. He thought, Just wait till I grow up. Then I'll beat Halvor, beat Anton, beat Embret—then I'll beat, beat, beat Halvor, then I'll...

But that was a long time from now.

He laughed with the others. Laughed with a stiff face. Oh yes, he managed it quite well. But sometimes he didn't get to eat. He kept busy trying to laugh.

They had been on the road for a long time. It went up-hill and uphill, everybody had grown quiet. There were dense spruce thickets and open heaths, there were dry creek beds, stretches of fen, and open places with tall ferns. There were long, steep hillsides with thick forest and lush blue-berry bushes, dark-blue at the top. They were deep into the woods by now, they heard the crash of a grouse once in a while, and they discovered moose tracks. It smelled of blue-berries, burnt evergreens and resin. The sun was scorching hot. Their path crawled with ants.

"Now we'll soon be at Vardberget!" Embret said.

At that very moment the forest was behind them, and they stood in an open, almost treeless area, a rocky flat with nothing but moss and a few crooked dwarf pines on it. They could see the sky on every side. Straight ahead lay a bog and a heath with red heather and green cloudberry leaves. The bog was strewn with crooked dead pines, looking like white corpses. They could see hill after hill on every side, one shaggy ridge behind another. And way, way down were the different hamlets, faraway and blue.

A small light-green square had been cut in the dark ridge far off. That was Møltemoen. The tiny cotter's plot re-sembled a little child who'd gone astray in the woods.

"Well, now we're halfway to Møltemoen!" Embret said.

They sat down to rest.

Hans whistled at a thrush and cackled like a frightened grouse hen.

Anders hesitated awhile. Then he did a headstand and crowed like a cock.

It grew quiet for a moment.

Then Embret started talking again.

"Møltemoen, you know—.

"Once a dairymaid was staying at the Muru summer dairy. Her name was Berte. She was made in such a way—well, she was so kind she could never say no. And when it got noised around, you know, all sorts of people began making trips up to the Muru dairy, both Saturday nights and in the middle of the week. For the girl was pretty and gay and likable.

"Then one evening in the fall—the evenings were dark already, it was late enough in the fall for that—Berte had gone to bed and the other dairymaid had gone to bed. Each had her own bed—Berte had seen to that—hmm! Then some fellow walked in through the door and groped his way over to Berte. Outside it was dark, inside it was even darker—the fire had been put out on the hearth.

"Berte wasn't one to say no, she couldn't. She didn't say a word, Berte didn't. Not the stranger either.

"He stayed for a goodly while, but not the whole night—when he got up to leave it was still dark.

"When he stood in the doorway, Berte said—and this was the first word that passed between them, 'Say, whereabouts do you come from—I mean, in case something should come up?'

"Then he answered, the man standing in the doorway:

> 'In darkness I came, in darkness I'm goin'.
> My name is Tjøstøl, my home's Møltemoen.'"

"My, what a blockhead!"

It was Grete who interrupted, clapping her hands and crying, "My, oh my, what a blockhead!"

Embret stopped and looked at her with narrow eyes. "Don't blame the sheep because it has wool, or men because they're stupid!"

"Hee-hee!" came from Gorinè.

Embret continued.

"And as it turned out, something did come up. And Tjøstøl married the girl. But when he had to go to the village, he locked the door from the outside. And he had the window nailed down. So his wife had to sit there till he returned. Before that time there wasn't a lock to be found on any door up in these here woods.

"But still people said that not a single one of her kids looked like any of the others, and no one looked like him who was supposed to have sired them. Except the first. But he, well, people said he looked like the whole hamlet."

"Oh, dear! Sure ain't easy!" Gorinè sighed piously.

Embret continued.

"People would ask Tjøstøl why he locked the door after him every time he went to the village—Tjøstøl was kind, you could ask him anything.

"'Why? What if a bear should come and take her!' Tjøstøl said.

"There were bears up around here in those days; and Tjøstøl's father, Kerstaffer—the one who carried his wife to the village in a basket—had a bout with a bear he'd never forget."

Embret pointed down the hillside.

"Down there it was. A tall spruce used to stand down there. A tree fit for a mast. That's where it was.

"This was after Kerstaffer had carried his wife to the village. It was before Tjøstøl got married. Kerstaffer was getting along in years, but he was still big and strong. He would often go after the birds at that time, with both gun and snare.

"He'd noticed that somebody was stealing birds from him. He was angry about it and thought that, if he caught the fellow, he'd pay for it—Kerstaffer had an awful temper.

"Then one day in the fall, a bit later than now, Kerstaffer was checking his snares. He had caught one bird, but noticed that another was gone. He was angry. Then he came to the snare he had set near the tall spruce—and there, under the branches, some fellow stood hunched over the snare. Kerstaffer got so furious he took the bird he'd caught and planted it smack in the stranger's back with all his might. 'I'll learn ya to snitch birds!' he said. At that moment the man straightened up and turned around sharply—it was a bear with a bird in his paws.

"Kerstaffer had his ax with him, and he held it up in front of him. The bear pressed on and Kerstaffer backed off. He thought he'd try to get the tall spruce between himself and the bear. And so he backed off there, but the bear grinned, snatched after him with his paws and pressed on. Kerstaffer waved the ax at him and the bear jumped back a bit, but then he pushed on again and Kerstaffer had to pull back. They walked around and around the spruce for half an hour this way—or a couple of hours, nobody knows— Kerstaffer in front and the bear after. They trampled a deep track around the spruce, you could see it many years later as a hollow in the ground. The bear didn't quite dare to attack, he was scared of the ax bit; and Kerstaffer didn't dare to strike, for if he were to strike he'd have to raise the ax, and then the bear would be at him. They say the bear is the fastest animal there is, ten times faster than the fastest man. In the end Kerstaffer saw no other way, he backed off from the spruce onto the summer-dairy road—he knew the whole area like the floor of his own kitchen. The bear after him. And that's how they walked all the way—Kerstaffer in the lead tail first, shaking and shaking his ax, the bear after, snatching and snatching at him with his paws. There were four creeks to cross, it's a touchy business to do it backward; but Kerstaffer knew the place like his kitchen floor, so he brought it off. Once in a while the bear would drop on all fours and snatch at Kerstaffer's legs. Then Kerstaffer brushed his muzzle with the ax bit, and he backed off a little. Finally they got as far as the fence around Møltemoen, and then Kerstaffer thought: Now I'm a goner, he thought. For to get over the fence, no, that would be quite impossible. But at that moment the bear started sniffing and sniffing—most likely it was the smoke from the chimney he didn't like. And so he stopped a moment, it was as if he'd come to think of something, because suddenly he turned around and padded off as quietly as a cat. But Kerstaffer, well, Ol' Kerstaffer sat right down—he was so overcome he couldn't make himself go through the gate for a long time. And after that day he was scared of the dark and didn't like to go out. You couldn't drag him off to the woods with a horse. But when people came, he liked to sit inside and relate the episode with the bear. 'Scared?' he said. 'I wasn't any more scared than I am right now,' he said. And then he began to cry sitting there. He would cry very easily after that day.

"Since then nobody has seen any bears in these woods."

At Møltemoen they found the wife and a young lad at home. The boy's name was Tjøstøl. Kerstaffer himself and Sjønne, the youngest boy, were over in the other village with blueberries and cloudberries.

The lad didn't say a word, just fetched wood and water, lighted the fire, and made himself comfortable again in the log chair by the fireplace. He was whittling an ax handle and looked at you with a wide-eyed stare. Later he went to the woods to fetch the cows. The wife set out a bowl of heavy cream. The lad returned and sat in the log chair without a word, the woman talked and asked questions, and Embret, Gorinè and Grete answered and chewed, swallowed and answered. The boy whittled and whittled at his ax handle, staring at Grete ever and again. His eyes grew bigger and bigger, then smaller and smaller, then again bigger and bigger. He whittled and whittled.

When they had finished eating, there was almost nothing left of the ax handle.

Grete glanced at him once in a while. She cocked her head and glanced at him from the corner of her eye.

The woman came down to the summer cow barn with them.

It was built into the fence, with the door facing the woods. Farther up there was a small pasture where a bull went moping around.

"We've kept this bull inside lately," the woman said, "he went after the cows like crazy, you see. And he ain't quite… he's a bit dangerous"—she flapped her skirt and shook her fist at the bull.

The cows were fine.

"We'll take'em out here, straight into the woods," the woman said. "Then we won't have to bother the bull."

At last they got under way again. But meanwhile Grete had been over in the cow barn with the young lad, she wanted to give the cows a bit of oats. She came running out again almost at once—rather out of breath and disheveled. The lad followed, with a queer look in his face. He kept loafing around by the fence with his eye on the weather—from the back he looked ill at ease.

They untied the cows and got them out quietly.

They had already let them out and were about to go when Raina stopped, damn stupid cow that she was, turned her head toward the pasture and mooed, just as if she was calling somebody. And she didn't have to call twice—the brush creaked and crashed and the bull came on at full tilt, snorting and roaring, and ran straight into the fence.

"Moo-oo-oo!" called Raina.

Crackling, snapping noises came from the fence. But it wasn't that easy to overturn, being fastened to the forest itself—the fence posts were live young spruce growing in serried ranks. The bull made another running start and butted at the fence, making a thumping noise.

"Moo-oo-oo!" Raina called, looking back. But, oddly, at the same time she got into such a hurry to run away, tripping and trotting down the road. Hans bent down, found a stick in the heather and dashed to the fence, and the third time the bull came rushing up Hans received it with a ringing blow on the neck before it got there. The bull roared, Raina mooed as she tripped along, and Hans stood by the fence whacking away at the bull. Grete ran ahead with Raina, Anders followed with the switch. He lashed out and noticed how good it felt to do so. He felt as if he was lashing out at all sort of things at once.

Now she'd get it! Now they'd get it! Now she'd—here they'd—get it! He whipped Raina, and Raina stuck her tail between her legs and ran.

Grete ran along with her, hanging on to her collar and running along.

"Poor bossy!" Grete stroked Raina as she ran.

"Poor bossy! Nothing to be scared about anymore! That naughty bull! Nothing to be scared about! Naughty, naughty bull!" She hung on, making the heather rustle as she ran swiftly and lightly, patting Raina and talking sweetly to her—in the end she nearly bent down and hugged the stupid red cow. She nearly hugged Hans, too, when he came running after them, sweaty and winded. She turned furiously on Anders, who gave Raina's rump another smack on the sly. The idea of beating poor, sweet Raina!

"But she mooed!"

Grete didn't seem to hear what Anders was saying.

"Poor bossy! Are they mean to my poor bossy!"

"But she mooed!"

Nobody listened to him.

The road back home was long. Everyone walked in silence.

It had just started to grow dark when they got home. A shadow detached itself from the dusk by the wall of the cow barn, it was Halvor who'd been waiting there. He helped put the cows in their stalls. It was nice and warm in the cow barn. The other cows gave their familiar friendly lows. Raina mooed longingly, "Moo-oo-oo!"

When the others came out of the cow barn, they noticed that Grete and Halvor remained in there. Grete was doing her evening chores and Halvor was helping her. They could hear his deep, low voice. They heard her voice too, but not gayly mocking as so often—rather a bit anxious and timid.

Hans stood nearest the door of the barn. He bent down, lifted a big stone lying there, lifted it high up as if he meant to hurl it at something—then dropped it again. He appeared pale in the dusk. Embret and Gorinè were a little way off. They were just waiting for Grete to join them, before going in for supper. The evening chores sure took a long time. They were getting more and more impatient.

"I wonder how it must feel to be like that." Gorinè's voice sounded furiously angry.

Embret's answer came a bit more quietly. "Oh—you know—it must feel like having an inflamed finger all the time, I guess."

Oh well! Here they were, the three who'd been showing off to Grete all day. And in there was the one who simply went and took her.

Anders stood for a moment—then he ran off. He seemed to run for his life—he rushed around the barn and down the green field, threw himself down in the grass, got up again as though possessed and rushed on. He didn't know what was driving him. He had only one thought: When I grow up! When I grow up! When I grow up!

He ran through the green aftermath, along the yellowing grain fields. Finally he had no more strength left and threw himself in the grass again.

He didn't know what was the matter with him, he was unhappy, he was strangely unhappy. He was so lonely, no, he wasn't lonely enough. He had to get up and rush on....

Darkness was falling. The dew was falling. It was no longer day, it was not yet night. The sky was a steady blue.

The First One

"Y OU'RE SO STUPID!" she said.

¶ He didn't answer.

"My God! You're so stupid. You should say, 'I love you!' And then I'll say, 'I love you!' And then you should kiss me. You'll have to. It says so in all the books."

She looked at him.

He didn't say anything.

"Say, 'I love you!'"

"I—," he said. He couldn't possibly say it. It was impossible.

"Ugh! What a peasant. You're a real peasant!"

She sulked a little; but then something occurred to her.

"Say, 'I'm fond of you!' then."

"I'm fond of you!" he said. That was no problem.

"It'll have to do!" she said. "It isn't right, but it'll have to do. Now you can kiss me."

— — — — — — — — —

"What? You don't want to? My God, you don't know *how*? But really—don't you kiss your mother?"

"We don't do such things," he said. He was red as a beet and felt like howling.

She was shocked.

"Oh, you peasants!" she said. "It's part of good breeding, after all. Look here—"

— — — — —

It was so strange. He felt strange long afterward.

She, for her part, grew quieter. She stood looking at the ground.

"Am I the first one you're fond of?" she said.

"Yes!" he said.

It was a lie.

"Ha-ha! Anders goes with girls!" Ole cried, slapping his knees and sniffing with his nose like a rabbit. And Gunder, Erik and Per slapped their knees: "Ha-ha! Anders goes with girls! With city chicks!" And Erik sniffed with his nose like a rabbit. Gunder and Per didn't know how to.

They'd been snooping on him. Perhaps they'd been eavesdropping, too, and heard what she and he had said.

When he pictured that to himself, he flew straight at Ole.

Gunder, Erik and Per looked on. Erik hollered, "Ah! There he got socked one," each time one of them was socked one.

"Am I the first one you've been fond of?" she asked.

"Yes!" he said. "Oh yes!"

She was constantly asking about that, though the book said almost nothing about it.

He was about to answer again, but she stopped him.

"No. I don't believe you. You should think it over. I'll give you five minutes to think it over, then you can answer me. Meanwhile I'll go sit down on the beach. Five minutes."

She looked at her watch. Yes, she had a watch, with a long chain around her neck, though she wasn't any older than him.

The first one...

He clearly remembered the first one. When Tora and Kari teased him about her—as they did for years—he said it was a lie. But he remembered her quite well.

It was at Christmas long ago, and her name was Anna.

They were all in the living room, the hanging lamp sparkled and there was a fire in the stove. The lamp shone on her. He became fond of her because she had brown eyes and because she had smooth, round cheeks that were red like apples. She was sitting on somebody's arm, it must have been Mother's, but he wanted to get over on the arm to her. She liked him well enough, but then the others laughed at her, his sisters—or it could have been someone else. It was probably someone else who laughed at her, for he could remember that both Tora and Kari sat stiffly in the sofa, having gotten their wish to be present. When the others laughed, she didn't like him anymore and didn't want to have him. He stretched out his arms after her, and when she drew back he cried and moaned, he *would* have her. The others laughed, she liked him less than before, and he stretched out his arms and cried.

She let him down because the others laughed.

She was the first one.

The second one—that was much later. At least a year, perhaps two. That was also at Christmas. Tora had a friend visiting her, her name was Guri. Tora, Kari and Guri were to go mumming at the nearby cotter homes and went up-stairs to put on their costumes.

He scrambled up the stairs after them. He was fond of Guri because she had big cheekbones and slanting eyes, and he wanted to look at her when she undressed.

He got to the door and stood up to peek through the keyhole. But Tora had heard him. He managed to see only a small glimpse of Guri before Tora came and tore open the door—and there he was.

They thumbed their noses at him. "Boo to you! So you peek through the keyhole, do you!"

They laughed at him, all three of them.

That was the second one. It hurt a long time.

The third one—she was let down by *him* because the others laughed.

This was much later, he'd started school already.

Her name was Eva, and she was pretty.

Tora and Kari said she was bad. But he understood quite well that they were envious and that Eva could never be bad, pretty as she was.

Eva often whispered to him in class when she didn't know what to answer. She sat in the same row as he but on the other side of the aisle. He didn't dare to answer, but didn't dare not to either.

She called him every day to ask about the homework, and little by little he understood that she was fond of him. That is, he wasn't completely sure, because she was rather stupid, well, in fact terribly stupid, so perhaps she really didn't remember the homework.

But Tora and Kari were sure, especially Tora. She laughed

when Eva called, teased him and told stories about how bad
Eva was. She had a brother who was so naughty they didn't
know what to do with him, because he would walk around
calling people names...

And now Eva called him every day! Ha-ha-ha-ha-ha!

Kari took her cue from Tora, and she too laughed,
Ha-ha-ha-ha-ha!

They danced around him. Ha-ha-ha-ha! Eva called him
every day! Ha-ha-ha-ha-ha!

He felt ashamed. They were laughing at him, and he
understood it was shameful and felt ashamed. When Eva
called, he could tell by her voice that she wanted to ask him
if they could meet and go skating together. He wanted to very
much, but Tora and Kari were tittering maliciously, and he
felt ashamed, became angry with Eva and said nothing.

"I really think you should tell her to stop calling you!"
Tora said one day.

Later she said it every day when she was through laughing.

Mother said the same. Tora had told on him.

He understood he had to think up something. And one
day when she called and both Tora and Kari were around,
he said it, "I really think you should stop calling me!"

Eva didn't say anything. She said, "Oh," into the mike,
and then nothing.

He just stood there, receiver in hand.

Tora and Kari had become so quiet.

"Why don't you put down the receiver!" Tora said, without looking at him.

Then she said, "Serves her right! The way she's been
calling you..."

They went their separate ways for the rest of the day.

She never whispered to him afterward. She never looked at him. She never called.

Later her parents moved, and he never saw her again. But he couldn't forget her.

Every time he'd done something cowardly he couldn't help remembering her.

Gunvor may not have been the fourth. No, definitely not, there had been others in between. But who could remember everything? Not he. Now and then he would remember things, then he forgot them again. You couldn't go around remembering girls all the time.

Gunvor wasn't the fourth, not the fifth either. But she was the only one while it lasted. Or the tallest one, in any case.

She never knew about it.

Or did she?

He wished she did—no, that she didn't.

Pity he could never bring himself to tell her or show her…But it was so impossible. She was more than a year older than he—at school she sat way over, three seats to the left and two rows up. He always remembered her from the back and slightly from the side—her cheek and the nape of her neck. And once in a while her fine curved nose, when she turned around for a moment during class, or when she stood turning and twisting because she had to recite and couldn't. That happened often. She was fairly stupid.

There was nothing unusual about her, as he knew very well. He knew it from the very beginning, but that didn't make it any easier. Only still more difficult.

On the other hand, you couldn't find any great faults with her either. She just wasn't very smart or remarkable. She wasn't even bad. She never said anything unexpected. When she began a sentence, you always knew the whole sentence right away, often many sentences to come as well— and then she would say them, over again, sort of.

But she had such a lovely voice.

It didn't help that she was stupid. It didn't even matter one way or the other.

He had started to read novels and knew: it was fate.

Others were also in love with her. Sometimes they would fight over her till the blood flowed. Some of them lived in the same neighborhood she did and used the same road to school. It was so painful to think about. They could walk with her every day.

What did they talk about with her? What in the world did they talk about?

When he pictured himself walking with her and trying to think of something to say, he felt cold shivers running down his spine.

She? She would just look at him with her lovely stupid eyes and wait for him to say something.

It was almost a comfort to know that this—just this— would never happen. He would never talk to her. She sat at such a safe distance—three seats to the left, two rows up— and they didn't have the same road to and from school.

When he ran into her every once in a while, outside in the breaks and such, it wasn't possible to say anything. Because it was impossible. He would start to sweat and wish he were dead. And so he thought up something and walked away—or ran. Sometimes he would run.

And then came that trip to the summer dairy last summer.

How could Father get the idea of lending the summer dairy for a school excursion!

He remembered that day from beginning to end. Remembered her and all the boys around her.

On the way down she was suddenly walking beside him. He was taller than she, something he hadn't known before. She didn't look at him. It occurred to him that perhaps they weren't so stupid after all, those lovely eyes of hers.

She smiled. "You don't say much, do you?"

In despair he cried, "I've forgotten something!," turned and ran uphill again. Up the long, steep summer-dairy road, all the way to the dairy.

He hadn't forgotten anything.

He ran till he was about to burst.

He dragged himself through the gate, threw himself on the meadow near the chalet cabin, on a hillside there. It was as if he'd found something—at any rate a refuge. He felt the salty taste of blood in his mouth. He lay there till he felt calm, sat up, plucked some sorrel.

Then came that everlasting, tiresome feeling—that this had happened before. That it had happened long ago…he had lain here and she had walked down there, had smiled when he turned and ran uphill again, and had walked over to the others. He saw it. He'd seen it.

He lay there till he could breathe calmly. Then he ran at a comfortable pace down the road again.

Relieved, despairing and ashamed, he saw whom she had paired off with. That guy, sure—he knew it from before.

Did he know it? Perhaps he'd only wished it.

A couple of weeks had gone by since then.

"Well," she said. "Have you thought it over now?"
He'd forgotten her.
So, now the five minutes were over.
"Yes," he said. "I have—."
"Well? So?"
If she was the first, she would throw her arms around his neck, press herself up against him and kiss him.
She stood looking at him with her calm big eyes.
"You're the first one," he said.

He was her knight. He would build a castle for her and buy a saddle horse for her. And a falcon, a gyrfalcon.
She was very keen on that saddle horse. It must have a flowing black mane and would speed along dim paths in wide forests. But then it occurred to her that *he* couldn't be the one, after all, for her mother had said that you couldn't get married on less than eight thousand, because you must have at least three rooms and a maid's room and kitchen. And he, who was a peasant, probably didn't even know what a maid's room was. And eight thousand!
She often spoke about peasants and was so stupid that he would have liked to slap her.

Those city people who'd stayed at Berg left yesterday! they said in the kitchen.
They left yesterday.
She hadn't showed up. She hadn't said a word.
The kitchen floor became so tremendously large. He made his way across it and slipped out.

The same day he received a letter from her.

Dear Anders!

We are leaving now. I am going back for the beginning of school, and I am worried about it. I am
starting my third year of middle school and will write
a lot of German, but you don't understand that. I will
think about you. You have to think a lot about me
and must never think about anybody else.

Your Alfhild.

It was the first letter he had gotten by mail. He would
walk with the letter in his trousers' pocket, close his hand
around it, take it out and read it, then close his hand around
it once again, until it was nothing but a thin black roll.

Later it was lost, and he didn't know what had become
of it.

The Snake

"GOOD LUCK WITH IT," Father said and laughed. ¶ And now Father had to be off, his horse and carriage were waiting already. He turned to Anders once more before he left.

"When you're good enough you can shoot a crow for us. You know, the crows keep flying around here and stealing both eggs and chicks. But promise to be careful while we're away, will you."

The carriage rumbled down the road. Anders stood behind the servants' quarters, alone. Alone with his new rifle. He began to understand it was true—he'd gotten a real gun, a fine small-bore rifle. He owned it. And it was Sunday with fine sunny weather, and it was his birthday. He was happy. Oh, he was so happy!

He weighed the rifle in his hand. He looked at the brown rifle butt. It was hickory—the finest wood in the world. The one the great skiers made their skis from.

He looked at the gun barrel. Shimmering, dark-blue steel. Oxidized steel, Father had said. It looked cold and dangerous—he remembered the adder killed by the washhouse many years ago. Afterward it lay on the stone slab all evening long, shimmering, dark-blue, dangerous. Finally a crow came and picked it up, rose heavily and flew away, the snake dangling from its beak and the awful three-cornered head pointing toward the ground.

He looked down the muzzle of the gun. It seemed to stare back at him with a black eye.

A gun…A murder weapon, some said.

Anyway, he wouldn't shoot anything alive. No crows. Not other animals either. He recalled what had happened in the hayloft during the summer. He was watching Embret turning over some old hay with a long pitchfork. Then he heard a very thin cry, not much more than a whistle, but painful and piercing nonetheless. Embret had run the prong of his fork clean through a mouse inside the hay. Impaled, it let out its thin death cry, while its little feet raced like arrows in midair. He felt sick just looking at it.

He would never kill animals.

But he could do targetshooting. He had twenty-five cartridges in his pocket.

Twenty-five cartridges. He would use five of them here, on the wall of the servants' quarters. Or maybe ten. Yes, ten. Then five on some old potatoes, which he would impale on a fence post. He would use five more for the cones on the big spruce down by the river. There were still five left. He would have to think about that.

He went over to the wall and put up a new target, a cardboard disk with circles and a black spot in the middle. Then he walked back to a distance of twenty meters.

He took aim and fired. There it was—that little nudge against his shoulder, the smell of powder, the bullet mark in the cardboard disk, the smell of sun-burnt timber and old tar as he stood by the wall looking at the bullet mark. Everything was fine, the sun was shining, it was his birthday and Sunday—all good things at once—he'd got a gun, he was happy.

He had fired three shots and just pulled out a cartridge— it lay on the ground in front of him, with a thin blue jet of gunsmoke spiraling into the air—when he heard a step behind him. Quickly, he put a cartridge in the barrel, turned his head and looked around.

It was Amund.

Anders had often met Amund since that time down the slope. But he'd never talked much with him.

Amund was even bigger now and nicer-looking than ever. Tall and broad, bigger than his own father. The biggest fellow in the whole neighborhood. The strongest one too, no doubt.

And that wasn't all.

He played the fiddle. And he had an air about him. When he came walking down the road in his slouching, cocky manner, you could tell it was him more than half a mile away.

Anders became stiff and dumb and clumsy when Amund was around. Afterward he always felt upset and unhappy.

But here was Amund.

"Well, well, so you're the one who's shooting," Amund said. It sounded as if he'd thought differently.

He walked over to the target and looked at it. One shot had hit near the center of the black spot. Then he came back.

"Fire a shot and let me see what you can do."

Anders fired. His hand trembled, so he missed the target. Amund laughed.

"Hand me the gun and I'll show you," he said. "How many cartridges have you got?"

"Twenty," Anders said.

He had twenty-one, he knew. But what he said was twenty.

"Hand over two or three then," Amund said.

Anders pulled the cartridges from his pocket. One, two, three—. It hurt. But here was Amund wanting to shoot with him. He counted out five cartridges and gave them to Amund.

Amund loaded and fired, loaded and fired again. The bullet marks appeared here and there among the circles, but none in the black spot at the center.

And then the five cartridges were used up.

"You'll have to give me five more," Amund said.

Anders took out five cartridges and handed them to him. He thought, Tomorrow I'll get some new ones, tomorrow it won't matter. Not at all, not at all.

Amund loaded and fired. Anders hadn't thought it possible to use up so many cartridges so quickly.

Now they were used up, all ten of them, and still Amund hadn't hit the black spot in the center. He stood for a moment, seemed to hesitate. Anders thought, This is impossible, he can't do it, this is impossible...

"You'll have to give me five more cartridges," Amund said. "And put up a new target. There must be something wrong with this one."

Anders gave him five cartridges. Anders put up a new target. Amund loaded and fired. Shot after shot. A sharp crack, a puff of smoke from the muzzle, a slight smell of burnt powder and a bullet mark on the disk.

He didn't hit the black spot. One of the shots didn't even hit the target. He didn't know how to shoot. He was a poorer shot than Anders.

And then the cartridges were used up.

Amund stood for a moment.

"Do you have more cartridges in the house?" he asked.

"Yes—that is—." Anders couldn't get himself to say that his father kept them locked up.

"Good. Then you must lend me five more. I really must find out if it shouldn't be possible to hit the bull's eye."

And so Amund fired again. He turned redder and redder in the face with each shot. But he didn't hit the bull's eye.

After the fifth shot, which missed the target altogether, he flung the rifle on the ground.

"Take your wretched rifle!" he said.

Anders bent down and picked it up.

"I'll buy some cartridges for you," Amund mumbled. Then he left.

Anders stood there following him with his eyes.

If only he hadn't made that remark about the wretched rifle. It was so pitiful.

Anders walked around all afternoon unable to make up his mind. He had one cartridge left, he kept his hand in his pocket and fingered it all the time. He didn't dare take his hand away. For what if the cartridge should get lost in the meantime! If there was a hole in his pocket or—.

He roamed about with the gun on his arm and his hand in his pocket, his fist clenched around the cartridge. But he couldn't find the one thing that was good enough for this last cartridge.

He went inside and placed the cartridge on the table in the living room while he cleaned the gun. He thought he might get an idea while cleaning it. But nothing came to him.

The day was passing. Evening wasn't far off. Soon it would begin to get dark. When it grew dark it was too late. If only Father and Mother had been back. But they were at a party and not likely to come home till late in the evening.

He roamed about restlessly—in the garden, across the field, down to the pasture. He didn't find anything. An old cone was hanging from a branch. It was a fine mark, but what if he should miss. It was too risky.

The sun had set. It was beginning to get dark already.

He was standing in the living room with the rifle on his arm. The window was open. He made up his mind. He would go down and shoot at that cone anyway.

Then he noticed something.

Down by the fence, near the gate, sat a crow. It was facing him. Whether it saw him or not was impossible to know. He was inside after all, almost hidden behind the curtains.

"When you're good enough you can shoot a crow," Father had said.

He hadn't meant to shoot any animals. But it was so long-range, at least fifty meters. He was sure to miss.

He put the cartridge in the barrel, bent down cautiously, supported the rifle on the windowsill and took aim.

He was sure to miss.

Now the rifle sight covered the crow's breast. He pulled the trigger.

A sharp little crack, a nudge against his shoulder. The crow was gone. But it hadn't flown away. It was—it must be lying behind the fence.

He got outside. He rushed down to the gate, the rifle in his hand.

The crow sat on the ground. It was quite still.

He, too, remained still.

He could see only one of its eyes. A black eye staring at him.

The crow supported itself on one leg, and on the wing that was on the same side as the leg. The other leg and the other wing had gone limp.

The eye kept staring at him.

He didn't know how long he stood like this. But finally— he must have been there a long time—he grabbed the gun barrel with both hands. This had to end.

The blood throbbed in the vein on his neck, he felt each thud like a blow to his body. Then he raised his gun and leaped forward.

The crow hopped away. It limped down the road toward the lake on one leg and one wing. It was incredible how fast it made progress. He ran after as fast as he could but was unable to catch up with it.

He ran and ran, his heart pounding in his throat. He clasped the gun barrel with both hands. The butt rested on his shoulder, ready to strike. But the winged crow hopped away.

And now they'd reached the lake.

At the shore he caught up with it. He swung the rifle butt.

Then it hopped again, straight into the water. And for the first time it cawed, hoarsely and piercingly.

One moment only. Then it hit the water and disappeared under a crooked branch.

But from a spruce nearby there was an answer. And from another spruce a little farther off. Two grayish-black birds came winging their way out of the forest, screeching with hoarse, furious crow's cries. Two more came from farther away. And still more. Black birds were coming out of the black forest. Far away he could see more and more, nothing but dim shadows in the twilight. But they were all coming closer. And they were all crying, wailing and crying.

He dropped the rifle and took off up the road.

He didn't look up. But he realized they'd soon be upon him. He glimpsed their shadows in the semi-darkness, he heard their cries—furious, greedy cries.

He ran. One flapped its wings straight over his head. Now there were more. He raised an arm to cover his head and ran. The stroke of a wing grazed his arm. Then he was inside the gate and was saved. The flock had stayed behind the fence.

He made it into the house. Then he sank down on the floor.

He lay there awhile, lacking the strength to rise. Nor did he dare to—it was dangerous to rise.

At last he managed to get up anyway and slipped over to the window.

They were gone. Not a crow in sight.

He sat down. He kept sitting there, motionless.

He heard a rumble down the road. The carriage. Suddenly he knew *this* was what he'd been waiting for. And now he couldn't wait any longer, he must be off—down through the woods to the lake, down to pick up the rifle.

Rushing out, he grabbed an old yellow rain cape in the hallway and threw it over his shoulders—then they might not recognize him if they should sit and wait for him.

It was almost dark. He didn't see anybody. The road was lined with underbrush, leafy trees and low spruce. They could have hidden there.

He didn't dare look about him.

He stared straight ahead.

Now he was almost down by the lake. He slowed his pace, forced himself to stop, looked around him. What if it had come out again and sat there waiting for him. Oh, rubbish! He didn't believe in such things. Where was the rifle?

Suddenly a crow rose from a nearby spruce, flew heavily into the forest and disappeared. He made a high jump and began to run. Where, where was the rifle—?

There it was, right by the water's edge. He saw only the barrel. He bent down and grabbed hold of it.

He couldn't explain what the reason was. The cold steel perhaps.

"Adder!" he thought. And before he knew what he was doing, he'd flung it into the water. It splashed and sank.

He calmed down immediately. It was done. Now all he had to do was to walk back and tell about it.

Tell about it—he couldn't. He had nothing to tell.

He'd lost it in the river. That was what he would say.

Father would get up. "How in the world—how could it occur to you—explain yourself!"

He had nothing to explain.

Couldn't—just couldn't explain.

Under the Cuckoo Tree

"THOU SHALT NOT commit fornication!"

¶ He said it with a long *o*. "Thou shalt not commit fo-o-o-rnication!"

They were sitting in the old courtroom. The boys in three long rows along one wall, the girls in three rows along the other. He was rushing back and forth between them. Suddenly you would feel his eyes staring at you.

It was semi-dark inside; from outside came a long menacing roar—the first thunderstorm this year rumbled over the hills.

He rushed back and forth along the row of boys, along the row of girls, from the table farthest down to the pulpit farthest up. Staring at one, then at another. There was a booming noise when he banged the table. The carafe and the glass jumped and clattered. Another roar came from out there, like a vast echo.

"Thou shalt not commit fo-o-o-rnication!"

And then, sharply, making them start, *"What does this mean!* Gunder Holtet—*what does this mean!"*

Gunder stood up, pale. "We should fear and love God so that we—so that we—."

Gunder always got muddle-headed when he was scared.

There was a flash of lightning. The parson's glasses

glinted. His white face gleamed. His glossy, pitch-black beard glittered. The thunderclap shook the building.

"Sit down, you ought to be ashamed!"

Over in the girls' rows he could make out pale faces in the semi-darkness, with big staring eyes.

They had known about this day in advance. They whispered about it from year to year. Two years ago one of the girls fainted and sank to the floor.

He saw Martha's face and yellow hair over there in the second row. She was very pale, and her eyes had such a deep luster. She was always so easily scared. She could take it into her head to faint, all right. She'd been born again when she was thirteen. Then she spoke in tongues.

This parson had brought about tremendous revivals in his former parish, they said. Here nothing much had happened yet.

All of a sudden it was over. It was as if the parson collapsed and became calmer. He blew his nose and looked up a hymn. They stood up and sang and were through for the day.

They hung around for a while outside the courthouse. The boys in one group, the girls in another. Nobody said anything. Not even the worst ruffian among the boys.

The pit of lust. Writhing in lustful pleasure. Writhing in infernal pain. When every point of pleasure on one's body would become a point of pain.

It was sultry. A dry heat in your body. The thunderstorm rumbled over in the hills, it wasn't coming closer. A sweltering, stifling summer heat and not yet the middle of June.

The girls were dressed in light colors. Girls' bodies in their dresses. The place of sin. They stood there turning and twisting. Stealing a glance at the boys and then look-ing away again.

The thoughts of the flesh are the thoughts of sin and the work of the devil.

Nobody said anything.

They used to go home together, all who came from his village. But today it didn't turn out that way. They kept hanging around. Finally the girls got started. The boys went strolling after.

Nobody said anything.

"Awfully angry, wasn't he!" Gunder said, pretending to take it lightly.

Nobody answered him.

The girls walked ahead of them, a bright flock. The dark thundercloud loomed above the hill.

It was so sultry.

They glanced over their shoulders there in front. They were snickering and laughing.

Now they turned off the road and down toward the lake. They were going down to take a swim.

They glanced back just before disappearing in the bushes.

"Let's steal after them and peek!"

It was Erik.

Nobody answered. They glanced back. There was no-body behind them on the road. Nobody could see them from any of the farms.

They jumped across the ditch and the fence.

The dense leafy wood stretched all the way to the lake here. Nobody could see them. They sneaked their way down.

Anders remembered something—actually he'd thought about it every minute. Mother had taken sick yesterday and had to go to bed. She was in bed today. Seemed to be worse, if anything. He'd meant to go straight home, instead of loitering on the road or rowing out on the lake, as they often did the days they'd been to the parson.

This was where they had to turn and walk through the alder wood.

They walked on tiptoe. Had to look out for rotten twigs. They shook their fists at one another.

"Ssh!"

"Ssh!"

Ole broke a twig. Everybody stopped.

"Ssh! Ssh!"

Now they glimpsed the lake. They knew where the swimming hole was. They had come out next to it, on the left. There were some thick alder scrubs along the fence here— if they could get that far, then...

Gunder broke a twig. They stopped again and held their breaths. There they had a glimpse of the girls, who seemed to be undressing already.

They'd gotten so out of breath from creeping along like that.

Impossible to stand still. He was all aquiver.

"Ssh!"

He was going home, to Mother....

They sat down among the bushes. They heard the voice of Olinè, she always talked so loudly, "Where are the boys, you think?"

"Ssh!" came a girl's voice. Somebody snickered.

Erik's breath was so short—as if he were asleep and lying in an awkward position.

They crawled forward along the grass-covered ground the last few steps. Per, that duffer, hit a branch.

"Ssh!"

They didn't even dare whisper, only said ssh! with their lips and gestured angrily with their clenched fists.

Something white flashed over there. They'd almost finished undressing. Just now Olinè pulled her shift over her head.

They pressed themselves closer to the ground.

Olinè was almost a grown woman. And Martha—there she undid both her braids, shook her hair down her back, it covered her shoulder blades—there she turned around— all the way.

Somebody gave a tickly laugh.

"Where are the boys now, you think?"

"Ssh!"

Erik's breath was so short.

One of the girls whispered—but the air was so still, they could hear it, "Is it such a terrible sin?"

"Ha—you know it is—."

"You heard, didn't you?"

"Ah!" someone sighed—it was Ragna, she was bending backward in an arch, her hands on the ground near her feet. She was so unusually lithe, Ragna was.

"Come on, then!"

Splashes in the water and yells. They spattered each other with water.

"Come, let's undress!"

It was Erik. Nobody answered, they all started tearing off their clothes. With numb fingers—Gunder couldn't unbutton his vest and ripped it open, making the buttons fly.

Home to Mother…

Erik had stripped already, and then Gunder and Per and

Emil—he tore off his last stitch and rushed forward through the brush with the others.

Now they started squealing down there. "Help— he-e-elp, the boys are coming and…"

They squealed and ducked—but they didn't squeal terribly loud.

"Go back, you pigs!" Olinè said, spattering water.

They splashed their way toward them. The girls squealed, looking offshore for rescue but seeing nothing but deep water.

He steered straight for Martha—was terribly scared that somebody else might get there first. But the others headed for other places. She was submerged to her chest; she hunched her back a little and kept her arms folded over her breasts, but didn't try to get away. She closed her eyes, then opened them again.

"Shame on you!" she whispered.

"How wicked of you!" she whispered.

He stood right in front of her, without moving.

She had yellow hair and brown eyes, it was so strange. She was Emma's sister.

It had grown so quiet, as if there weren't anyone but them.

They stood looking at each other.

Her arms fell and her eyes became so strange—it was as if some metal melted in her eyes and spread outward. She went slack around the mouth.

"Come, let's go into the bushes!" she whispered. "No, no, no, no!" she whispered instantly at furious speed, putting her arms over her breasts again. "No, no, no, don't, don't—."

He hadn't moved.

It didn't seem to be cold, but his teeth were chattering.

Suddenly her teeth began chattering too.

"Oh—w-w-we have to—g-g-go ashore—w-w-we m-m-must…"

A sound of cracking twigs came from up the woods. A gruff woman's voice—two women's voices.

They rushed ashore, raising jets of spray, reached dry land and pushed into the bushes; the others were right behind them, crashing forward so hard that twigs and branches snapped.

The other girls had found their things, only Martha had ended up in the wrong place, and now it was too late—they could already see Maria Teppen and Gunda, her daughter, come their way with a clothes basket between them, they were going to wash clothes. Martha whimpered, curled up into a ball, turned her back to the boys and wriggled over to the fence.

"Olinè!" she whispered. "Olinè!"

Olinè saw her and snickered. She held her hand over her mouth and laughed, but sat down in such a way that she screened Martha's clothes so Maria couldn't see them. The girls were peeking and tittering over there. Martha lay curled up, crying softly, her head shielded by her hair and hands; her back was twitching, she'd become so small. Without a word, the boys took their clothes and sneaked off a little way.

They could hear Maria and Gunda talk a bit with the girls. The girls had some difficulty answering, they were so full of laughter.

Now they seemed to be putting the caldron over the

stones. You could smell the smoke from the fire already. There came Olinè with Martha's clothes in a bundle under her arm. Shortly, all the girls were there, keeping Martha covered while she dressed. They poked each other, bent over and giggled. They could hear Martha crying and sniffling. The smell of smoke from the fire became stronger and stronger. Now Martha had dressed, and there came the girls; Martha had grimy streaks down her cheeks but was smiling. The others were brimful with laughter, whispering eagerly and stopping again and again to double up and laugh softly behind their hands.

They stole up through the woods in a pack. Now and then they had to stop, clutch their stomachs and laugh. Something or other was so terribly funny, it seized them like a spasm beneath their chests.

"Oh!...Oh!...if Maria...had seen...!"

They had to stop again.

He found himself with Martha, who had fallen into stride beside him. They went up the slope couple by couple.

"How wicked of you to come after me like that—." She was still panting, her mouth twitched when she smiled.

He didn't say anything.

"On Midsummer Eve we're going out to Geitholmen to have a bonfire—are you coming?" she whispered.

"Yes," he whispered, as if it was something wrong.

They were approaching the road and had to be on the lookout.

"Ssh!"

Erik turned around and shook his fists back at the others.

There was nobody on the road.

The others had to go on. He took the short cut and raced across the knolls.

When he was halfway he remembered the hymnal, his collection of Bible stories and the catechism explanation—he'd forgotten them all down there.

They would have to wait till later. He ran faster.

Once through the gate, he slowed his pace. Soon he would see the board where they tied up the horses. Now, soon. He slowed down.

There was the doctor's horse.

The doctor came out, bag in hand. He walked with his eyes on the ground. Father was with him, his eyes on the doctor.

The doctor got into his carriage. Father said something and looked at the doctor. The doctor answered, without looking at Father.

Impossible to hear what they said.

"Ssh!" Gina said in the kitchen. Her eyes were so red.

He wanted to go into the bedroom. She barred his way.

"Nobody can go in!"

She was crying.

"What is it, then?"

"Ssh! "

"What is it?"

"I don't know!"

She cried.

Father came in, he didn't see anybody and went straight to the bedroom.

There was no danger. Common pneumonia—there wasn't a bit of danger. Only old people died of pneumonia, so there was no danger. The telegrams to Tora and Kari were only a precaution. Just in case. They were going to come home soon anyway. On holiday. Tora at any rate—and Kari could only benefit from a trip home. Torvald Norset and Randi Hoff were both old. There was no danger, it took nine days and nights, then the crisis came, and afterward there was no danger, then it was just a laughing matter and no danger—Lord, how they would laugh, and no danger—then came all the years afterward, they would sit laughing and he'd tell her lots of things he hadn't gotten around to telling her all these years—since that time...

He would take her along to the summer dairy and show her his shelter of evergreen branches and the fox burrow— they would row on the lake together, fish, and sit and talk— and laugh at the time when they thought there was danger.

It was just absurd. It was so absurd that there were no words for it—walking around on tiptoe and saying ssh and ssh and ssh! It was absurd, simply absurd. Father was absurd. Gina, Embret, Åse, he himself—simply absurd.

It was only because of the fever, you became like that from the fever—her skin wasn't more sallow than that of other people who had such a high fever, it was only because of...

All sick people had eyes like that, also because of the fever, it only looked that way, as if they came from far away and knew everything—it was only stuff and nonsense that he couldn't bear looking at those eyes, it was only...

What did they have to howl about, Tora and Kari? Coming back home like two drowned rats and blowing their noses time and again! They could have stayed where they were, not come here to howl and play the fool, they could have remained where they were! Coming here and behaving like…

If only they would stay away, all of them.

"Anders," she said.

"Yes, Mother?"

She drew a couple of breaths. There was something she wanted to tell him and he could see it was difficult, her fingers were fumbling with the sheet, she had a word on the tip of her tongue, drew another breath with that un-pleasant whistling sound—and then Kari burst into tears, subdued but piercing, leaning her head against the table and her whole body shaking, from her shoes to her braid. She was making the table shake, and a glass with a spoon in it standing on a red tray in the middle of the table started jingling.

He had to brace his legs against the floor not to rush over there and remove the glass. Tora and Åse, who sat on the other side of the table, both started crying, trying to cry a little louder than Kari and still acting as if they were more restrained.

He wanted to scream, "Ssh!"

He felt a clear, distinct, and quite cold desire to kill.

Mother turned her eyes away from him, toward the other three. She drew another couple of breaths, tight and whis-tling, and a film settled on her eyes; she was far away again. The moment had passed.

Three days, the doctor had said.

If only she could hang on for three days.

It depended on her heart—on whether it could hold out.

One could also say it depended on her lungs. On whether they would get completely clogged up.

Three days.

Sixty times sixty equals three thousand six hundred—times twenty-four equals eighty-six thousand four hundred—times three equals two hundred and fifty-nine thousand two hundred. Two-hundred-and-fifty-nine-thousand-two-hundred seconds in three nights and days. Two-hundred-and-fifty-nine-thousand-and-two-hundred. Count slowly—one, two—three—four—five—six—seven—eight—nine—ten seconds. If only they would leave her alone. But they were constantly sticking their hankies in their mouths, sat all in a tremor on their chairs, got up and went out because they couldn't bear sitting there any longer, and came in again because they couldn't bear staying away anymore. There wasn't one moment's peace.

Father was so quiet. He was the worst. Sat quite still, staring. Staring and staring, without a word. He was so quiet. You felt like screaming, "Talk, why don't you! Cry! Do something!"

If only one could scream, "Out of here! Out!"

Take a whip and drive them out.

Alone with her.

There was something called strength. Transference of strength. The important thing was to *want* something, so hard that—faith moves mountains—.

Nonsense. Superstition.

Two-hundred-fifty-nine-thousand-two-hundred.

Embret came into the kitchen.

"How's the old lady?"

"No change."

He went out again. Went out into the yard and down toward the woodshed.

Midway he would stop.

He stood quite still, looking at the ground. Would stand this way for a long time. Then he suddenly turned around and came into the kitchen again.

The same question.

The same answer.

He went out again.

He would stand still like that, now here, now there. You could see him standing anywhere out in the fields. As if he tried to remember something or other he'd quite forgotten.

Father, bowed, up at her pillow.

They down by the foot of the bed.

They were quiet for a moment now—catching their breaths a bit. Only dabbed their noses with their handkerchiefs.

Kari's swollen red nose.

They were ready to start. Waiting for a signal—then they would take off and race each other—to see who could howl the loudest. They were just catching their breaths, waiting.

Ssh!

Father raised his head.

His face a grayish-white, his red, strained eyes squeezed tight between swollen, blue eyelids. How many nights now since he'd slept?

He bent down again.

…no, he mustn't do that…

…mustn't do it…

There he took the mirror and put it to her mouth. Straightened up.

"She's dead."

This was the signal. They burst into a loud wail, grabbed the bed, trembling, and screamed: "Mother! Mother!," throwing themselves forward on the blanket, shrilling and weeping. Tora was the fastest, but Kari screamed louder.

Father stood by her pillow. He didn't move.

Sweep them away. Stuff their mouths with something.

That they couldn't even understand *this* much—to keep silent.

Drive them out with a broom.

To stand here screaming and wailing—disturbing, defiling—to stand here screaming and carrying on—forcing him to have mean thoughts just now.

He would pay them back for it.

Chase them out. Kick them.

Alone with her.

Quiet, damn it.

Ssh!

Father stood stock-still.

To scream—it would help. Scream so that he couldn't hear the others. Clench his fists, suck in air and scream—scream till the world cracked, scream till his eyes popped out of his head, scream to make them jump, to make them shut up, gape, withdraw into the corners like frightened mice—scream, scream…

He and Father were quiet. The other three cried and screamed, throwing themselves about and posturing.

In three days, the funeral.

Many things to attend to. Father was so forgetful.

Ole had hit him on the nose the day they fought down in the pasture. He bled heavily—but that wasn't what he remembered. But that his whole face became numb. It started at the nose, then spread across his whole face—didn't hurt at all, almost tickled a little. He bled heavily and thought, Now you can hit me wherever you want, now it doesn't matter.

People sitting everywhere, staring.

Never alone. Never a moment alone.

Kari and Tora and Åse.

He thought, You've got to pull yourself together. There must be something wrong with you. You can't know for sure that they are play-acting. They are heartbroken, remember. They kept you from talking to Mother, but now they are heartbroken, remember. Remember that. They don't reflect…They are heartbroken, remember.

Kari had a new attack of tears, it made her shake. She leaned forward and supported herself on the bench in front of her, shaking both benches. Tora wept louder and more piercingly, and jumped up and down on the bench. Everybody turned around to look.

"And now we'll sing the first verse of the hymn, 'I know a sleep in Jesus' name.'"

Kari's red nose.

Grab hold of them. Shake them till they shut up. Completely.

You must pull yourself together. There seems to be something the matter with you.

The wind rushed across the churchyard, stirring up the young leaves. A warm summer wind, most likely. It felt so bitter, so dry and cold.

He stood at her grave without a tear in his eyes.

He felt repudiated by God, united to the devil in all eternity. To be standing here so bitterly dry and cold. He looked at his sniffling sisters and felt an intense pride, it seized him like a spasm.

God or devil—he didn't recognize either of them. Hadn't done so for many years. Not since that time when he was six, actually, and Father—and Mother…

He felt as if he were walking an old road. It ran backward, he didn't know where it was taking him. Only saw it as a line ahead of him and followed it.

Through a dim hallway, looking neither left nor right.

"Anders," she said.

Suddenly he was crying.

A strange sound. He heard it and kept wondering, shaken by his sobs.

A strange sound from many long years ago.

People packed tight around every table.

They were eating, swallowing large pieces, talking and laughing.

Pull yourself together, yes, pull yourself together.

He made his way out.

He headed for the gate and went down through the pasture. He knew a spot there, among those birch bushes, almost at the lake.

It had become so quiet. The wind had subsided, the birch leaves were still and had a bright new luster. The birds were busy. And there was the cuckoo.

Cuckoo. Cuckoo.

It reminded him of the willow flute Embret had carved for him once. He remembered it so vividly—the rough, grayish-green bark and those two hoarse notes that affected him so strangely: Whoo-oo! Whoo-oo!

He recalled how she walked past him once as he was blowing it. She stroked his hair as she walked by.

"How are you, Anders?"

"Oh, I'm fine."

"You seem to be so quiet," she said.

"I? Oh no."

"There's nothing the matter with you?"

If he wasn't mistaken, there was anxiety in her voice.

"Something the matter with me? No, nothing."

He understood he had to be careful and appear happy.

How often had this happened? Many times, probably.

He remembered those times when she'd tried to get closer to him—cautiously, almost as if she was afraid. He remembered how he'd turned her away, coolly and calmly—had never understood what she meant.

He remembered well that look of hers—a bit surprised, a bit helpless. It had given him a cold joy every time.

When he had slipped away and enjoyed himself and laughed and been happy and she looked at him—"It's nice that you're happy, Anders"—and he ran off to hide.

This last time—was it that day in the hallway she'd wanted to talk to him about?

Had she remembered it at all?

Had she done anything at all which she needed to remember or be sorry about?

He would never know.

From the lake came the sound of oars, song and accordion music. People were going out to Geitholmen to have a bonfire.

It was Midsummer Eve.

The cuckoo had come closer. How loud it sang. Cuckoo! It sounded so clear and so nearby. He'd never heard it so near.

It was silent.

A gray bird came flying and alighted in the birch straight over his head.

Cuckoo!

It was the cuckoo.

It crowed time and again, clearly, extremely loud; the echo came back from the hill.

Here he was, sitting under the cuckoo tree. Now he could wish what he wanted.

That he would never know.

He buried his head in the grass there at the foot of the birch—buried his head as if he wanted to bury himself in the earth.

Embret

EMBRET WAS CROSSING THE YARD with his ax in the crook of his elbow. "He's grown old now, Embret has," someone said.

He felt as though a veil was torn aside. Anders was standing by the kitchen window, and suddenly he could see it himself. Embret was crossing the yard with his ax in the crook of his elbow—his woodcutter's ax had become his last sweetheart, people said—looking his old self from top to toe, just the same as ever. But suddenly he noticed that Embret had grown old. Bent back, a thin wreath of hair under his hat, stiff knees—and so small and frail.

How often had he stood here by the kitchen window, watching Embret cross the yard with his ax in the crook of his elbow? It was strange—a twinkling, no time at all—it was like flying across years and days and all manner of things and coming down again here at the kitchen window where he'd been standing all along, and then it turned out to be *now* and many years had gone by.

He'd grown old now, Embret had.

It was summer, the first days of July, with the haying season approaching. Father went around looking worried.

"I guess I'll tell Embret he can take it easy this haying season," he said.

But he didn't tell him anything. He had so little initiative lately.

"He won't be able to walk the swath with the others anymore now," he said another time.

"What about Nils, then?" somebody said.

That was just it. Nils—it was impossible to let Nils go with the others and then tell Embret that he was too old. Embret, who was the same age as Nils and at any rate didn't have to go to the privy in the middle of every work period. Everybody would understand that. Father understood and wandered from room to room without saying a word.

But then Nils got pneumonia and died. It went so fast, like everything where Nils was concerned—a dog wasn't faster at getting rid of its fleas, people said.

Death didn't make a fat catch that time, people said. He'd become so thin and light, Nils had, and almost faster than before. When he'd been rushing down the road lately, it almost looked as if he didn't touch the ground; it was like seeing a leaf from last year being picked up by the wind and wafted away. And now he was gone. People cocked their heads and said, "Well, I guess his time had come—good he could pass on, I'd say...."

One day the church bells rang, and a small company ambled down the road toward the bridge-hills and the churchyard, behind Martin Teppen's dun-colored mare. Nils had sat behind that mare many a time, waving his birch whip—he was hard on the horses, Nils was, he thought they ought to be as fast as he was. Now he was quiet for once, Nils too, Embret said, sounding very cheerful. Then he got up with his stiff knees and walked out of the kitchen.

"He's getting old now, Embret is," someone mumbled. Wasn't possible to make out who. It was in the air, sort of.

The following day he came inside in the middle of the work period, his ax in the crook of his elbow. He had to talk with *the boss*.

Oh yes. He had discovered he was too old to keep up with the young fellows in the swath. It probably didn't matter very much—there was plenty of trash mowing for an old man.

Nothing came of his trash mowing. Before the haying season got under way, Embret would sit all day long on the stone outside the servants' quarters.

In quiet villages it happens now and then that the deaths come in flurries, as it were—without grave illnesses, without any rule, as far as people can tell. After long periods when nobody dies, the bells may toll every day for weeks for people going to be buried.

It was like that this summer. And whether it was because of this or something else—nobody was surprised when a message came that Gorinè was dying at the old folks' home. She had moved there with her mother when Maren died.

Now she was dying. If she could talk with Embret. Those were the words the messenger brought.

"What do you think?" Embret said to Father. "I feel sort of poorly."

Father thought perhaps he'd better go. They could take the carriage.

Embret dressed up and trimmed his beard. He also put on his black hat—his funeral hat, as he called it. He looked even older as he sat in the carriage, washed and with his beard newly trimmed and combed. He almost looked like a sweet, patient child. But extremely old.

About an hour later they were back again.

Gorinè died and was buried. Embret's legs were so shaky that he couldn't go to the funeral. He sat on his stone looking eastward, he could see the churchyard from there. He probably also heard the singing, his hearing was good.

When they got back after the funeral he was still there, looking east. He turned around.

"It was a nice funeral, I noticed," he said. "I saw a fellow carryin' something under his arm—that was the horn with her mother, I expect!"

Gorinè's mother was over ninety now and still alive. Embret claimed, and nobody could change his mind about it, that she hung in a horn on the wall of the old folks' home.

Oh yes, the old lady had saved her daughter from marrying misery, people said. When Gorinè got sick and took to her bed, her mother forgot her rather quickly. That is, she thought the director of the old folks' home was Gorinè. And every day the director had to promise not to marry under her station. And that she could probably promise quite safely, they said, for to find the like of this sixty-year-old shrew you'd have to travel seven parishes.

"You're up and about, Embret!" they said to him.

"Well, yes. The bed can wait, no need to hurry," he said.

If people came he tottered along with them to the servants' quarters. He would sit there in the evenings, putting in a word now and then. When everybody had left, he walked out and sat down on his stone again. The sun went down, night came, and he would sit there looking out over the field. At sunrise, when people came walking past, he was there again, they said. When did he sleep?

"You never sleep, do you, Embret?"

"Well. Old people don't need much sleep."

He was getting older from one week to the next—indeed, almost from day to day.

The stone where he used to sit was on high ground. In fact, the entire servants' quarters were on high ground, on a shale rock. He could see far and wide from where he sat. He could see down the road to the bridge-hill and on to the church and still farther. He could see down to the lake and across the lake, and still farther. He could see the whole west field and the south field, the pasture and a bit of the east field, and still farther.

On the east side of the lake was Rud, where he had been head servant nearly thirty years ago. The barn appeared a glowing red, the farmhouse a shiny yellow. They were dead now, all those who'd been there in his day.

He looked old and small sitting there on his stone. At a distance he looked almost like a part of the earth itself. Well, close up too.

His homespun trousers were black once but had turned greenish with age, they were covered with dirt and looked like an overgrown plowed field. His work blouse was blue and weatherworn, like the sky itself. His hands and face were wrinkled like old aspen bark. His beard and his few tufts of hair had lost all color and looked like wisps of last year's grass, the kind that you see fluttering in the wind on heathery moors. His blue eyes had become very pale lately, a bit milky and dim, as sometimes happens with the old.

When he sat there on his stone, he looked like he belonged there.

There was nothing wrong with him, as far as he knew. It was simply that his strength had left him. He was sure to get better in the fall, he said, turning his eyes away.

He couldn't sit idle. He got himself an ax and a saw and some birch materials. One day he was surrounded by a heap of old rakes. Nobody had seen so many rakes on the farm before. He'd remembered the whereabouts of every one of them, some a good generation old, and had gotten Anders to fetch them. For several days he was setting teeth into these rakes and seemed to get a bit younger again.

But one day all the rakes were in order. Anders had to walk another round but it didn't help, there weren't any more.

The haying took its course. Every evening he asked if any teeth had been broken during the day. As you might expect, one and all raked a bit recklessly on purpose, causing the teeth to snap.

This way he had a little to do, but not enough. One day he got hold of two staves and made his way as far as the woodshed, found a pine chunk and got somebody to saw it into suitable lengths and split it. When he'd managed to bring everything to the servants' quarters, he sat all day long carving bunches of long pine sticks for lighting. Such sticks were used a lot at one time. He carved and he carved, with hands like horn and pale eyes in the sunshine.

One day he'd carved it all up. He sat there helpless, his hands falling at his sides.

The following day he was whittling ax handles. This was heavier work, the birch wood was hard, and his hands fell at his sides more and more often.

Down in the fields the mowers walked one after the other,

whetting their scythes to a resounding echo, joking and laughing and moving forward in their swaths. The scythes hissed through the thin grass and shaved the thick meadow with a full sound.

Late in the evening, long after the haymakers had gone home and the sun had gone down, you could see in the twilight as midnight approached, if you were still up, a shadow creeping along the hay-drying racks down in the field. Embret had tottered down there to feel the hay. Small and gray, he could barely be made out in the dewy gray light.

The haying season went by and was gone. It grew quiet on the farm. No strangers, only the familiar people who went their familiar ways.

Embret kept sitting on his stone. In the nick of time they managed to break several rake's teeth, so he had something to keep him busy. Later he just sat there.

At dead of night, if someone on the farm took a walk around the buildings to the stable, the hayloft or the toolshed on some errand or other, he might unexpectedly bump into Embret. Small and noiseless, he shuffled around on two sticks. Lingered in the hayloft, to sniff the fragrance of the hay most likely. Or before the door to the stable. Inside stood the mare, Chestnut, munching or hanging her head, asleep; but from the warmth that streamed from the open stable window, you could tell that a large, trusty animal was near. Nobody talked to Embret at these times, and he talked to nobody—he was simply there, small and shadowy. He probably checked if the door was working, dropped in on the animals, hovered about—it was almost like having a brownie on the farm. You felt safe knowing he was there, though he could hardly have warded off a misfortune anymore, if misfortune were to strike.

One day he no longer sat outside on his stone. He was inside the servants' quarters, lying in his low, red-painted bed, with pale, strengthless hands that met on top of the blanket. The room had only one window, with small panes and old green glass in three or four of the panes. They were rather overgrown, he'd never allowed anyone to dust in there, they were barely allowed to wash the floor. The world looked strangely gray and dim when seen through those panes—through all the dust that had been stirred up by a thousand scraping boots, a thousand tall tales, nasty cracks and bursts of laughter for many a long year.

He lay in his small, red-painted bachelor's bed, looking out at the world with his faded old eyes, through all those little gray and green panes with their coating of working-men's dust. But most times the door was open, and then he liked to look out that way. The ground was green outside his door. The aftermath was on the way, lush and fresh like cabbage. Down in the garden, the branches of the apple trees were laden with fruit, there were glowing reds and yellows among the dull-green leaves. The sky had taken on that limpid, pure-blue fall hue. A fresh wind, full of fragrance, streamed in through the door.

He lay still, watching it all. He could see well, age had not taken away his eyesight, only drained him of his strength. He was sure to get better when fall came, he said, looking at the wall.

People were dropping by. "How are things, Embret?"

Things were fine. Then they would get up and leave.

One day Andrea came by. She'd become a real wife with a potbelly, sagging breasts and four kids. Her husband, Anton, was nothing to write home about, but still.

How were things going?

Things were going fine.

Andrea sat down. The chairs made a crashing noise now when Andrea sat down.

"Do you want anything, Embret? Can I do something for you?"

"No."

He thought about it for a while.

"No," he said once more. "I would've liked some water. But the boss will come by soon. So I'll just wait till he comes."

"How are you doing, Embret?" Father asked.

"Well, you know, I'm doing fine now," he said. He smiled and didn't turn his eyes to the wall.

Had they had a talk, those two?

Of course they hadn't, anybody could see that. If they couldn't understand each other without having a talk, it wasn't worth much.

One day Embret said something all the same.

"The hay in the east field turned out very nicely."

"Yes," Father said. "You were right there."

They'd had a silent battle over it the year before, and Father had given in.

It turned out to be a quiet summer on the farm this year—as it must when someone has died and everybody knows that someone else is on his deathbed. Less banging of doors than usual, less clatter of pots and pans. People talked more softly and walked more quietly past one another.

The evenings grew quiet. Each went his own way and the farm remained—quiet and hushed, as if even the wind had made a detour and passed it by.

Everybody knew that Embret would die. His time was up, there was nothing more to be said about that. And as if it was something everybody had always known, as if it wasn't even necessary to speak about it in whispers, people in the kitchen and people on the road said, "Sure enough. Now that the old lady has died, Embret won't last much longer."

Gorinè had long since been buried and forgotten.

There was almost no change in any of this when Embret died one morning in August. It was as though even Embret himself didn't change much.

It was a fine day, with a blue sky. He was looking out through the door. Nobody but Father was up there, except for Anders, who used to sit with him. Nobody said anything. Then they noticed that one more film had settled on his eyes.

They placed him on the threshing floor, as was the custom. He looked basically unchanged. His badly worn, horny hands rested piously one against the other; their color, turned grayish-yellow, was also like horn now.

There had been no sense of uneasiness when he was dying, there wasn't any uneasiness now when he was dead. Nobody was afraid of the threshing floor because he was there. Not even late at night. It almost made you feel safe to know he was lying there when you went to pull a little hay for the horse in the pitch-dark nighttime hours.

Funeral

IT WAS A NICE FUNERAL. Embret wasn't really regarded as a servant, he'd been on the farm for so long that he'd become a kind of master beside the master. And so people showed up from the neighboring farms, from Berg and Haugom, Nordby and Millom. It was the second time the master at Berg came to the farm this summer. The second time in twenty years, they said. The first time was at Mother's funeral.

From Millom there was nobody but Martin himself; he was alone on the farm now, his youngest daughter and his only grandson died last spring. It was almost creepy to look at Martin now, they muttered. He'd become so thin and seemed to be even taller than before. With his bristly hair and beard and white face and hands, he recalled one of those dead spruces that have neither needles nor shoots and haven't had any for a long time—nothing but naked bristly twigs, where the bark has flaked off so that the naked, white dry wood shines through.

He never said a word. He was like an entire funeral by himself, someone remarked.

In addition, there were people from cotter country, men who had sat with Embret in the servants' quarters all those hundreds of evenings. Hans and Erik Fallet, both woodsmen with springy knees. Martin Teppen with his fiery-red beard and Hans, his son, already taller than his father; Ole Hagaen with his stiff, crooked leg, nicknamed the Hobblehack; Edvart Saga, Tørjer Lykkjen, Mons Bru and Kerstaffer Nust. Anton, who was no stranger to the farm and was usually called Andrea's Anton. Per Myra, Tøsten Vedlia, Amund Inngjerdingen, Hans Grina, and Even Oppi, the shoemaker, who was nicknamed Even Pitchatwine. Sjønne Høybråten, Hagebart Oppom, and Halvor Bakken, Grete's husband; Krestian Kvennstuen and his son, Fredrik, who'd been to the city and returned as a fool with press in his pants, saying he was a socialist and calling himself Møller. And then some young boys and girls, and a great many old women with kerchiefs on their heads.

And then, of course, there was Andreas Elstad, the son of Embret's sister, with a pointed nose and wary face, an old man judging by his looks—though he couldn't be much past confirmation age, around forty or so, Martin Teppen remarked. He'd already begun to go around making inquiries where Embret kept his things.

"You know, that's what we're all thinking about, just wait till we've gotten him well below ground, then we'll begin to talk about it," Martin said—he'd taken a dislike to this sneak from the beginning.

The men wore black homespun clothes, which looked as if they'd been cut with an ax. Some had given their faces a scratch with the razor, others had combed their beards, one and all had spent a good, long time scrubbing themselves, some were almost unrecognizable—Ole Hagaen had become so spotlessly clean and bright you could scarcely believe your own eyes; some of the fellows walked circles around him, not quite sure if it was him, he seemed to have become so much smaller.

Some were a bit taciturn and subdued, they shook hands as if they hadn't seen each other for ages. The women wept a little, as is customary at the beginning of a funeral. Andrea had gotten away from her nursling and wept awfully. Emma was there too. But Grete was missing today, she'd stayed home at Bakken to take care of the twins. Three kids in two years—there wasn't very much left of Grete, people said.

The new schoolmaster was there to give the funeral sermon. He hadn't known Embret and talked about something else.

They slowly pulled out through the gate. A long black procession which made the sunny day look less bright.

They came back at a slightly faster pace. Some of the old dash had returned, some of the accustomed tone. But they were still subdued—they teased each other a lot in front of the door, pushed each other back and forth and nudged each other. They kept standing in a bunch inside the living room, one and all trying to get to the center of the bunch, where it was safe and you could crack a joke. There was loud laughter in the middle of the bunch; those who were at the edges didn't laugh. But everything was put right when Amund Inngjerdingen slipped and fell trying to force his way to the middle. Someone in the middle said, "'There you are,' said old man Lisett, he shit in the soup!," and that saw was a good and familiar one, everybody laughed, and they felt at home at once. They found their way to the table, and soon there was a buzz and a roar of laughter, as behooved a proper funeral. When they got up from the table an hour or two later, everything was as it should be, they were all laughing and talking at the same time: "Oh yes, Embret knew how to find the right words!" Ole Fallet slapped his thighs and laughed and laughed at something Martin Teppen had said, but when several people came over and wanted to hear, he'd quite forgotten what it was. Ole Hagaen had taken a couple of extra drinks and remained at the table, laughing jerkily, "Haw-haw, haw-haw!"

And all the women had become so friendly.

They hung around the stoop and below the stoop and were well-contented. It grew a bit quieter when the new schoolmaster and the old man at Berg came out on the stoop and stayed awhile, stroking their beards and talking about the crops. But things livened up again when they went with Father to the cow barn to look at the pigs.

They drifted over to the meadow north of the storehouse and settled down. Before long, Erik Fallet had gotten some-body to wrestle "fox hook" with him—it was none other than the son of Krestian Kvennstuen, and he was wheeled around and to the ground with a bang. "You're a lightweight, you've only got bran in your bag!" someone yelled. Sjønne Høybråten positioned himself, and Erik bragged, "Around you'll go, even if you're so full of beer and schnapps that it pours off you."

Sjønne was wheeled around and Erik stayed down, yell-ing, "Are there any more who'd like a ride? Here's a bout to make your knees tremble and your assholes crow like a cuckoo!"

Per Myra, with his big, heavy shoulders, came up and lay down, and this time it was Erik who got wheeled around.

"They're light, those big shots from Fallet!" said some-one in the crowd, most likely Krestian Kvennstuen.

They continued to wrestle fox hook for a while—heavy

when one of them missed the mark. Some of the women and girls had found their way out, their white shawls made them look like a flock of magpies around a huge flock of crows. Some of the older fellows stood by themselves, talking and laughing: "Do you remember the time he met the farmer from Opstad on the road? 'Whereabouts, should I say, does a fellow like you hail from, then?'—he was so snooty and never wanted to recognize people. 'If someone were to ask you, just tell him you ain't sure!' Embret said. Oh yes, Embret knew how to find the right words, he did!"

Inside there was toddy to be had, and it beckoned. But—nobody really knew how it came about—more and more people were drifting up toward the servants' quarters. The young fellows first. They settled on the stoop and talked. There was Amund, there was Martin, red-haired and freckled, there was Hans Teppen, and there—Lars Tuven, friendly as ever, rather small in his get-up but looking bigger than usual now that he was sitting down. He had incredibly short legs, Lars did, and Anders, who stood listening and watching, happened to remember that at one time he'd thought it was because Lars had sucked his mother for so long—till long after he'd started school. Even now he thought there was something odd about Lars, he couldn't help remembering something Embret had said once: "I believed it when I was small, and when it's real dark I still believe it."

More and more people came drifting up to the servants' quarters, soon most of those who'd been used to dropping by there through the years had showed up. They walked in, glanced around the room—. Embret's bed was empty, the corpse straw had been burned. Nobody went to sit there, but they did sit on the other bed; they went out and found a board and a couple of logs, and soon they sat thick as flies on a lump of sugar. They left the door open. They talked and laughed.

"Oh, yes, Embret…"

What about that time with Marius Moen? Marius asked Embret in for a drink. And Embret liked a drink. But a squelcher was more important to him than a drink. So when Marius had poured him a drink and talked dirt about everybody he knew, and many he didn't know, and wanted to pour another drink, Embret said, "'A drink is the best thing I know,' he said, 'I don't know anything in the world as good as a drink,' he said, 'but if I have to sit here looking at your ugly mug,' he said, 'and listen to your filthy talk,' he said, 'just because you offer me a drink,' he said, 'then I'd rather be without the drink,' he said, and with that he got up and left!"

Andreas Elstad came sniffing around—it was here Embret used to stay, wasn't it? Martin Teppen noticed him outside the door and spoke up in a loud voice, "If somebody here hasn't gotten anything after Embret, he'd better speak up!"

Andreas Elstad sniffed a little, then he disappeared.

The talk went on. They forgot Embret, then edged in on him again; they forgot him once more. The old man at Berg and the master at Haugom came in and settled down—it was getting dark outside, but here they were many, they felt at home, their pipes glowed and murmured, and there were sallies of ringing, whinnying laughter. Good old tales were brought out again and given another turn. The stove shook when the laughter was at its worst—it stood there rust-colored with age, with a crack the length of the entire door which radiated a cozy glow on winter evenings. The table stood on three legs, the fourth would hit the floor with a little tap once in a while. The tobacco smoke, thick as stuffed cotton, rolled out through the door. Ole Hagaen, who'd made a couple of trips to the toddy table, sat there shaking with laughter, "Haw-haw-haw!" Nobody knew what he was laughing at.

…Kari and Mari…

…Listen, do you remember the time…

It was as if nothing had changed, as if Embret had merely gone around the corner a spell, when Gina came to call them for supper.

Next day the servants' quarters were empty.

Ashes and piles of matches on the floor, a forgotten pipe over on the table. The bed saggy from all that sitting, a couple of empty tobacco tins left on the board. Around the walls, in the half-open table drawer, in the corner cabinet, hung up on nails and spikes, was everything that collects in a man's room throughout the years: gapingly empty knee boots and regular boots and shoes, lasts and axes, a knife wedged into a crack in the wall, harness and patches of leather, an old lap rug, a couple of hames, a saddle pad, a box of nails and spikes and shoemaker's tacks, a hammer and pliers and a sledgehammer and a small anvil, work blouses and work pants and a red-checked Icelandic sweater hung up on a hook, a brass tobacco tin on the windowsill, a fragment of a mirror on a shelf; under the bed, Embret's chest with its rose-painting trim and, inside, more precious items—a silk scarf, a couple of flowered mittens, a black, glossy hat bought that time nearly forty years ago when Embret made his long journey, saw the world, lived one summer at Lillestrøm and worked one winter on the Smålenene Railroad. This and more the man from Elstad would come to pick up today.

Through a dusty windowpane came a slanting sunbeam, it lighted up the whirling dust in the empty room.

And Now Goodbye

As he stood beside Embret's grave—that dark, square hole with yellowish-brown dirt and clay on the sides and, next to it, a group of men and women dressed in black, along with the parson and the sexton who were going about their business—it occurred to him that he'd stood beside the same kind of grave countless times by now. He felt as if he'd done nothing else all his life than this: standing beside a grave, then standing beside another grave.

He was dressed in his black confirmation suit, doing duty a few weeks ahead of time and so new that his body could feel it. He was flanked on both sides by men in stiff black homespun, slightly taller than he and much broader. They were so quiet and so patient. How many times had they stood like this before? He had only done it three times, that he knew very well. But this thought carried no weight and fell quietly to the ground inside him.

Standing beside a grave and going on. Standing beside a grave and going on.

"…but from the earth thou shalt rise again!" came in a deep, ringing voice.

Embret had asked Anders one day—it was just before he took to his bed, "You're going out into the world, aren't you?"

"Yes. No." Anders didn't know.

Embret sat by himself, just breathing.

"There are many curious things—out there in the world. Many curious things will happen to you. Oh yeah…

"And afterward—well, then you'll understand that everything had happened to you before you were ten years old. Yeah…"

He drew a breath.

"Afterward it just happens over again."

And what did he say later?

"All paths lead to the same place…"

Then he was talking less to others than to himself.

He said it over and over again.

Anders looked at him. He understood that what they were saying was true—he'd grown old now, Embret had. Old—his thoughts going in circles. Old—seeing only his own things. Old—sitting around dreaming in the middle of the day.

Everything happened to you before you were ten years old?

Nothing had happened to him yet.

All paths…

All paths led out into the world.

He remembered something that had happened to him a long time ago. He'd been far away—had taken somebody to the station. Actually, it was his father he'd taken there. When he was almost home again, going into the last turn and seeing the buildings, he had to stop the horse. He had to sit and look for a moment. He had the impression that the place and the buildings were quietly watching him. And he felt he understood something. That everything came to have a meaning because the buildings and the entire place were watching him—yeah.

That was long ago now. Sometime last spring it was.

Everything had become different since then. Things had gotten turned around, somehow. Now it seemed to him that it was the world out there which had to give a meaning to it all. Here everything was so confused, nothing was connected. The connection was in the world out there.

Of course it was.

All paths led out into the world.

"Would you come with me up to the summer dairy?" Father asked one day. "I'd like to drop by there before the frost sets in," he added, by way of explanation.

The woods had a tang of fall. Here and there a yellow birch among the funeral-dark evergreens. The little moors were pale-brown, like stripped-off horse's hides.

A storm bird followed them for a while, portending rain. Afterward it was still. No birds, no sounds in the forest.

It was cold and damp inside the semi-dark chalet cabin, as always when nobody had been there for a while. Ashes and half-burned sticks in the fireplace. The two bunk beds looked unmade, with hay and gray burlap rags in them. The sheepskin blankets were folded over the crossbeam and flapped against their faces as they walked about tidying up. Anders took them down and threw them onto the beds. It became a bit cozier when they'd lighted a fire. The flames licked at the pine root, made the semi-darkness come alive, and gave a luster to the ax, the bucket and the spoon in the wall crack. The personal marks and letters that had been carved everywhere were all lighted up.

While they were eating, Anders noticed that his father looked at him on the sly several times.

The silence was oppressive.

Father sat down on the low chimney ledge and looked into the fire—then he turned his back to it and picked up a stick of wood which he started whittling. He was terribly busy with it for a while.

Anders sat on a stool, looking out through the open door.

"Anders—there were a few things I'd meant to talk to you about...."

There it came—just as he'd thought.

Father stammered a little. "About—different things. About your mother and—about your mother and me and..."

A gust of wind came down the chimney, the smoke swept in a blue arc under the chimneypiece and out into the room. Quickly, Anders got up.

"I'll go and put up the slab against the wind," he said. They'd found a broad, flat slab that they kept on the roof; when they put it up between the chimney and the wind, the draft improved a bit.

He was busy up there for quite a while, took precise note of the direction of the wind and put up the slab with care.

When he came down again, Father sat on the chimney ledge as before, whittling at the stick—it had become eight-cornered now.

"I guess I'll have to begin with the beginning," he said. Then he was silent for a moment.

Anders tried to think fast but could see no escape.

"Oh, look at that bird!" he called, jumping up from his stool and pointing down at the tall spruce.

Father got up, came over and looked.

"Where?"

"Over there—in the tall spruce—I think it was a grouse."

"You don't say," Father said. He went back to his seat again and said nothing for a while.

What if he started telling him about himself and Mother!

He'd taken her away—from everybody—put her in his pocket—made her *his own* so that she didn't notice anybody else—her eyes sought him wherever he was in the room—if he really wanted to start telling him about that, then…

He didn't want to hear—he'd sooner run, straight through the door, right down to the village, right out of the village—he didn't want to hear a single word—about that…

"You know, the master at Berg was at your mother's funeral," Father said. "Perhaps you don't know it was the first time he was in our house in more than twenty years."

…Well, so that was what he wanted to talk about…

Father had gotten started. Talked about his early days in the parish, as an agronomist at Hoff. About his early days as Grandfather's steward. About the master at Berg, who'd figured he would get hold of the farm when Grandfather died…About all the gossip in the hamlet—that Father had married for money—only to get his hands on the farm…

"While in reality—," he said and stopped.

"While in reality—." He stopped again.

Then he continued, about the master at Berg and his shenanigans. He talked a long time. About a lot of quarrels and squabbles—about the master at Berg who'd managed to egg on the neighbors—one night they had sneaked into the stable and tried to mutilate his horses, both of them—one man was badly mauled that time—.

He stopped. "Have you heard any of this before?"

"Oh yes—some," Anders said.

He'd heard it all before. Many times over.

The man who was badly mauled—that was none other than old Ole Hagaen, the Hobblehack, who got a horse shoe planted in his knee that time. Nils on the Slope got out through the stable window, light-footed then as always— though you couldn't be sure that Father knew it was Nils on the Slope.

And afterward the two of them had been day laborers on the farm for many a day. Oh yes—but people *were* like that—in this parish anyway, no doubt in every parish.

Old things. That somebody could have the patience to torment himself with such old things!

In the end they'd really become fond of Father, in their way. Both of them. Talked dirt about him, sure, but—. The world wasn't any different. Nils sent for him when he was dying—he had more faith in Father than in the parson— however badly he'd slandered him throughout the years.

"Where have you heard it?" Father asked.

"Oh—in the kitchen—in the servants' quarters—"

"Yes, of course," Father said.

He sat for a while.

"I guess I haven't talked enough with my children. But there were so many other things to do—"

He laughed, embarrassed.

"You needed food and clothes too, you know—."

He had turned red.

Grownups shouldn't be embarrassed.

Father spoke again. There were several things he wanted to explain. Several important things.

Old things all of them.

Old things—Anders happened to remember the murder up here a hundred years ago—Kristian who was executed in the Murderer's Field—at that time also a farm was involved—it was a cotter's daughter he killed, wasn't it? Because she was going to have a child by him, but *he* would inherit a farm and could have a girl with one.

It was always farms they fought about—farms and girls—that is, girls with farms.

He gave a start. Father had stopped, he was looking at him. Had probably noticed he wasn't listening. Ought perhaps to have thrown in some questions.

Father sat on the chimney ledge without saying a word.

A small shower passed across the chalet meadow. The storm bird had given the right omen.

Only a small shower. It went away.

Father got up.

"Well, I'd better go and take a look at the fence," he said.

Anders was wandering about on the chalet meadow.

He felt he'd been hard but wasn't sorry.

Strong and hard, as behind an armor.

Oh no. They wouldn't get near him. Wouldn't ever get through his armor.

Strange how clumsy the grownups were.

So helpless, in a way.

There came Father—wanted to show him confidence. Clumsy, embarrassed.

He wanted to worm himself into *his* confidence—that was why.

But it was too late. It didn't really matter now anymore.

He'd managed to pretend he didn't understand anything. Even Father hadn't been able to get through!

He felt a cold joy standing there.

To come to him like that, begging for his confidence!

It was too late. It didn't matter now anymore.

You'll be sorry about this, someone said.

You'll be sorry about this. You're just scared. Scared, scared, scared. You're scared, you're bad, you're running away—you'll be sorry for this. Everything returns. Everything returns. When it's too late, you'll be sorry.

This everlasting inner voice. All right then, he would be sorry!

He looked around him. He stood on a slope where tall, spindly sorrel was growing.

It was here, wasn't it, last summer…

It was here he lay catching his breath, after running away from Gunvor.

He stood and looked around him for a moment.

There was something special about this hill. Must be because of the sorrel.

Was someone there? Up on the crest of the hill? Someone who was laughing? Didn't he stand here, small, looking down at the ground—?

Amund—now he remembered.

Anyway, Gunvor was his sister.

Gunvor—she'd gone to America. Dropped by last summer to say goodbye.

He'd barely seen her the whole year. Hadn't exchanged a word with her.

"Goodbye," he said, shaking hands. He avoided her eyes; but he noticed a sort of questioning look in her eyes.

Had she understood anything? Did she know anything? That he would never know.

Father sat inside the chalet cabin. He'd packed his bag, thrown the sheepskin blankets over the crossbeam again, and was putting out the fire on the hearth. He didn't look up as he said, "I've been thinking—I suppose I'd better let you go and start at that school."

It had become so quiet on the farm. Once the potatoes were out of the ground, there wasn't a living creature left. So it seemed. The people gone, the birds departed.

Tora and Kari were both away. How long would it be before he saw them again? In the meantime they might all be changed. He felt no qualms about Kari, though. Tora was something else. Tora and he seemed to be too much alike—he didn't know what to expect from Tora.

Åse was home. But she was going to school, or whatever it was, he hadn't seen her in quite a while.

It was strange to walk around knowing you were going to leave. He saw everything and did a lot of different things, but he didn't seem to be touching anything any more. Wasn't really touching the ground either. He was gliding. Leaning forward on the air and gliding, as when he dreamed he was flying.

Many things became so different, now that he was to part from them.

The sawhorse, that damned sawhorse—he'd hated it like a living thing he was chained to, he'd reeked with hatred when he stood there sawing and fretting, every thrust of the saw reminding him of the clock, which never stopped ticking off lost time while he stood there fretting away— he'd brought himself to the point where he knew exactly all the delightful things he could have done during one, two, ten, twenty thrusts of the saw. And now it almost hurt to part from that damned sawhorse.

He met Åse in the pasture one day and was astonished. He was astonished every time he hadn't seen her for a while. She had become so tall each time—he always remembered her as short and chunky.

"You're walking here alone?" he said—it sounded so odd, almost as if he were talking to a stranger.

"Yes," she said.

"Are you often alone, Åse?"

"Oh, well," Åse said, laughing, "I have all the animals, you know. And then I have a brother who looks up and notices me at least once a month. By the way, I've just been seeing my aunt, Ma's sister, for a couple of weeks. Did you notice?"

"You've grown, haven't you?"

Åse dropped a curtsy.

"I can well believe it. Since you deigned to look in my direction."

"Don't be saucy, Åse. Remember, you're almost grown-up now."

Åse gazed at him with that calm, maternal look she'd had since she was small. She gave a short laugh.

"Almost grown-up? I'm much, much older than you are," she said.

Everybody had said that confirmation was a great and solemn thing. They said it repeatedly, until you almost felt like doubting it.

But it was probably true. Even Tora had wept. So he knew he had to be solemn. It seemed strange, but he actually *did* feel solemn as they started out. Everybody was solemn. Even the weather was solemn—heavy, gray, late fall weather as stern as the Old Testament.

The trip to church was solemn, with all the horse-drawn carriages on the road, all those serious people in their Sunday best.

The church was solemn—all those people, the candles at the altar, the organ, the singing.

All of it—until he noticed he was thinking about *one* thing only, the most solemn of all. And that was the new silver watch he had in his vest pocket. It had been given to him today. He had held it in his hand time and again, so heavy and so fine, with those bright gold hands which pointed and pointed at the black numbers, and that small second hand which was so busy. He'd seen it right away—the second hand, that was him, the minute hand was Mother, and the hour hand, which almost didn't move at all, was Father. It ought to have been the longest. He thought of Mother and put the watch in his pocket again. But then he thought of the watch and had to take it out again.

The second hand was a bit absurd perhaps, still it kept running around saying ticktock, ticktock, giving life to it all.

He had opened the cover and peeked. Inside it said,

½ Chronomètre
15 Rubis.

Afterward he'd opened and closed it many times to hear the tiny snap.

Now he was sitting in the aisle, facing the long row of

girls in their white dresses. It was solemn—but he wasn't thinking about that.

It was supposed to be the sin against the Holy Ghost, some people said—having dirty thoughts about girls in church on the very day of your confirmation. He'd talked to people who boasted they'd done it. Martin boasted of it. Others, too.

But *he* was thinking about something else. He kept two fingers in his vest pocket, by chance as it were, and was touching the watch all the time. He could hear it ticking, too, all the time, except when the organ was going full blast. It was singing so sweetly in his pocket: ticktock, ticktock. He felt like trying something: if he removed his fingers, would he still be able to hear it?

He could hear it then, too. Once in a while it disappeared, but then it returned again: ticktock, ticktock, here I am!

The organ pealed, they all stood up, everything was drowned in a tempest of sound. It was so solemn—all the girls were in tears and Martha, who stood face to face with him, cried as though she were being whipped. He himself felt a lump in his throat.

But when things quieted down, his watch was singing so sweetly in his pocket: ticktock, ticktock, here I am!

Perhaps it was this that was the sin against the Holy Ghost.

No, he couldn't possibly believe that. Anyway, it said in the catechism explanation what sin it was; he didn't quite remember, but it was something else.

One day in October he left. Martin Teppen drove him. Father came along a little way. It couldn't be far, he had a meeting in the bank. He could probably have gotten some-body else to show up instead, he told Anders. All in all, he could probably have managed to take the day off and go with him. But—.

"I want you to take your first trip on your own," he said. "I remember myself—. Oh yes, it's quite strange, you'll see."

They didn't talk a great deal.

At the top of the hill, where the forest started, Father stopped the horse and got off.

He stood beside the carriage for a moment, looking into the distance.

There was a rowan tree at the roadside where they had stopped. It was loaded with red rowanberries. The leaves were also beginning to turn red. It stood out so vividly against the gray sky. Lots of rowanberries—that was sup-posed to mean a wet fall, Embret used to say. Or perhaps it was a dry fall. It meant some sort of fall or other.

It had been wet this year.

Embret.

"And so I ran away from the parish," Embret said.

"I understood I'd run away, because I had to go home again."

Why did he come to think of that?

He wasn't running away from anything.

Not from the parish, anyway.

He knew this parish inside out. It was like chewing por-ridge.

Some day when he would be real old, perhaps—then he might come home again....

Now Father stood looking down. He'd started doing that

lately. Would often walk stooped, with a sharp bend in his back, as if looking for something on the ground.

Anders hadn't really taken a good look at Father since Mother died. Now he noticed that his red beard wasn't red anymore. It had turned gray this summer.

Father straightened up.

"Well, goodbye then!" he said.

"Goodbye."

Father turned around and left. Martin said gee-up to Chestnut; but it was taking its time.

He felt heavy and light at the same time. Like an arrow on its way. Alone and moving swiftly.

He turned around and followed Father with his eyes.

He didn't seem to be in such a great hurry now. He was walking slowly. Tall, bent and thin down the dust-colored road, between borders of yellow fall grass.

He looked utterly alone.

SIGURD HOEL

Born in 1890, Sigurd Hoel was one of the most influential literary figures in Norway between the wars. An intellectual of wide learning, he trained in the sciences but chose a literary career, serving as an incisive literary critic, a vigorous cultural commentator, and a distinguished editor at Gyldendal Publishers, as well as writing some dozen novels.

As the poet André Bjerke said at the time of Hoel's death in 1960: "If he had written in English, he would have had a world-wide reputation." Among his novels are *Sinners in Summertime* (1927, translated 1930), *One Day in October* (1931, translated 1932), *Meeting at the Milestone* (1947, translated 1951), the last of which probes the psychology of the Nazi collaborators in Norway. Among his most noted novels are *The Troll Circle*, published by the University of Nebraska Press in 1992. *The Road to the World's End* was originally published in 1933.

SUN & MOON CLASSICS

This publication was made possible, in part, through an operational grant from the Andrew W. Mellon Foundation and through contributions from the following individuals and organizations:

Tom Ahern (Foster, Rhode Island)
Charles Altieri (Seattle, Washington)
John Arden (Galway, Ireland)
Paul Auster (Brooklyn, New York)
Jesse Huntley Ausubel (New York, New York)
Luigi Ballerini (Los Angeles, California)
Dennis Barone (West Hartford, Connecticut)
Jonathan Baumbach (Brooklyn, New York)
Roberto Bedoya (Los Angeles, California)
Guy Bennett (Los Angeles, California)
Bill Berkson (Bolinas, California)
Steve Benson (Berkeley, California)
Charles Bernstein and Susan Bee (New York, New York)
Dorothy Bilik (Silver Spring, Maryland)
Alain Bosquet (Paris, France)
In Memoriam: John Cage
In Memoriam: Camilo José Cela
Rosita Copioli (Rimini, Italy)
Bill Corbett (Boston, Massachusetts)
Robert Crosson (Los Angeles, California)
Tina Darragh and P. Inman (Greenbelt, Maryland)
Fielding Dawson (New York, New York)
Christopher Dewdney (Toronto, Canada)
Larry Deyah (New York, New York)
Arkadii Dragomoschenko (St. Petersburg, Russia)
George Economou (Norman, Oklahoma)
Richard Elman (Stony Brook, New York)
Kenward Elmslie (Calais, Vermont)
Elaine Equi and Jerome Sala (New York, New York)
Lawrence Ferlinghetti (San Francisco, California)
Richard Foreman (New York, New York)
Howard N. Fox (Los Angeles, California)
Jerry Fox (Aventura, Florida)
In Memoriam: Rose Fox
Melvyn Freilicher (San Diego, California)
Miro Gavran (Zagreb, Croatia)

Allen Ginsberg (New York, New York)
Peter Glassgold (Brooklyn, New York)
Barbara Guest (Berkeley, California)
Perla and Amiram V. Karney (Bel Air, California)
Václav Havel (Prague, The Czech Republic)
Lyn Hejinian (Berkeley, California)
Fanny Howe (La Jolla, California)
Harold Jaffe (San Diego, California)
Ira S. Jaffe (Albuquerque, New Mexico)
Ruth Prawer Jhabvala (New York, New York)
Pierre Joris (Albany, New York)
Alex Katz (New York, New York)
Pamela and Rowan Klein (Los Angeles, California)
Tom LaFarge (New York, New York)
Mary Jane Lafferty (Los Angeles, California)
Michael Lally (Santa Monica, California)
Norman Lavers (Jonesboro, Arkansas)
Jerome Lawrence (Malibu, California)
Stacey Levine (Seattle, Washington)
Herbert Lust (Greenwich, Connecticut)
Norman MacAffee (New York, New York)
Rosemary Macchiavelli (Washington, DC)
Jackson Mac Low (New York, New York)
In Memoriam: Mary McCarthy
Harry Mulisch (Amsterdam, The Netherlands)
Iris Murdoch (Oxford, England)
Martin Nakell (Los Angeles, California)
In Memoriam: bpNichol
Cees Nooteboom (Amsterdam, The Netherlands)
NORLA (Norwegian Literature Abroad) (Oslo, Norway)
Claes Oldenburg (New York, New York)
Toby Olson (Philadelphia, Pennsylvania)
Maggie O'Sullivan (Hebden Bridge, England)
Rochelle Owens (Norman, Oklahoma)
Bart Parker (Providence, Rhode Island)
Marjorie and Joseph Perloff (Pacific Palisades, California)
Dennis Phillips (Los Angeles, California)
Carl Rakosi (San Francisco, California)
Tom Raworth (Cambridge, England)
David Reed (New York, New York)
Ishmael Reed (Oakland, California)
Tom Roberdeau (Los Angeles, California)

SUN & MOON CLASSICS